Don't miss BJ Hoff's first two books in
THE RIVERHAVEN YEARS SERIES...

RACHEL'S SECRET

With the first book in her compelling series The Riverhaven Years, bestselling author BJ Hoff introduces a new community of unforgettable characters and adds the elements you have come to expect from her novels: a tender love story, the faith journeys of people we grow to know and love, and enough suspense to keep the pages turning quickly.

When the wounded Irish American riverboat captain Jeremiah Gant bursts into the rural Amish setting of Riverhaven, he brings chaos and conflict to the community—especially for young widow Rachel Brenneman. The unwelcome outsider needs a safe place to recuperate before continuing his secret role as an Underground Railroad conductor. Neither he nor Rachel is prepared for the forbidden love that threatens to endanger a man's mission, a woman's heart, and a way of life for an entire people.

WHERE GRACE ABIDES

In the engaging second book in the Riverhaven Years series, BJ Hoff offers an even closer look at the Amish community of Riverhaven and the people who live, love, and work there. Secrets, treachery, and persecution are only a few of the challenges that test Rachel's faith and her love for the forbidden outsider while Gant's own hopes and dreams are dealt a life-changing blow, rendering the vow he made to Rachel seemingly impossible to honor.

Many of the other characters first introduced in *Rachel's Secret* now find their gentle, unassuming lives of faith jeopardized by a malicious outside influence. At the same time, those striving to help runaway slaves escape to freedom through the Underground Railroad face deception and the danger of discovery.

All the elements you have come to expect from author BJ Hoff—romance, drama, and great characters—join together to fill the pages with a tender, endearing love story and a bold, inspiring journey of faith.

The RIVERHAVEN YEARS

RIVER OF MERCY

BJ HOFF

HARVEST HOUSE PUBLISHERS
EUGENE, OREGON

Cover by Koechel Peterson & Associates, Inc., Minneapolis, Minnesota

BJ Hoff is published in association with Books & Such Literary Agency, 52 Mission Circle, Suite 122, PMB 170, Santa Rosa, CA 95409-5370. www.booksandsuch.biz

RIVER OF MERCY
Copyright © 2012 by BJ Hoff
Published by Harvest House Publishers
Eugene, Oregon 97402
www.harvesthousepublishers.com

Library of Congress Cataloging-in-Publication Data
Hoff, B. J.
River of mercy / BJ Hoff.
     p. cm.—(The Riverhaven years ; bk. 3)
     ISBN 978-0-7369-2420-7 (pbk.)
     ISBN 978-0-7369-4052-8 (eBook)
     1. Amish—Fiction. I. Title.
PS3558.O34395R58 2012
813'.54—dc22

                                                    2012012455

ACKNOWLEDGMENTS

I'm thankful to so many people who helped bring this book to fulfillment, and especially to...

My husband, Jim, who knows all the important stuff I can never figure out and doesn't make *too* much fun of my helplessness. (He can actually read maps and calculate how long a buggy would have taken to get from point A to point B.) He also puts up with my Irishness and smiles through it all.

My daughters, Dana and Jessie, who pray for me, cheer for me, and put up with me during deadlines and disasters. They also make me smile—a lot.

My grandsons, Noah, Gunnar, and Caleb, who enrich my life and crack me up on a regular basis.

Special friends—Cheryl, the bravest and most resilient woman I know; Sara, a true Steel Magnolia who never ceases to surprise me; Charlotte, who saves me from frumpdom, prays for me, and on occasion, feeds me; Wennie, who storms heaven with a velvet hammer and is known well by the Father; and Edith, who simply does too much for me to list. Bless you all!

My long-suffering editor, Nick Harrison, who wears a mantle of patience and shows the grace of a saint and rolls his eyes only when I'm unaware.

Shane White, indefatigable encourager and optimist supreme.

As always, my agent and friend, Janet Kobobel Grant, who never gives up on me.

Kelli Standish, friend and wizard who teaches me something new at least once a week and holds my hand through the nightmarish maze of cyberspace, Facebook, and The Media.

Harvest House—a publisher of the highest integrity that treats its authors like family and friends. Every one of you is such a blessing!

And my readers. I am blessed to have patient and kindhearted readers who continually encourage me with their messages and ongoing prayers. "I thank my God through Jesus Christ for you all."

Thanks be to my God, who always brings me through in spite of myself.

TOO MANY LONG NIGHTS

I feel like one who treads alone
Some banquet hall, deserted.

THOMAS MOORE

Amish settlement near Riverhaven, Ohio
November 1856

Rachel Brenneman had always liked to walk by the river at twilight.

There had been a time during the People's early years at Riverhaven when she gave no thought to walking alone, day or night. After she and Eli were married, the two of them liked to stroll along the bank of the Ohio in the evening, discussing their day, planning the workweek, dreaming of the future. After Eli's death, however, Rachel no longer went out alone after dark, although sometimes she and her ten-year-old sister, Fannie, took a picnic lunch in the early afternoon and sat watching the fine big boats and smaller vessels that traveled the great Ohio to unknown places.

Now though, venturing away from the community no longer felt safe, even in the middle of the day. In truth, there was nowhere that felt safe, not after the deadly attack on Phoebe Esch and the other troubles recently visited upon the People. At night, especially, Rachel stayed inside, sitting alone in her bedroom with the window scarcely open in deference to the weather, which had recently turned cold.

November was a lonely month. Rachel still loved to listen to the river from inside her home, but the nighttime sounds—the distant lapping of the water, the blast from a boat's horn, the night creatures in communion with one another—never failed to set off a stirring of remembrance and an ache in her heart. Yet she couldn't resist sitting there night after night, watching and listening, trying not to let her memories struggle to the surface of her thoughts, trying not to let new hope ignite the ashes of her dreams...

Trying not to think of Jeremiah.

But how could she *not* think of him? How did a woman love a man, even if their love was forbidden, and not see his face in her mind or hear his voice in her ear or remember the imprint of his smile upon her thoughts?

Common sense seemed to tell her it should be easy to put the man out of her head. They couldn't be alone with each other. They couldn't even pass the time of day unless they were in the company of others. If they happened to meet by accident, they were expected to separate as quickly as possible.

Yet even with all the rules and restrictions that kept them apart, Jeremiah Gant was still a part of her life. He flowed through her heart and traced the current of her days as surely and completely as the Ohio flowed through the valley, winding its way through the land, coursing through the days and lives of Rachel and the other Plain people.

Lately, there had been talk of leaving. Two years and more of unrest and harassment and threats—even death—had begun to wear on the Riverhaven Amish. It was rumored that talks were taking place among the church leaders, discussions of whether to remain in this once peaceful valley that had become home to the entire community or to consider moving on.

There was no thought of fighting back, of seeking out the unknown adversaries and taking a stand against them. Even if the People could identify their tormenters, they would not confront them. The Amish were a people of nonresistance. They would not fight, not even to protect their own lives. It wasn't their way. To strike out at another individual under any circumstances was strictly against the *Ordnung*, the unwritten but strict code that guided how they were to live.

The only person Rachel had ever known to defy the rule against fighting, even in self-defense, was Eli, her deceased husband. He'd gone against the Amish way when he defended Rachel against those who ambushed them on another November night, now four years gone. He had fought with desperation and all his strength, only to die at the hands of their attackers while allowing Rachel to escape.

She knew it was a grievous sin to have such a thought, but many had been the time she wished she could have died alongside Eli that terrible night rather than live through the grief-hollowed, barren days that followed his death. She had been totally devoted to Eli. Their marriage had been good, for they had been close friends as well as husband and wife. Rachel had thought she could never love another man after losing Eli.

And then Jeremiah Gant had come to Riverhaven, turning her life around, enabling her to love again—only to have that love forbidden. Even though Jeremiah had made it known he would willingly convert to the Amish faith, Bishop Graber refused to grant permission, once again leaving Rachel with a lost love and a broken heart.

Perhaps it would be better if they *were* to leave Riverhaven...leave the fear and the dread and the pain-filled memories behind.

Leave Jeremiah...

The thought stabbed her heart. Could she really face never seeing him again? Never again hear him say her name in that soft and special way he had of making it as tender as a touch? Never again see the smile that was meant for her alone?

In truth, it wasn't only Jeremiah she would miss if they were to leave this fertile Ohio valley. She loved the land, the gentle hills, the singing river. She had come here when she was still a child, come from another place that had never truly been home to her. Here in Riverhaven though, she had felt welcome and accepted. At peace. At home.

At least for a time. It was almost as if she had become a part of the land itself. Even the thought of leaving made her sad beyond telling.

She sighed, knowing she should stir and make ready for bed, even though she felt far too restless for sleep. Would this be another of too many nights when her thoughts tormented her, circling like birds of prey, evoking an uneasiness and anxiety that would give her no peace?

Finally she stood, securing the window to ward off the cold, even though she sensed that the chill snaking through her had little to do with the night air. All too familiar with this icy wind of loneliness, she knew there was no warmth that could ease its punishing sting.

1

A Visit to Riverhaven

I used to think that love made people happy,
but now I know it can also make them sad.

FROM THE PERSONAL DIARY OF FANNIE KANAGY

Even though a heavy sadness lay behind this visit to Riverhaven, Rachel couldn't help but take pleasure in the music streaming from one of the two churches on the main street.

It was unusually mild for a late morning in November. Someone must have cracked open the church door or a window, for the hymn singing was clear enough to make out most of the words. Even though it was church music, Rachel knew she probably shouldn't give it too much of her attention. Music tended to take her mind off everything else, and today she didn't want to be distracted.

The Amish held worship services on alternating Sundays, and the other Sundays were usually spent calling on family and friends. Rachel didn't know Ellie Sawyer very well, but on this particular day she felt the need to pay her a visit. It was early to call on someone who wasn't family, and the newly widowed Mrs. Sawyer was probably in church, so Rachel had agreed to Fannie's suggestion to go sightseeing first at the Riverhaven Park with its nice picnic grounds. There was a beautiful view of the Ohio River and the sloping hills that bordered its grounds and pier.

Rachel and Fannie's widowed mother had recently married Dr. David Sebastian, and the couple had traveled by train to Baltimore to meet the doctor's son and family, so only the two sisters were visiting Ellie Sawyer today. The poor young wife and mother had only recently learned of her husband's tragic death from a farm accident in Indiana, so no doubt she would be grieving deeply.

To make matters worse, Mr. Sawyer had been buried for nearly two weeks in another state before Ellie learned by post that he was gone. The awful news had come too late for her to travel and attend her husband's funeral.

Rachel couldn't begin to imagine how difficult that must have been. At least when she lost Eli, she had been there to prepare his body for burial and had known the comfort of her entire family and community of friends. The People gathered close around one of their own during such a time to help and console in any way they could. Death was always a hard thing, but having loved ones close by to share one's sorrow helped ease the pain, at least a little.

The church and its music now behind them, Fannie nudged Rachel. "The *Englisch* hymn singing is real pretty, isn't it, Rachel? I like music, don't you?"

Rachel nodded. "*Ja*. But we mustn't let it distract us today or any other day for that matter. And let's be sure to give Ellie Sawyer all our attention while we're there."

"Does Mrs. Sawyer know about Eli? That you're a widow too?"

The road to the park was in sight now, so Rachel slowed the buggy before replying. "I doubt that she does. And I wouldn't want to mention it to her, especially now. She doesn't need to be thinking about anyone's loss but her own these days."

"I just thought it might help her to know someone else understands what she's going through."

Rachel glanced at her sister. For such a young girl, Fannie sometimes showed surprising insights. Was she right? Would Ellie Sawyer feel better knowing that someone nearby could understand and even share her grief?

"Well," Rachel said before stepping out of the buggy, "if the time ever comes when I feel I should mention it, I will."

Even as she said the words though, Rachel hoped the time wouldn't come. Despite the years that had passed since Eli's death, it was all she could do to speak of it. The memory of that awful night still seared her heart.

Rachel and Fannie stayed considerably longer at the park than they had planned. The mild weather encouraged walking along the riverbank, and the view was worth the time they spent admiring it. By the time they drove back into Riverhaven to visit Ellie Sawyer, it was almost two o'clock.

"I wonder if it's too late to stop at the boardinghouse," Rachel said. "I wouldn't want to wake the baby if she's napping."

"Oh, Rachel, I really want to see the baby! Please, let's stop for a few minutes at least."

Rachel looked at her. "All right, but we won't stay long." She slowed the horses, intending to park across the road from the boardinghouse.

"Captain Gant!" Fannie cried, standing up in the buggy. "Look, Rachel, there's Captain Gant!"

Rachel reined in the horses a little too sharply, easing up as she saw Jeremiah step down from the porch of the boardinghouse. At Fannie's cry, he stopped by the side of the road and returned her wave, waiting while Rachel parked the buggy before walking toward them.

Irked by the way her heart raced at the sight of him, Rachel sat still as a stone, still grasping the reins as he approached. His first words were for Fannie, who was practically squirming with excitement. As always, he charmed the girl by sweeping a bow and breaking into a huge smile.

"Well, now, if it isn't Miss Fannie Kanagy. This is a nice surprise."

When he turned to Rachel, his smile softened. "Rachel," he said quietly. The look he gave her was as warm and intimate as if he'd laid his hand along her cheek. "How are you keeping?"

It was all Rachel could do to choke out a greeting. He unnerved her at the best of times, but coming upon him unexpectedly made it almost impossible to keep her composure.

Tall and casual in his shirtsleeves—although the weather wasn't quite that mild—while a faint November breeze ruffled his dark hair, he was handsome enough to make any woman go weak-kneed and take a second look.

Only the awareness that she didn't dare look at him too closely made it possible for Rachel to drag her gaze away. Even so, she allowed a quick, forbidden thought that the roads of Riverhaven would be far safer if men like Jeremiah Gant were confined indoors.

She finally faced him to find him studying her with one raised eyebrow and a hint of a smile. She cleared her throat, saying, "I'm doing well, thank you."

"It's a little unusual to see you in town on a Sunday," he said. "Are you looking for Gideon?"

"We came to visit Mrs. Sawyer and her baby," Fannie put in.

"We did see Gideon though. He was out at the farm to help me feed the animals while Mamma and Dr. David are gone," Rachel added.

"Have you heard from them?"

"No, but they should be home by the end of the week."

"Well, I'm sure Ellie will be glad to see you," he said, darting a glance behind him toward the boardinghouse. "I just came from there. You'll find her and Naomi Fay downstairs. She's back at work, helping Marabeth in the kitchen."

"Oh—so soon?" Rachel said.

He nodded, his expression turning solemn. "I expect she needs the money. It's going to be hard for her with a baby and no husband. Besides, it's probably best if she can keep busy."

"She surely won't stay here, will she? Doesn't she have family she could go to?"

He shoved his hands in his pockets, frowning. "She says not—she grew up in an orphanage. And apparently she and her husband weren't close with his family, so she seems to be on her own."

The sting of an unidentifiable emotion caught Rachel off guard. She couldn't help but wonder how it was that Jeremiah knew so much about Ellie Sawyer. And he seemed so...concerned about her.

But of course he'd know something of her background. After all, her husband had worked in Jeremiah's carpentry shop before moving on to Indiana. And it was only natural that he'd be concerned about her situation. Jeremiah was a kind man. He'd care about anyone in such difficult straits.

"How awful for her," she said, meaning it.

"We'll help her," Fannie said. "Lots of people will, won't they, Rachel?"

"I'm sure they will," Rachel said, smiling at her sister. "Well...we'd best be going in now before it gets any later. Get the pie, Fannie."

Fannie hopped down from the buggy and retrieved the basket that held the apple pie they'd baked the evening before. "Will you be out to visit us soon too, Captain Gant? I know Thunder would like to see you. And so would we," she quickly added.

"I'd like that too," he said quietly. "I expect he's grown quite a bit since I saw him last."

"*Ja*, he's getting real big. Mamma says he's going to be big enough to haul the hay wagon if he doesn't stop growing soon."

He laughed. "Let's hope he doesn't get *that* big!"

As Rachel started to step out of the buggy, Jeremiah quickly took her arm to help. In that instant their eyes met and held. Heat rose to her face. Unnerved by his closeness and intense scrutiny, she clenched her teeth until her jaw hurt in an effort not to react. He tightened his grasp on her arm, holding on to her for what seemed an excessive length of time. Only when Rachel made a small tugging motion to free herself did he drop his hand away.

She mumbled a hurried goodbye and started across the road toward the boardinghouse. With every step Rachel imagined him watching her. It was all she could do not to turn and look.

"Fannie," she said just before they went inside, "you can't be inviting Captain Gant to visit us anymore."

Her sister gave her a quizzical look. "But he's our friend."

Rachel drew a long breath. "But he's also an *auslander*."

The word tasted bitter on her lips. Calling Jeremiah an outsider seemed so wrong.

Fannie stood staring down at the porch. "He doesn't seem like one." She lifted her face to look at Rachel. "Captain Gant's been good to us. He cares about us. It doesn't seem fair that we can't be friends with him."

"We *are* friends, Fannie, but we can't be...too friendly."

"Maybe you can't, but Mamma and Dr. David don't feel that way."

"What?"

"They treat Captain Gant just like they do anybody else. They have him for dinner sometimes, and he and Dr. David play checkers at least every other week."

"Well, that's different."

"How is it different? Dr. David is Amish now too, but he and Captain Gant are still friends."

Even as Rachel struggled to reply, she saw her sister's expression change, clearing as though she already had her answer. "It's because he likes you too much, isn't it? But you can't get married because he's not Amish, so you're not supposed to be friends, just the two of you."

Caught off guard by Fannie's perception, Rachel swallowed against the dryness in her throat. "Something like that, *ja.*"

Her little sister—who, Rachel suddenly realized, had nearly caught up with her in height—reached to take her hand. "I'm sorry, Rachel. I didn't mean to make you sad."

"Oh, no, Fannie, it's all right. I'm not sad."

Fannie watched her. "Your eyes are."

Rachel knew she shouldn't be discussing this with her sister—or with anyone else. Even so, she felt compelled to ask. "Who told you…about Captain Gant and me?"

"I heard Mamma and Dr. David talking." Fannie dipped her head a little. "I wasn't eavesdropping, Rachel. Honest, I wasn't. I was just picking some burrs off Thunder right outside the kitchen, and I heard them. I went the rest of the way into the room so they'd know where I was. I didn't hear all that much. Besides, I knew before then that Captain Gant liked you an awful lot. And I knew that lately it made him unhappy."

Rachel waited, sensing there was more to come.

"Used to be," Fannie said, "that the only time the hurt ever left his eyes was when he looked at you." She paused. "But now when he looks at you, it's as if that's when he hurts the most."

Rachel stood there, stunned and speechless, her eyes burning. Finally, she managed a ragged breath, opened the door, and waited for Fannie to step in first before following her inside.

2

A Future and a Hope

For I know the thoughts that I think toward you, says the Lord, thoughts of peace and not of evil, to give you a future and a hope.

Jeremiah 29:11 NKJV

As Rachel watched Ellie Sawyer standing over her sleeping baby in the back of the boardinghouse kitchen, she thought the recent widow was likely the prettiest young woman she had ever seen. Her features were delicate and perfectly molded, and wisps of flaxen hair curled softly around her face. Her large blue eyes, though sad, brimmed with love for her child.

They'd had a nice visit, if a brief one. They arrived before the baby fell asleep, and Mrs. Haining insisted that Ellie take a break with her visitors in the kitchen. Fannie was absolutely delighted with the opportunity to hold little Naomi Fay. Rachel also enjoyed snuggling the sweet warmth of the precious infant against her shoulder, though a wrench of regret seized her when she thought of the babies she might never have.

The only awkward moment came when Ellie expressed disappointment that they had just missed Captain Gant.

"I know you're good friends," she said. "I'm sure he would have liked to see you."

Rachel managed to choke out an inane reply, to which Ellie responded, "The captain is such a good man, isn't he? I don't know how we would have managed without his help!"

"It was so thoughtful of you to come," she went on as she walked them to the front door of the boardinghouse. I think Naomi Fay really likes you, Fannie. I hope you'll come again soon."

"Oh, we will, Mrs. Sawyer!" Fannie said. "Won't we, Rachel?"

Rachel nodded, meeting Ellie's smile over the top of Fannie's head.

Outside, after they said their goodbyes, Fannie glanced back at the door. "She's nice, isn't she?"

"Very nice." But even as she agreed with her sister, Rachel was aware of a certain edge of reserve in her feelings about Ellie Sawyer. For no good reason, she couldn't quite warm to her, not as she knew she should, given Ellie's tragic loss and now uncertain future.

Without warning, the memory of Jeremiah's expression when he'd voiced his concern about the young widow squeezed its way past the fringes of her mind. Rachel actually closed her eyes for an instant against the image. She was unfamiliar with the strange emotion that struck her, but she recognized it for exactly what it was—jealousy.

The realization struck Rachel like a blow. Shame surged up in her. She hadn't known she was capable of such a petty, childish feeling. Hadn't she been taught ever since her childhood that jealousy was a vicious, corrosive sin? She was to rejoice in the well-being and good fortunes of others, not resent them.

If Jeremiah should come to care in a special way for the attractive young widow, and in time, Ellie for him, well, that would be a good thing for both of them, wouldn't it? Hadn't she prayed about that very thing not so long ago, prayed that he would find happiness with a wife and family of his own someday, just as she had prayed for Ellie Sawyer as well, for God's comfort and peace to fill her emptiness and ease her sorrow?

Jeremiah was free to love whomever he chose, and in all likelihood, Ellie would eventually find her way to love and happiness again as well. It would be a most grievous sin to not wish them exactly that, even if the thought of Jeremiah looking at another woman with the same softness in his eyes that had once been there for her sliced at her heart with an icy knife.

"Rachel?"

Her sister's questioning tone brought Rachel sharply back to her surroundings.

"Shouldn't we be going now?" Fannie asked.

Only then did Rachel realize she'd been sitting in the buggy, staring at the road ahead without making a move to drive on.

"*Ja*," she said, her voice shaky. "We definitely should."

"You've been awfully quiet tonight," Asa said, clearing the table of the supper dishes. "Something troubling you?"

Gant felt his friend's eyes on him but avoided meeting his gaze. There was plenty troubling him all right, but he didn't feel up to talking about any of it. Instead, he got up from the table and went to the stove, where water was heating for washing the dishes.

"Nothing in particular," he said and then changed the subject. "Have you seen the boy today?"

"Young Gideon?" Asa scratched his head as if to consider. "No, as a matter of fact, I haven't seen a sign of him all day. Have you?"

Gant shook his head. "No, but that's not unusual for a Sunday. He goes out to the farm sometimes on Saturday evening and stays through Sunday."

"Didn't you say his mother and the doctor are out of town?"

"They are, but Gideon looks after things all the same. He still does quite a bit to help out around the farm whenever he can."

Asa nodded, waiting while Gant poured the hot water into the sink. "He's a good boy. A good son."

"He is," Gant said, "but I think his mother would be a sight happier if he'd come home and be a good *Amish* son."

"It's my night for the dishes," Asa said, waving Gant out of the way. "Do you think he'll ever go back to the Amish settlement?"

Gant shrugged, standing back while Asa rolled up his shirtsleeves and plunged his hands into the sudsy water. "I'll dry," he said, going in search of a clean dish towel. "There was a time when I would have thought he'd be unlikely to go back. Now I'm not so sure. I suspect there might be another attraction out that way besides the farm."

Asa shot him a glance as he scrubbed a plate. "Oh?"

Gant grinned. "I've seen him talking to a certain young Amish lass every now and then when she comes to town, and he gets this spoony look on his face every time he manages to get within speaking distance of her."

"Aha! So if he should go back to his people, do you think you would lose him from the shop?"

"Not necessarily, unless he wanted to return to farming full-time. A few Amish men are beginning to work elsewhere besides their farms. Not many as yet, but I wouldn't be surprised if more don't follow suit in the future."

"Why? I thought the Amish preferred to stay mostly to themselves."

"Oh, I'm sure that's their preference. But I wonder if the day won't come when land will be too scarce for them to make a living from farming alone. Huge sections are being grabbed up all over the place these days, and there's also the way the Amish pass land on to the families. Sooner or later they may have to branch out into other areas."

Gant hung up the towel after drying the last dish. "In any event, I'd hate to lose Gideon. He has a natural flair for the wood, and the longer he works for me, the more conscientious he seems to be."

Asa muttered something that sounded like "Probably afraid to be anything *but* conscientious."

"I heard that."

"Never was anything wrong with your hearing," Asa said.

After that, Gant made an effort to be better company. As always, Asa had picked up on his dark mood. Ordinarily, Gant probably would have confided in his friend about what was bothering him. But he wasn't willing to discuss Rachel, not even with Asa.

And of course, it was Rachel who was troubling him.

Long after Asa went to bed, he sat up, thinking about the day. He'd been feeling pretty good after visiting with Ellie and the baby in the boardinghouse kitchen. The little one had a way of smiling her way into his heart, and Ellie, despite the loss of her husband, somehow always seemed to have a bright way about her. Ironic that she, who had endured such a terrible tragedy, should be responsible for lifting his spirits.

In a way, Ellie Sawyer puzzled him. She was almost childlike in her cheerful mannerisms and behavior. True, she was young—little more than a girl—but she was also a widow and a mother. Yet she had a way about her, a kind of innocence and optimism that didn't quite fit the hard life she'd apparently lived. Raised in an orphanage, obviously not much more than a child when she'd married, and now widowed with an infant to take care of, she still found it within her to make the best of what she'd been given.

It was entirely peculiar that he never left her without feeling a bit more lighthearted—but confused. That had been the way of it today.

And then, right after leaving the boarding house, he'd met up with Rachel, and the old ache had started up in him again. All he had to do was look at her, and the possibility that they would never be together brought a sadness that came rushing in on him like the winter wind.

No, not with Asa or anyone else could he talk about Rachel. But he couldn't stop thinking about her either, no more than he could stop loving her. And he couldn't quite bring himself to give up entirely on the hope that they might still have a future. Folly though it might be, a part of him deep within still clung to the hope that a new bishop would eventually be chosen for the Riverhaven Amish, and a new bishop could make all the difference for him and Rachel.

Recently it had come to light that their current bishop, the elderly Isaac Graber, would be retiring. Apparently his mind was going bad, and he also had a number of physical problems related to a long battle with diabetes. As Rachel had briefly explained the day of her mother's wedding to Doc Sebastian, a new bishop would eventually be chosen by lot from among their own.

Bishop Graber had refused to allow Gant to convert to the Amish church and marry Rachel, but Gant hoped that a new bishop might be more open-minded. Of the three men eligible to be included in the lot, Abe Gingerich or Malachi Esch might reconsider Bishop Graber's decision. Unfortunately, there was another man who might be considered for the position of bishop.

A man who had pursued Rachel for years with the intention of marrying her. A man who seemed to have appointed himself Gant's personal nemesis. A man who would take great delight in making certain that Gant and Rachel would never be free to wed.

If Samuel Beiler should be chosen as the next bishop, any hope Gant might ever have had for a future with Rachel would be forever lost.

3

A WOMAN GROWN

Sad are our hopes, for they were sweet in sowing,
But tares, self-sown, have overtopp'd the wheat.

AUBREY THOMAS DE VERE

Tuesday was Gideon Kanagy's usual day off from the carpentry shop. Typically, it was also the day he spent working at the family farm—the farm that would be his whenever he wanted it.

If he ever wanted it. As the only son of a deceased father, he became the owner of the farm. Gideon, however, had no intention of settling down to a life of farming for a long time, if ever. So instead of his mother living in the nearby *Dawdi Haus*—a residence provided by the Amish for their retired parents—she remained in the main house for now while Gideon lived in Riverhaven above the carpentry shop.

He wasn't living Amish, and he didn't know if he ever would again. He sometimes dressed Plain—when he attended an Amish event with his mother, for example—but for the most part he lived *Englisch* and had for some time.

Even so, he still spent some of his time at the farm, doing what needed to be done, especially those tasks he thought too demanding for his mother. Today was no exception.

Although his recently married mother and Doc Sebastian had been in Baltimore paying a visit to Doc's son, they would be returning by train tomorrow. Gideon wanted to have the house in good condition when they arrived. He had spent the better part of the day doing inside work.

He did his best to keep the house and other buildings on the property in good repair on a regular basis, but he'd still found a number of jobs that needed doing: patching here and painting there, fixing the stubborn handle on the pump in the kitchen, securing the threshold at the back door, and a few other things. He planned to spend the night in order to keep the fires going so the house would be toasty warm for Mamm and Doc the next day.

By two o'clock he'd managed to finish up most of what he had hoped to accomplish and was headed back toward Riverhaven in the shop wagon Captain Gant had let him use for the day. He wanted to stock up on some supplies for his mamm and Doc so they could enjoy their return home without having to make a trip into town right away.

The day before had brought sleet and wet snow to the area, which then turned sloppy and slippery, freezing overnight to leave a coating of ice on top. The road was treacherous in places, so he let Duffy, the shop horse, take his time along the way.

He was nearly to the crossroads when he spied a buggy in the ditch on the opposite side of the road. After another moment he realized that the young woman standing alongside was Emma Knepp.

He saw Emma fairly often, sometimes in town with her *dat* or a brother. Seldom did he meet up with her alone. When he did, she always seemed awkward, hesitant even to carry on a conversation. He hated that. Their families had been friends for years, and he and Emma's older brother, Joe, had spent a good amount of time together.

But of course the Knepp family would disapprove of him these days for living *Englisch*. They were civil if they chanced to meet—Gideon had never joined the church, so he wasn't under the *Bann* for living outside the community—but they showed no real warmth toward him. He sensed that Emma might like to be friends but was too reserved to respond to any gesture he might make in that direction.

When they were younger, some of his friends liked to tease him about Emma Knepp having a crush on him, but he'd never thought much about it one way or the other. At the time, she'd simply been Joe's little sister. And even if there had been something to their teasing back then, that was obviously no longer the case.

He was surprised to realize that the thought brought a faint twist of regret.

Relief warred with anxiety as Emma watched Gideon Kanagy pull his wagon to the side of the road and jump down, starting toward her. Stranded as she was, relief won. She wasn't sure what it was about Gideon that flustered her so and made her feel like an awkward schoolgirl, but at the moment she couldn't help but be glad to see him. Everybody knew that Gideon Kanagy could fix just about anything, and she wasn't so proud that she wouldn't be glad for his help.

He smiled as he came toward her, his coat collar hiked up against the cold. "Emma? Looks as if you're having a little trouble."

Emma nodded, avoiding his gaze as she pointed to the buggy's right front wheel. "I don't know exactly what happened. I hit something pretty hard and skidded into the ditch."

His smile faded. "Are you all right?"

Emma waved off his question. "*Ja*, I'm fine. It was just a bump."

She watched as he appraised the buggy and then went to soothe Sugar, the chestnut-colored mare, who was growing more and more agitated.

"We need to unhitch her," he said. "I'll tether her to that maple tree for a bit."

After seeing to the horse, he came back and, going down on one knee, took a closer look at the wheel.

"It's not that bad," he said, straightening. "Just bent a little. I can fix it, but I need to get into town first, before the stores close. I've got to pick up some things for Mamm and Doc Sebastian. I'd better take you home for now and fix the wheel on my way back."

Emma fumbled for a reply. "Oh…that's not necessary. It's not that far. I'll just walk."

He frowned. "I don't think you want to do that, Emma," he said. "You're a good mile away from home, and this wind is pretty cold."

What to say? She couldn't let Gideon Kanagy take her home! Her *dat* would have a stroke. To be seen at all with a rebel like Gideon, much less to be caught riding in his wagon with him, would taint her reputation and maybe even mark her to be as wild as Gideon himself.

"Oh, but I'm…I'm used to walking in the cold," she stammered. "It doesn't bother me."

His mouth twitched, and the glint that flickered in his eye made Emma feel as though he knew the reason for her discomfort—and was enjoying it.

"Well, Emma," he said, his tone dry, "it would bother me. Why, my mamm would never let me hear the end of it if she found out I'd let you walk home in weather like this when I had a perfectly good wagon. Come on now and get in. I'll let you out a little ways from your house so you won't be disgraced."

So he *did* know!

Emma felt heat stain her face. "Oh, it's not that…"

She stopped, realizing that in her unwillingness to hurt his feelings she had come close to lying. Truth be told, it was exactly that. She was loath to be seen with Gideon because of his reputation among the People.

And yet she liked him, had always liked him. And what had he done so bad anyway, to deserve the malicious rumors spread about him? True, he'd prolonged his *rumspringa* and hadn't joined the church and was living among the *Englisch.* But from all she knew of Gideon, he was a good son, helpful to his widowed mother and his sisters, hardworking, and kind to the younger children and old people in the community. He wasn't under the *Bann* despite his no longer living Amish.

When they were younger and Gideon still lived among them, she'd had a terrible crush on him. She had daydreamed—fanciful as it might have been—that one day he would actually court her and even ask her to marry him. Now, of course, she didn't dare let herself imagine such foolishness. Not with Gideon living *Englisch.* Even so, if she were to be completely honest with herself, she still felt a strong attraction to him. Sometimes, before she could rein in her imagination, she would catch herself wishing he would come back to the community, that he would realize she was no longer Joe Knepp's little sister but was all grown up and of courting age.

Then she would realize the treacherous path her thoughts had taken and quickly yank them back to a safer place. Even if Gideon were to return to the People and the Amish way of life, he wouldn't be likely to be interested in her.

Once while she was in town, she had seen him with the fancy *Englisch* girl everyone said was his girlfriend. She was strikingly pretty and had made him laugh long and loud. She must be exceptionally bright and clever, to charm Gideon Kanagy in such a way. Why would he ever look twice at a Plain girl like herself?

She hated the rumors and unkind stories that followed him around like an angry swarm of bees. And he was right—it was too cold to be walking around outside for any length of time. Besides, he had offered to drop her off before reaching her house, so why not let him take her home? *Dat* would never need to know.

She bit her lip. What was she thinking, even considering the idea of hiding something from her father just so she could get out of the cold? Was that all there was to it? Or was the idea of sitting next to Gideon Kanagy in his wagon so tempting that she would actually deceive her father to indulge herself?

Emma decided she could never enjoy the experience if she were to resort to shading the truth. "All right then," she finally said. "I mean...I'll take you up on your offer." She hesitated for just a moment. "But you don't need to let me out before we get there. You can take me all the way home."

He lifted one eyebrow. "You sure about that, Emma?"

Without meeting his gaze, she nodded, but even as Gideon helped her up onto the wagon bench, Emma knew her words were stronger than her backbone.

Gideon found himself enjoying Emma's company. Truth be told, it was a downright pleasant experience, her riding along beside him on the wagon bench, talking to him as though she wasn't afraid of being tarnished by his supposedly unacceptable lifestyle.

Not only that, but he discovered a quick mind and a substance to her thoughts that he wouldn't have figured her for. But then, what exactly *would* he have expected from her? Emma wasn't a little girl any longer, and he hardly knew her.

Now, in talking with her, he learned that she helped her *dat* keep the books for the farm and small dairy business that had been in the Knepp family for years. He even detected a surprising interest in events outside the Plain community.

He did know she wasn't hard on the eyes. The small dimple that creased with every smile intrigued him more than it should have. For that matter, when he managed to coax one of her smiles, he felt as if he'd accomplished something pretty special.

Just her luck. *Dat* was standing in front of the house when they pulled up, his sturdy arms crossed over his chest. By the time Gideon came around and handed her down from the wagon, her father had made his way to the road.

"You're late, daughter," he said, his voice gruff and laced with unmistakable irritation. "And what's the meaning of this?" He jerked his head toward the wagon. "Where is our buggy?"

His eyes were hard as he looked from her to Gideon.

"I'm sorry I'm so late, *Dat*, but the buggy broke down. The wheel bent and slid into a ditch, and—"

She held her breath as Gideon broke in.

"I told Emma I'd fix the wheel, Levi, but it was too cold to let her wait while I worked on it. I insisted on bringing her home."

When her father made no reply but merely kept his stony glare fixed on him, Gideon added, "I'll bring your buggy back yet today."

Levi Knepp's mouth turned down even more. "You needn't bother with the wheel. I'll send one of the boys to take care of it."

Gideon's expression didn't waver. "I don't mind, Levi. It shouldn't take all that long."

"My sons and I will see to the buggy. You've done enough by bringing my daughter home."

Emma felt shamed by her *dat*'s sharp tone and distasteful stare. Couldn't he at least acknowledge that Gideon had done her a kindness?

She turned her face away from both of them, unwilling to let her father see how angry she was with him and unwilling to look upon Gideon's almost certain humiliation.

But Gideon's response surprised her. He seemed to ignore the censure in her father's attitude. "I hope it was all right...my giving Emma a ride home. Things being what they are, it isn't safe for a young woman to be walking alone."

Emma drew in a long breath. Who could hear those words without remembering what had happened to Phoebe Esch only weeks ago?

Right on the heels of that thought came another: Gideon had called her a *young woman*! Was it possible he'd finally realized she was grown and no longer the child he remembered?

Unfortunately, *Dat* seemed unmoved by Gideon's words. "There are many dangers to our women in these troubled times. Their protection is the responsibility of their families and close friends."

Emma had to bite her tongue to keep from pointing out that families and close friends had failed to save Phoebe Esch's life and that families and close friends weren't always nearby when danger lurked. She kept her silence, knowing that any defiance on her part would only provoke her father and probably make things worse for Gideon.

She glanced quickly from one man to the other. Gideon's jaw tightened while her *dat*'s eyes remained hard and wintry. Neither uttered another word, and after a moment Gideon's eyes met hers with a look that was both knowing and gentle. Then he turned back toward the wagon and walked away.

Emma could have wept at the unfairness of it all. Finally, Gideon had taken notice of her, had treated her with attention and what seemed to be genuine interest—and her father had spoiled everything by acting as if Gideon had committed some forbidden act against her.

She sighed and started toward the house. One thing for certain: *Dat* wouldn't have to worry about Gideon Kanagy paying her any mind in the future.

4

NIGHT WATCH

What is this, that keeps watch over me
When I thought myself to be alone?

ANONYMOUS

Gant had a sparse supper, cooking for just himself with Asa having been gone the better part of three days now. He wandered outside and began walking with no particular destination in mind. It was good to just get out and exercise his still less than agile leg. Perhaps Doc was right, and the slight limp would be with him for the rest of his life. No matter. Being able to get out and around as he was doing tonight was enough. An inconvenience, but enough.

He came to a stop on the crest of the hill behind his house. He lifted the lantern a little higher, using his free hand to hike up his collar around his neck as he stood thinking.

A man who couldn't find some wonder in a night like this was either blind or numb. The November wind had blown its way down the mountains and moved on, leaving a stillness behind in which even the softest night sound seemed to echo. Fog hung heavy over the trees up here and even thicker on the valley below. Only the thinnest of the moon's light managed to squeeze its way past the clouds, spraying a fine, shimmering mist over the woods and the small settlement of Riverhaven.

From here, the smell of the river retreated, overcome by the spicy scent of pine and falling leaves and wood smoke. Every now and then the mournful sound of a boat's horn could be heard.

Gant felt a little guilty about leaving Mac back at the house. The great hound loved their nightly walks. But with Asa gone and more fugitives due to show up any day now—in addition to the runaways who arrived the night before last and were now lodged in his barn—he felt more comfortable with Mac on the premises to alert him to visitors. He'd saved him a beef bone from supper to help make up for any perceived neglect.

In any case, he should be getting back. He'd been gone long enough.

He almost always delayed going indoors after a walk, especially at night. He loved the nights here. After years of living on the crowded, noisy streets of New York and working in the nearly deafening clamor of a Brooklyn shipyard, this quiet, idyllic little river valley settlement was a balm to his spirit.

Even during the days of piloting his boat on the river, he had never known the gentle peace he'd found here in Riverhaven, the healing calm of this place that so subtly but surely nourished his soul. In this blessedly tranquil valley, he could live and work and breathe in cleanliness and purity and freedom and simply *be*.

His life had taken on a previously unknown clarity and purpose. Most days he felt nothing lacking, nothing wanting.

Except for Rachel. His want of her, his love for her, was like a raw and open sore that burned continually within, as if to remind him that his long-sought peace was a fickle, fragile thing.

He pulled in a long breath and started walking again, only to stop dead at a rustling sound somewhere behind him. He glanced up, peering into the stand of trees that lined the rise of the hill.

He waited, and the sound came again, this time with a low rumbling.

Gant stared hard into the dense fringe of woods. He saw movement, a shadow—and then the glint of eyes looking into his.

His throat went dry, and he thought to run. Instead he remained still as a stone, watching the thing that stood watching him.

If it was what he suspected, should he back off or stay as he was and make some noise? Maybe a lot of noise. But he still wasn't exactly sure what he was seeing, so he waited.

Suddenly a cloud passed across the moon just enough to give him a better look. At the same time the shadow emerged from the foliage around the trees and became real.

He'd seen wildcats before, but never one this big. It was easily forty or more pounds of muscle. Had to be a male. A *big* male. Those steady, staring eyes measured him intently, and Gant measured the cat right back. Clearly he was trying to decide whether the human creature was prey or just a nuisance.

Wildcats—*bobcats* they were called around here—weren't known for attacking people. They were more elusive and sometimes downright shy. This big fellow, however, looked anything but timid.

He could also be rabid, and then all bets were off. Still, rabies was rare among the big cats. Gant held the lantern up and out a little, not liking the way it flickered from the slight trembling of his hand. It was too dark to tell much about the creature other than his intimidating size. His coat looked to be gray with dark spots. He would be fairly young because the spots hadn't faded yet. Black bars wrapped his forelegs like mourning bands.

The cat gave another low growl, but somehow Gant didn't feel threatened. The sound seemed almost halfhearted, as though he'd been judged and deemed not worthy of any real attention. He wouldn't have been surprised if the creature had yawned at that point. Clearly, he was a lot more impressed with the cat than the cat was with him. And despite that menacing stare, Gant did find him impressive. He was an intimidating but handsome animal.

He had the oddest feeling the animal was waiting for him to leave. After another moment, and keeping the lantern high and well in front of him, he started to back away. Slow steps, carefully, quietly, taking his time. The cat's gaze held steady, watching his every move.

Finally, when he was almost convinced the creature wasn't going to lunge and run him to the ground, Gant turned his back on the cat and started down the hill toward the house. He resisted the urge to turn and look back, intent on feigning indifference.

Unnerved and still a bit shaken from the encounter, he wasted no time going inside and throwing the bolt on the back door, inordinately glad for Mac's loud and eager greeting.

"Make all the noise you want, pal," he said, stooping to rub the big hound's ears. "We've got company out there, and I'd just as soon he knows I'm not alone."

He straightened and went to get the beef bone he'd left on the stove after supper. With Mac watching his every move, Gant put the bone on the rug by the back door and gave a nod, at which point the dog licked it indifferently a few times as if to show a lack of interest. Only when Gant walked over to the sink and began washing the supper dishes did the hound snatch up the bone in his powerful jaws and begin to attack it.

When the dishes were done, Gant was still too keyed up to sleep. He took his fiddle out of the cabinet and played for a solid hour. He stopped twice to listen for any sound coming from outside, but he heard nothing. Yet somehow he sensed their visitor hadn't moved on.

Later that night Gant heard its screech. From his place beside the bed, Mac stirred and gave a low growl. The chilling sound clearly came from somewhere close by, yet Gant felt no real threat at the cat's presence.

He lay completely still, listening, but it didn't call out again. Finally, he fell into a fitful, restless sleep, only to dream about a creature with a large, whiskered face and black-tufted ears pacing back and forth on the hill behind the house, keeping watch.

→5←

MISSING RACHEL

I had a beautiful friend
And dreamed that the old despair
Would end in love in the end.

W.B. YEATS

By four o'clock Gant gave up trying to sleep. He'd tossed and twisted for hours, so he decided he might just as well make some coffee and start work early.

Mac stirred and lifted his head with a grumpy look as Gant lighted the lantern. "No need for you to get up too, lazybones. Go on back to sleep."

The big dog needed no coaxing. With a somewhat exaggerated sigh, he turned over and was snoring again before Gant was out of the room.

In the kitchen, he set the lantern on the table and looked out the window. There was nothing to be seen. No doubt their night visitor was long gone. All the same, he didn't step outside the door to brace his lungs with cold air as he usually did first thing in the morning.

He wasn't hungry, so he settled for a leftover biscuit and a hot cup of coffee for breakfast. Later he'd need to take some food out to the runaways in the barn. Maybe he'd fix something more for himself then.

He sat idly at the table, drinking his coffee and wondering what had kept him sleepless for most of the night. Surely not the bobcat. He should pose no real problem, after all. And even if he hadn't moved on by now, he probably wouldn't come any closer to the house or the barn. Not if he was a typical cat.

And if he wasn't typical?

Gant shook off the thought. He'd been in a strange mood for a couple of days now. Restless. On edge. Even a little jumpy. His imagination seemed to be working overtime, and last night was no exception. Something about the cat had spooked him, as though the creature was out of the ordinary.

He'd been alone too much lately. That must be it. Not that he'd ever much minded being alone. Most of the time he preferred it. He'd always been a loner, guarding his privacy and feeling far more comfortable with himself than in a crowd. But being alone didn't always mean being lonely. At least it never used to.

Too often of late though, his state of mind bordered on loneliness. For one thing, until recently, Asa had been around more than usual. But now with Asa somewhere near Zanesville, familiarizing a new conductor with the territory and several of the safe houses, Gant felt his absence. Then too, he gave Gideon a day or two off every now and then to do some extra work out at his mother's place, so at times the shop was quieter than normal.

Well, Asa would be back soon, and so would Gideon. Then there would be a bit more life about the place.

Of course, if he were to be completely honest with himself, he knew it was Rachel who really accounted for his melancholy these days. When the loneliness moved in on him, as it often did lately, Rachel was the one he wanted to be with. Sometimes her absence felt like a weight crushing his spirit; other times like a cold, black night heavy with rain. He missed her and wanted to be with her every minute of every day. At times the missing made him ache as if he carried a fever.

Thinking about Rachel inevitably led to the thought that the new bishop would soon be chosen—a thought that never failed to make his heart race. The harder he tried not to think about what this change in the Amish community might mean for Rachel and him, the more he couldn't tear his mind away from it.

If the two of them would ever have a chance to be together, this would most likely be it. Should a new bishop approve his conversion, the door would be open to the possibility of their marriage. Beyond that...he refused to let himself speculate.

But the waiting was hard. And worrisome. Especially knowing that one of the men to be considered as bishop was Samuel Beiler.

He started to take another sip of coffee but found his cup empty. For a time he sat staring at the flickering lantern on the table, but finally he got up and headed for the shop.

While it was still dark, Mac sauntered into the shop and stood watching Gant as if waiting for their usual morning routine to begin.

"I suppose you want your breakfast," Gant said without looking at him as he tightened the bench vise a little more.

Out of the corner of his eye he saw the big hound's tail start wagging.

"All right, then," he said after a moment. "We'll tend to you first. Then we need to get our visitors fed."

He was almost finished planing Web Brighton's cabinet door, but he decided to feed Mac and the folks in the barn first. The door would wait. Hungry stomachs shouldn't have to.

"Okay, chum," he said, wiping his hands. "Back to the kitchen."

Later, Mac followed him to the barn, no doubt lured by the aroma of the fried ham and biscuits Gant had packed in the basket. "You just ate, you big oaf. Don't expect to filch any of this."

The dog continued to press himself as close as possible to Gant, keeping a sharp eye on the food basket all the way. "And stop drooling. I told you, you've had your share. No more. These folks are hungry. You can't possibly be."

The hour before sunup was cold with a heavy mist. Gant continued to dart glances toward the hillside at his left and the road in the distance to his right, carrying his lantern low and close. He was far enough removed from the road that he didn't worry much about anyone watching him. Even so, you never knew when there might be slave catchers in the area, keeping an eye out for runaways and those who harbored them. And the bobcat was never far from his mind.

At the barn, he set the basket down just long enough to unbolt the door.

"No," he warned Mac when the dog brought his nose a bit too close.

The hound checked out his owner as if to make certain he meant business, and then he stood at attention until Gant picked up the basket and motioned Mac to follow.

Inside, the barn smelled of hay and leather harnesses. Flann, the big ginger-red gelding, roused and puffed at the sight of Gant and the dog. "I'll feed you in a minute, fella. Be patient."

Gant started with the basket to the people at the far corner of the barn, glancing back once at Mac and the gelding, who stood watching each other. The two seemed to have struck up an odd kind of friendship in which no audible conversation was necessary. They clearly enjoyed each other's company. Even when Gant hung the lantern on a pole and set the basket of food on the log table he'd rigged for the runaways, Mac made no move to leave his station by Flann's stall. Apparently he'd finally accepted that there would be no seconds on breakfast this morning.

The family perched against the wall—a young black man called Nate, his wife, and their small son—had obviously been waiting for him. As soon as the lantern cast its light into the corner, they clambered to their feet.

The woman, named Mercy, rubbed the sleep from her eyes and then helped Gant empty the contents of the food basket. "Oh, my, Cap'n Gant, this be a feast!" Immediately she put food in front of her little boy and helped him eat.

Her husband held back, his gaze intent on Gant rather than the food. "Any word yet, Cap'n?" he asked, rubbing his hands together as if they ached.

Gant shook his head. "Nothing yet. But don't worry. You're safe here for now. It won't be long until you'll be leaving. Just as soon as Asa gets back."

"This Asa—he your overseer?"

Gant looked at him. "I don't have an overseer, Nate. There's no plantation, not even a farm. I'm just a carpenter with a shop, where I work. Asa is a friend and one of the men who'll be helping you on your trip north."

Nate nodded, but Gant could see that he was still on edge, still concerned for his family's safety. And why wouldn't he be? If they should be captured, they would almost certainly be brutalized. At the least, he and his wife would be beaten. They might also be separated and sold downriver. Their child might even be taken away from them.

"Heard tell you used to be a river man, Cap'n. Folks talk a lot about you. Say you used to take runaways to the north on your boat."

Folks talk too much. Gant didn't acknowledge Nate's remark one way or the other. "You'd best have your breakfast," he said. "You'll have to go down below before sunup."

With Asa's help, Gant had dug a kind of root cellar beneath the barn where runaways could hide during daylight hours, supplying it with blankets and staples and what comforts he could. But he didn't like them spending nights that far below ground. Instead, he insisted on them staying in the barn at night, where it was warmer and dryer.

Nate regarded him with a searching look but said nothing more.

Gant didn't stay with them long. Mercy's almost servile gratitude made him feel awkward. He'd always hated being dependent on anyone for anything. That a man and his family were forced to depend on others, even for their very lives, just because of their skin color, smacked of degradation. He didn't want anyone feeling beholden to him for what was nothing more than simple human decency. It wasn't right.

He'd felt that same discomfort often, from his early days as a conductor transporting runaway slaves on his boat, right up to today. He detested being the recipient of another human being's feelings of indebtedness. So after another brief exchange of questions and answers, he left the barn.

By ten o'clock that morning Gant had finished Web Brighton's cabinet door and started the rocking chair Ben Roberts had ordered for his mother's birthday. He was in the back washing up a little when he heard the bell over the door chime.

Strange. Mac was in front but had made no sound. He usually alerted Gant to someone's entrance.

Still drying his hands, he walked into the shop to find Doc Sebastian standing just inside the entrance, his hat in hand and a broad grin on his face as he rubbed Mac's ears.

By now, Gant considered Doc as thoroughly "Amishized," having converted and married Rachel's mother, Susan Kanagy, a few weeks past. These days he sported an Amish man's beard and the dark, plain clothing of the People.

Gant had finally grown accustomed to Doc's change in appearance, gradual as it had been. In fact, it seemed to suit him, just as most everything about the Amish lifestyle seemed to be a comfortable fit for his friend.

"Well, it seems I made fresh coffee just in time." Gant motioned him toward the back of the shop and then told Mac to stay. "So how was your trip to Baltimore?"

"Couldn't have been any better," Doc said, following Gant to the back room. "I particularly enjoyed Susan's reaction to the train."

Gant poured Doc a cup of steaming coffee and another for himself. "That's right. You said she'd never ridden one before. What did she think of it?"

"She loved it." Doc shrugged out of his coat and sat down at the small table where Gant usually ate his noon meal. "Oh, she was a little on edge at first, but that didn't last long. Her eyes were fairly popping most of the way. I think she enjoyed herself immensely."

"And your family? Everyone doing well?" Gant sat down across from him.

Doc nodded. "The new baby arrived two days after we did. A little girl. Susan was beside herself. She'd been hoping all along we'd be there for the birth."

"Did you deliver her?"

"I assisted. My daughter-in-law and Susan did most of the work without much help from me." He took a sip of coffee. "Speaking of babies, how's the Sawyer infant coming along? Have you seen her?"

Gant smiled a little as the image of wee Naomi Fay came into his mind. "She seems to be thriving. Growing fast."

"And Mrs. Sawyer? How is she?"

"Doing all right, I think. She stays busy in the restaurant and keeps the baby with her. You're going to call on them soon, I expect?"

Doc looked at him, and Gant said, "I forgot. You won't be doctoring anymore outside the community."

"And even there, on a limited basis only," Doc said, his expression sobering. "Nothing really too different about that, of course. A large number of my patients have always come from the People. But now it seems I'll be practicing primarily among the men and children."

Gant frowned. "That's something new, isn't it?"

Doc Sebastian had been a friend and physician to the Amish for years, but after his conversion, Bishop Graber ruled that, although the doctor could continue his practice among the People, he would have to give up his patients in the outside world. The Amish would be his only patients.

Doc didn't seem to mind all that much. Gant supposed he would have given up just about anything to marry Susan.

Gant understood that feeling well enough. Had the bishop allowed him to convert and marry Rachel, he would have given up everything he owned. That hadn't changed. Unfortunately, neither had the prohibition against his conversion.

"Not really. I've been expecting it," Doc said, drawing Gant back to his surroundings. "I'm perfectly fine with it, actually. Susan has assisted at a number of births and a few emergencies among the women over the years. If the situation warrants it and a woman prefers her to an *Englisch* doctor, why not? She's had plenty of experience. She's more than capable of helping out. And we may soon have a new doctor in town."

"You've found someone?"

Doc had been sending out letters over the past few weeks in search of a doctor who might want to take over his *Englisch* practice. "I believe I've found just the fellow. I've invited him to come and look us over, so we'll see if he's interested. He's supposed to visit not long after Christmas."

"Well, it didn't take you long to find someone."

"Actually, if this fellow doesn't decide for us, it could take quite a while. Small town, fairly isolated...no one's going to get rich here." He stopped. "Except for clever carpenters, of course."

Gant ignored the jibe. "Sounds as though all that should work to his patients' advantage, if not his. At least it's a safe bet he wouldn't be setting up practice to make big money."

"Quite."

Doc spun his hat around on his index finger for a few seconds and then looked up. "So...any news since we've been away?"

Gant didn't have to think long. "Seems as though some of the vandalism might be moving closer into town."

Doc frowned. "How so?"

"Fred Scott found two of his chickens dead outside the coop the other day. Somebody wrung their necks in the night."

"You mean they just left them there?"

Gant nodded.

"Obviously not someone looking for food then. Just meanness. Sounds like youngsters to me."

"That's what I thought too. At least that's what I'd like to think. But who knows?"

"Yes, who knows?" Doc sighed. "Anything else happen?"

Gant thought for a moment. "Nothing like that. I had an interesting visitor last night though."

"Oh?"

"Bobcat. On the hill behind the house. Got a pretty good look at him."

"That's a bit unusual, isn't it? Don't they typically stay out of sight?"

"That's been my experience. But this fella didn't seem too shy about checking me out."

"Best stay your distance. They're strictly meat eaters, you know," Doc said, his tone light.

Gant pulled a face. "But not human meat."

"So far as you know."

"Aye, so far as I know."

"Well, I'd best be on my way," Doc said. "Oh…Susan said she'll expect you for supper one evening soon."

"Just say when. Can't be too soon to please me."

"I told her you'd be hard to convince. So how does Friday sound?"

"Hadn't you better ask her first?"

"I can't think why. She cooks enough for a barn raising with every meal."

Gant grinned in anticipation. "Friday it is then."

After Doc left, he fell into wondering if Rachel might be at Friday night's supper. She was Susan's daughter, after all. It wouldn't be all that unusual for her to join them, would it?

On the other hand, Rachel seemed set on avoiding him most of the time. He was beginning to wonder if it was altogether because she was attempting to obey the bishop's stipulation that they not spend any time in each other's company, or if she was deliberately trying to cut herself out of his life because of the seeming hopelessness of their situation.

He hoped that wasn't the case. If Rachel truly felt that a future together was hopeless entirely, it would only make it that much more difficult for him to believe otherwise, and it was hard enough already to keep a remnant of hope alive.

Still, he wasn't about to give up. Not yet. Maybe not ever.

6

THE MAN WHO WOULD BE BISHOP

I know myself a man,
Which is a proud, and yet a wretched thing.

JOHN DAVIES

Samuel Beiler knew he shouldn't want to be bishop.

Most men would lament the idea, groaning at the very thought. The responsibility was overwhelming—a burden to dread, not to covet. But in his secret heart of hearts, Samuel admitted that he did want the office. Badly.

He stood in front of the barn, studying his white two-story house and surrounding field. It was that quiet time of evening when the daylight was almost gone but darkness not quite settled. Somewhere in the distance a dog barked. The tree branches, November bare, cracked and whispered as the light wind lifted them.

Was it really so wrong, this wanting, this wish to be leader of the community in which God had placed him? After all, any Amish man baptized in the faith had to be willing to become a minister or even a bishop, should the lot one day fall on him. Still, it was a heart-heavy, serious responsibility and a lifetime commitment. No doubt if others knew he actually wanted the position, they would look on him with doubt or, more likely, disapproval or distrust.

That was for them to deal with. Truth was, few men among them were strong enough to be a good bishop. He could count on one hand the number fit for leadership.

A man must possess strength of character and discernment, and he must follow faithfully after the Lord God. As it was, only two other men besides himself were eligible to participate in the lot: Abe Gingerich and Malachi Esch. Both were good men, but Abe was slow and plodding, not a man to make insightful or even wise decisions. And Malachi, while an intelligent and physically strong man, was, in Samuel's estimation, too lenient with the People and sometimes negligent of tradition.

He suspected some would say that he was too young—and the fact of the matter was that he would be a young bishop. Others might point out that he was a widower and not presently a married man, but that would change soon enough once Rachel came to her senses.

And if she did not...well, he would make it his business to put an end to her dithering once and for all. When he took over as bishop, he would insist that she bend to his will and his judgment. She would be under his authority and subject to his decisions.

The next bishop would need to make many changes, not the least of which involved the foolish leniency some men allowed their wives and children. Amos Kanagy, for example, before his death, had been far too easy on Susan and Rachel. Indulged them to a fault, Amos had.

And just see the result. Rachel especially, with her willful ways setting a poor example for the other young women in the community. Headstrong and independent, she had developed her own business, selling her handmade birdhouses to *Englischers*. Worse still—outrageous, really—was her befriending of the *auslander*, that Gant fellow.

Everyone knew the sort of lives those river people led, lives of immorality and debauchery. Bad enough that she'd given him and his slave shelter, but to think she apparently hadn't discouraged his lust, which led him to seek conversion in order that they might marry.

Fortunately, Bishop Graber had refused the man's request.

Not that the bishop was without fault for some of the lapses in conduct and good judgment on the part of the People. Here again the dangerous sin of indulgence could be blamed for a number of their young people straying to the *Englisch* world and even leaving the community altogether.

There had also been whispered rumors for some time now that a few among the People were actually helping runaway slaves to escape their owners for the freedom of the North. Outright breaking the law, they were. If Bishop Graber knew of such things, he apparently was inclined to turn a blind eye. Some made allowances for the bishop though. He was old and getting soft in the head.

All the more reason the new bishop must be a man of great strength, a man who would not compromise under any circumstances. To stop any further lapses in the faith and quell any rumbles of division within the community, the new bishop must be a man continually involved with the People and willing to deal promptly and severely with any form of misconduct.

Samuel knew himself to be such a man. For proof, anyone could look to the sons he had raised. True, Aaron had seemed bent on sowing seeds of rebellion with his *Englisch* friends on occasion. That was of course due to this *rumspringa* tradition—a foolish and dangerous practice that Samuel would put a stop to once he became bishop. *Ja*, his eldest son did try his patience, but more often than not the boy recognized his father's authority and that of the church. So far he had done nothing to get himself in any real trouble. As for Noah, his middle son, and Joe, the youngest, Samuel had all he could do not to be prideful. No man could ask for more obedient *kinner* than those two.

Of course, he had worked hard and disciplined conscientiously to develop their obedience and submission to authority. All in all, his sons were living proof that it was unwise to spare the rod when raising one's children.

As for Aaron, Samuel never doubted the boy would come around in time. He would make certain he did. He must be broken of his sour-tempered moods and stubborn ways if he were ever to become a righteous man and a leader in the community.

Rachel becoming a part of their family would be a good thing. In addition to being a fine helpmate and mother to his sons, she would naturally assume many of the chores for which the boys were now responsible. This would leave him more time to train them up while teaching Rachel the ways of their household, and it would free up the boys' time considerably so they could be of more help on the farm.

Of course with Rachel's farm and property added to his own, there would be even more work to do, but they would manage. Everything would work out. Rachel was young enough that he should have no great difficulty molding her to fit into their family and teaching her the way he liked things done. She would make a difference in all their lives.

He found himself eagerly looking forward to that difference. Any necessary discipline to rid her of her faults and gentle her character should be well worth the effort.

So much depended on his becoming bishop. Sometimes he wished the community wasn't so dependent on the draw of the lot for these decisions. Wouldn't simply appointing a bishop be a more efficient way to make certain the best man for the position were chosen?

Immediately he dismissed the thought. To desire any change in God's ways would be sinful. After all, the Lord God would recognize and select the man most fitted to carry out His will for the People's good and for His glory. Samuel's part was simply to trust and wait with patience.

Admittedly, it was the patience that presented him with the greatest challenge.

7

MUSIC IN THE NIGHT

He who hears music, feels his solitude peopled at once.

ROBERT BROWNING

At first Gant thought he must be imagining it. But this was the fourth straight night it had happened, so it could hardly be his imagination or coincidence, could it?

The week had been uncommonly warm for November—so warm he'd cracked the kitchen window while having his supper. Later, as he frequently did when he was alone and finished with the nightly chores, he took out his fiddle, sat down by the window, and played awhile.

Even though he was given to fits of melancholy when he played— usually when he was thinking of Rachel or brooding over his earlier years in Ireland—he seemed to need the music. Ever since he was a boy, something inside him had groaned for release, an escape that he could never quite identify and that had remained undiscovered until he learned to coax music from an old fiddle. From then on, the music became a kind of healing balm to his spirit.

The more he was alone, the more often he played. Cheerless, even mournful melodies. A lament. Sometimes a love song.

He knew few tunes other than those from home, from the past. The Irish seemed to own a special fondness for gloomy airs. Occasionally a brighter mood spurred him to some foolish little ditty, but this week his frame of mind had been anything but sunny. Besides, the cheerful tunes kept Mac awake. His canine companion preferred the more subtle melodies as he dozed behind the stove.

Halfway through O'Carolan's "Blind Mary," Gant stopped to tighten a string. A screech pierced the night, causing him to jerk and Mac to pull himself up with a growl. Gant recognized the bobcat's cry and gauged it to be surprisingly close. Obviously, the cat had again wandered down from the hill quite a ways, even farther than before. He had to be close to the house, as close as the woodshed.

Another cry sounded, almost like an angry protest. Again Mac growled but only halfheartedly. As on previous nights, the moment Gant hushed him, the dog settled.

To Gant, that seemed even odder than the bobcat's visits. The big dog was almost always on alert. Asa swore the hound slept with one eye open. It was as if Mac tolerated the cat's presence because he sensed no threat.

Gant took up "Blind Mary" again. And just as he expected, silence fell. He went on playing for a few minutes before coming to a halt. When he heard the cat again, his throat tightened. The sound was closer now, a deep rumbling, almost like a heightened purr. The rumble grew louder as Gant played, but each time he stopped, the cat made a sound of protest. When he began to play again, the peculiar purr rumbled on.

It had been like this every night. When Gant played, the bobcat wandered in close to the house with his eerie purr. When Gant silenced the fiddle, the cat challenged him with a low hissing sound or even a screech.

Although sorely tempted, Gant never gave in to the urge to look outside. He wasn't altogether certain whether he resisted because the sight of the cat so close in would spook him or because the sight of him might spook the cat and keep it from returning. For some unfathomable reason, he wanted the odd creature to keep coming back.

In any case, he stayed out of view.

He played for a long time while Mac slept and the cat apparently listened. Later, long after he'd gone to bed, he couldn't sleep but kept thinking about the bobcat's curious behavior. He wondered where the animal went at night when it wasn't attending Gant's serenade.

They were nocturnal, of course, these cats who lived in the wild. They roamed, sometimes for miles. He wasn't sure, but he thought it must be unusual for them to show any kind of homing instinct. If they had young nearby, the males more often than not abandoned them and their mates to roam at will.

Yet for some reason this nightly visitor seemed to have made itself at home, at least for the present, in the woods on the hill.

If bobcats could think, Gant wouldn't mind a glimpse into what was rattling about in the big fella's head.

Gant managed a couple hours of sleep before getting up at two to help Fred Scott move the runaways out of the barn and onto the wagon, which he'd stocked earlier that night. Word had come down the line for a conductor to transport Nate and his family out of Riverhaven as far as Summerfield, where Asa would take over.

He needn't have worried about keeping the three of them quiet as they prepared to leave. Nate had already instilled in his wife and son the absolute necessity of making no noise whatsoever as they boarded the wagon and lavished their thanks in hushed voices.

After waving off their appreciation and hurrying them on their way, Gant led Mac back to the house, thoroughly scanning their surroundings before going inside and locking the door. Then, as he always did, he said a prayer for the safety of the folks who had just set out on what might well be the most dangerous journey of their lives.

For a short time, he stood looking out the window into the darkness-draped night. Finally he decided to go back to bed for a while. The day had been long, and his bad leg had begun to ache.

He stared out the window another moment before following Mac to the bedroom. Perhaps it was nothing more than simple fatigue. On the other hand, it might have been the relief of being freed from the responsibility for another family of fugitive slaves. In any case, he quickly fell into a deep and dreamless sleep for the first time in several days.

8

A Not-So-Cozy Evening

Unease comes not only from the outside.

ANONYMOUS

Susan, you've fretted yourself all week about this. It's only supper, for goodness' sake! Why don't you simply go along now and ask her to come this evening?"

David Sebastian was trying hard not to lose patience with his wife's indecisiveness. "Rachel will say either yes or no, and that will be that. Why are you having such a difficult time with this?"

From her place at the kitchen sink, Susan shot him an exasperated look. "Because I don't want Rachel to misunderstand and think I'm trying to throw them together. And more to the point, I don't want Captain Gant to think it! They're not supposed to be seeing each other at all."

"They're not supposed to see each other *alone*," David pointed out. "It's acceptable for them to be friends on a casual basis."

Susan shot him a sharp look. "There is absolutely nothing casual about the feelings those two have for each other, and you know it! So it's really not acceptable."

With a deep sigh, David took one last sip of coffee and set his cup down on the table. "But having supper with us and Fannie wouldn't exactly be a clandestine meeting, now would it?" he said, his tone dry. "I believe it could be considered quite harmless."

She uttered a low sound of impatience. "You just want them to be together."

"Don't you?"

"Only if it's right! I know you and Captain Gant are good friends, and I like him a lot too, but he's still an *Englischer*, and the bishop warned them they're not to be together."

"The bishop didn't forbid them to be friends."

"David, I don't see how they can ever be just friends."

His wife's woebegone expression went right to his heart. She wanted only the best for her children, and Rachel had already suffered a great deal of pain with the loss of her young husband and later her good friend Phoebe Esch. It was only natural that Susan would want to spare her daughter any more hurt if it were within her power to do so.

He got up and went to her, taking her in his arms. "You can't protect her from everything, you know. Rachel is a woman grown. You have to let her make her own decisions."

She looked up at him. "But, David, I know she still cares for Captain Gant. I see it in her eyes every time she looks at him. Surely being with him only makes it harder for her."

David took his time answering. "Perhaps it does," he said carefully. "But Rachel has the right to decide that for herself. And besides," he went on, "it's not for us to know whether God means to keep them apart forever. That could change."

"You're thinking that whoever becomes the new bishop might give in and let Captain Gant convert after all."

"It's a possibility."

Her shoulders sagged a little. "I try not to think about it one way or the other."

He tilted her chin to make her look at him. "But we can pray about it, can't we? Pray for God's will for both of them?"

He saw her hesitation before she nodded. "*Ja*, we can pray for them. And I do. You know I do. But I tell you, David, I try my best not to wish for something that might never come about."

He searched her eyes. "You're a good mother, Susan. A good mother and a good woman."

A light stain blotted her cheeks, and she glanced away. "Don't say that, David. No one is good except the Lord God."

He put a finger to her lips. "I say what I see, Susan Sebastian," he said, giving her a playful push as he released her. "Now go along and ask Rachel to supper. I can't be idling about in your kitchen and drinking coffee all morning. I have work to do."

She still looked indecisive. "I should have asked them for dinner. It seems strange to be having our main meal in the evening instead of earlier."

"Yes, I've grown used to an earlier meal too, and I rather like it now. But we decided that this would be best. Gant has a business to run, and with Asa still gone, it's awkward for him to leave the shop in the middle of the day."

"Gideon would lock up for him."

"No doubt he would. But Gant mentioned only recently that he's had more business than both he and Gideon can handle together. I think it's good of you to accommodate him. I'm sure he appreciates it."

"I wish Gideon would come too." Her mouth tightened. "I suppose he's still seeing that *Englisch* girl, and that's why he said he had other plans."

"As it happens," David said mildly, "it seems he's not seeing her at all anymore."

"Really? And just how would you know that?"

David shrugged. "Gant mentioned it. From what he's observed, Gideon has been trying to run into the Knepp girl as often as possible."

"Really?" she said again, her eyes widening. "Emma?"

Amused by her pleased expression, David worked to stop a smile. "I don't recall the girl's first name. But I know she's Levi Knepp's daughter."

Susan gave a satisfied nod. "That would be Emma. Oh, I'm so happy to hear Gideon might be interested in her! I hope Captain Gant is right."

"You're not going to turn into one of those matchmaker mothers, are you?" David said, feigning a stern look.

"Of course not! You should know by now that Amish parents stay out of their children's business, including their courting."

"Now, Susan, Gant didn't say anything about Gideon courting the girl—"

"I know, I know." She waved off his caution. "But it sounds as though he might be interested in her. That's good news, *ja*? If he should start seeing a Plain girl, he might eventually stop living *Englisch* and come home where he belongs."

David was tempted to point out that only Gideon and God knew where the boy belonged, but he thought better of it. He enjoyed seeing her so lighthearted and didn't want to dampen her spirits. Even so, he had occasionally wondered if Gideon would ever come back to the Amish community. For the most part, the boy seemed perfectly content where he was.

After another hesitation, Susan gave her *kapp* a pat and fetched her cape from the peg by the door. "When Fannie comes in from the barn," she said on the way out, "tell her not to go wandering off. I'll want her to help me with the pies."

David stood at the window, watching her cross the field that lay between their farm and Rachel's, smiling a little at her usual brisk, purposeful stride. Susan always walked as if she were on a mission.

But then, she usually was.

The moment Rachel walked into her mother's living room, she knew she'd made a mistake by coming. What had she been thinking anyway? That she could have a nice cozy evening, just sitting around the fire with her family and her "friend" as if everything was perfectly normal and uncomplicated?

For that matter, what had Mamma been thinking, inviting her?

She hadn't been in the house five minutes before realizing this evening would be anything but normal. She could almost feel Doc and her mother and even Fannie watching her and Jeremiah to see how they were going to act around each other.

And just how *were* they to act around each other? Like old friends, casual and altogether at ease with each other's company? Or like strangers, stiff and formal and proper, barely acknowledging each other's presence? Or just plain foolish, painfully aware that if one were here, the other should be anywhere else *but* here?

Oh, if only she hadn't wanted to be with him so badly. If only she hadn't let her longing to see him again overcome her good sense!

Jeremiah was looking at her in that way he had sometimes, as if he could simply take a good long breath and swallow her up. She found it impossible to meet his gaze—and impossible not to.

She finally escaped to the kitchen, where she spent most of the time before supper pretending to help her mother with the meal even though Mamma clearly didn't need her help. As always, her mother had everything taken care of and in good order. Rachel knew she was probably more of a hindrance than a help. Still, she wasn't eager to leave the cozy confines of the kitchen.

By the time they were ready for dessert, Gant thought Rachel was feeling almost comfortable. At least she'd begun to speak a few words now and then. She'd spent the first part of the meal sitting like a frozen rabbit, not looking at him, moving only to jump up like a jack-in-the-box to get something from the kitchen.

Seated directly across from her and Fannie, Gant took advantage of the opportunity to study her as much as he pleased. Not to the point of rudeness, and not to call attention to his feelings for her, but simply to drink in the sight of her as fully as possible.

Rachel was well worth studying, after all. She had the prettiest complexion he'd ever seen on a woman—*any* woman. She virtually glowed. And even though she carefully avoided looking at him directly throughout most of the meal, her incredible dark eyes could surely make a man take leave of his senses.

Only when Doc gave a somewhat pointed clearing of his throat did Gant realize he must be waiting for a reply of some sort from him.

"Shem Miller's barn? You're going to be there, aren't you?"

"Oh…I am, sure. Shem asked if I'd lend a hand. I've got his order ready to deliver early Saturday morning, and I'll be staying after I drop it off."

"Let's hope the weather holds."

Gant had to steel himself from asking Rachel if she'd be there helping with the food. The possibility of spending an entire day in the same place with her made him almost lightheaded. He reassured himself with the reminder that she would almost certainly be there. A barn raising among the Amish typically drew every able-bodied man and woman.

Not for the first time, he was grateful for the way the Riverhaven Amish had finally, albeit gradually, accepted him as a friend. Such friendships between the Amish and the *Englisch* weren't all that common. As an *auslander*, he had been suspect for quite some time after he first charged into the community on that storm-driven night a year ago.

A stranger to the Plain People, he was a part of the very world from which the Amish had chosen to distance themselves. But he was also a *wounded* stranger, and thanks to Rachel Brenneman and her family's willingness to care for him until he regained his health, he had been allowed to remain, at first within the community and later on the edge of it. Even after moving into the town of Riverhaven and taking over the area's only carpentry business, Gant had maintained ties with some of his Amish friends.

And right or wrong, he'd also retained his affection for Rachel and her family.

Still flustered by Jeremiah's insistence on driving her home in his buggy after supper, Rachel sat as far away from him as she could manage.

Clouds hung heavy over the moon, and even though a thin ribbon of stars still dotted the night sky, the scent of rain thickened the air. They were halfway to her house before either of them finally spoke. "This isn't at all necessary, you know," she said, not looking at him. "Going out of your way when I could just as easily walk across the field."

"You shouldn't be walking about alone after dark," he said easily.

"Mamma or Doc always watch me until I get inside."

"Lot of good that would do if there was trouble," he muttered.

Now she looked at him. "Really, Jeremiah, it's not as if I live in the middle of the woods. I have neighbors. I'm quite safe."

He startled her by putting a hand to her arm. "No, Rachel—you're not. No one is safe these days. I've told you and anyone else who will listen that you shouldn't be alone. Not until there's an end to this bad business."

The intensity of his words surprised Rachel. Although the harassment of the People had begun long ago, the trouble seemed to be strictly an Amish problem. A few of their *Englisch* neighbors had expressed concern but for the most part had left the People to deal with their difficulties by themselves. She wouldn't have expected Jeremiah or any other outsider to be all that bothered by the frightening incidents occurring among the Amish.

She felt a twinge of forbidden pleasure to think that he still cared enough about her to be worried for her safety. At the same time, however, his concern seemed to sharpen her own apprehension. The idea that he was actually afraid for her somehow made the situation seem more sinister.

"I'm always careful," she muttered. Although true, the words sounded flimsy, even to her own ears.

His pressure on her arm increased. "Being careful isn't enough, Rachel. I think you know that."

She looked at him.

He eased his grip somewhat but didn't entirely drop his hand away. "A woman alone this far out of town…it's not a good situation."

Although his hand still rested on her arm, he didn't look at her.

Rachel wondered if he might be thinking of Phoebe.

Then another thought struck her, and she took advantage of the moment to change the subject. "I've been wondering about Ellie Sawyer," she said, trying to keep her tone casual. "How is she doing now?"

Jeremiah darted a quick frown at her, abruptly releasing her arm. "Ellie Sawyer?"

Rachel didn't quite meet his eyes. "Well, she's alone too. And a widow I mean…you must be concerned for her as well. I know you probably watch out for her, living as close as you do, but still…"

Rachel let her words drop away as she watched him, waiting.

He appeared confused. Or was he merely trying to conceal his interest in the attractive young widow?

"I'm sure the other boarders keep an eye on her," he said.

"But you *do*…look in on her sometimes, don't you?" Why was she pressing him like this?

He looked at her as if he might be wondering the same thing.

When he made no reply, Rachel sensed she might have taken her questions too far, so she changed the subject again. "Dr. David told us about your late-night visitor," she said lightly.

He delayed his reply, as if her quick change of mood had thrown him off guard. "My...oh, the bobcat. Aye, it seems he's made himself a regular caller, that one."

They were near the house now, and Rachel was determined to keep the rest of the conversation entirely neutral. "What does Mac think of him?"

"Well, they haven't actually met yet. I expect they'll keep their distance from each other if they ever do."

"I suppose they'd be natural enemies," she said, thinking aloud.

The sudden thrust of his arm in front of her made Rachel whip around to look at him. "What—"

Jeremiah continued to block her with his arm, shaking his head as if to silence her. He stopped the buggy with such a jolt it raked gravel and shuddered. "Did you leave your front door open?"

Rachel answered before she even looked. "Of course not! Not anymore...not since—"

He jerked his head toward the house, his jaw tight as he sat staring.

Rachel turned to look. A shadow scurried across the yard, and the heaviness of the night seemed to draw in on her with a rush.

Her front door stood open on a gaping darkness.

→ 9 ←

BEHIND THE DARKNESS

'Tis not an easy thing to see the Truth behind such heavy darkness.

UNKNOWN

Gant waited only long enough to grab his gun from under the seat before leaping down from the rig and taking the lantern from its light box.

"Stay here," he told Rachel, his voice low.

She stared at the weapon in his hand. "You still have that gun? You carry it with you, even here?"

"Stay here," he said again, starting for the porch.

Before he reached the house though, he turned and saw that she was behind him, coming at a run.

"I told you to stay with the buggy!"

"I'm not staying out here alone. And stop telling me what to do."

He looked from her to the open door. Her stubbornness exasperated him, but she had a point. There was no way to know if someone was still inside—or out here, watching them.

He shot a look toward the trees at the side of the house. There was just enough moonlight to enable him to see the barn and other outbuildings, but there was no sign of movement. He found himself wishing he'd brought Mac along tonight. The big hound heard things Gant couldn't hear and saw things he couldn't see.

He took in the open front door and the darkness it framed. He debated with himself only another second or two before passing the lantern to Rachel. "Here, take this."

Finally, taking one cautious step at a time, his glance darting in all directions as he went, he stepped inside. Rachel came right behind him, extending the lantern so they could both see by its light.

A floorboard in the narrow hallway creaked and he stopped dead, causing Rachel to bump against him. The lantern dinged, breaking the silence. She gasped, but Gant warned her to silence with a shake of his head. He tracked the hall and then the front room with the gun, left and right. His mouth was dry with the bitter taste of apprehension.

Nothing.

He caught a breath and returned to the hall. With Rachel at his back, he headed for the kitchen, only to be met by more shadows and total silence.

Watching him, Rachel shook her head, confusion still glazing her eyes. "Why would anyone break into my house? I don't have anything valuable."

Good question, and one Gant had already asked himself. And just how did they get in?

"The door was locked?"

She nodded. "I remember locking it."

He checked the front door again but found no evidence that it had been tampered with. But the door off the room at the side of the house was a different story. The moment they stepped inside Gant saw how the intruder had gained entrance. Broken glass littered the floor from a shattered window. It had been so easy. Break the window at the top of the door, reach in and turn the key in the lock.

The door stood partly ajar. Whoever had broken in hadn't bothered to completely close it upon leaving.

This was Rachel's workroom, where she made the birdhouses she sold to the *Englisch* in town. The room had been wrecked. Wood strips had been flung everywhere, paint overturned and splattered, tools ripped from the board above her worktable and tossed randomly across the floor.

Anger.

No—not just anger. Rage.

Gant could feel it. Whoever had vandalized this room had been violating Rachel.

He turned to catch her, expecting her to fly apart. Instead she made only a small whimper, like that of a wounded animal. The lantern shook in her trembling hand. Pocketing his gun, Gant reached to take the lantern from her as she stood staring in obvious bewilderment.

Her husband had built this room especially for her before his death. Gant remembered the pride and love in her eyes when she'd told him how Eli had encouraged her craft, how he'd called the little birdhouses she made with such precision and care her "art."

He set the lantern on a shelf and then turned and caught her lightly by the shoulders. "It's all right, Rachel," he murmured. "It will be all right. Tomorrow I'll put in new glass and a new lock. And I'll help you clean up."

Her gaze moved to his. "Why?" she asked, her voice choked. "Why would anyone do such a thing?"

He didn't answer, didn't voice what he was thinking. Whoever had gone to the trouble of opening the front door after breaking in at the side of the house hadn't intended to hurt her. Just frighten her.

He continued to hold her for another moment, assuring her again that they would fix everything the next day and do a thorough cleanup. "We'll have everything back together in no time," he said. "You'll see."

Gently, he released her and again picked up the lantern. "I need to check the rest of the house. Why don't you wait down here for me?"

He tried again to get her to wait, but she wouldn't hear of it. On the way upstairs he took the steps two at a time but quietly, Rachel keeping up with him.

At the landing he stopped dead. Something turned in his mind. The feeling of someone in the house changed to a sense of nothingness. The house itself seemed to echo that it was alone, that whoever might have earlier stalked through its wide rooms and silent darkness was now gone.

A breathless quiet hung over the upstairs. Rachel came alongside him, her eyes still dazed with a combination of shock and questions. He squeezed her arm lightly but said nothing, continuing his search of the upstairs bedrooms until he was absolutely certain they were alone.

Downstairs again, he felt his pulse slow, but he didn't dare relax. He wasn't about to be caught off guard. Rachel stood watching him, and he tried to give her a reassuring smile, but it fell apart before he could say anything.

She was so hurt, so clearly baffled. Watching her, seeing her usually tranquil features pinched with fearfulness and pain, Gant again felt the gnawing, corrosive anger swell inside him. He bit down hard on the urge to release the fury burning inside him by smashing his fist into a wall or shouting. He knew that a display of anger would do nothing but upset Rachel even more.

He had to stay in control. For the most part, he had learned to suppress the rage that sometimes built up in him. He had seen too much trouble handled by fists and clubs in Ireland and on the docks of New York. But sometimes…sometimes when least expected, his own temper reminded him he wasn't immune from the same kind of destructive fury that fired others.

There had been a time when he thought little of settling his own conflicts with physical prowess, and he had even found a certain pleasure in using his strength and powerful size to put down an opponent. But Asa had led him to a different place, a place where Gant came to realize that the Christian way of resolving conflict wasn't with brutal confrontation, and that the measure of a man's character had nothing to do with physical strength or endurance.

Asa had taught him that a man of real strength could take a stand or make a point or settle a difference without ever lifting a hand against another human being.

"The real strength of a man," Asa told him, "is in the peace he fosters and the grace he offers."

Through the years, Gant had tried never to forget his friend's words. Asa was that kind of man, the kind of man Gant wanted to be, the kind of man he tried to be. It struck him in that instant that it was also the way of the Amish men he had come to respect.

"Jeremiah?"

Rachel's soft, questioning voice snapped him back to their surroundings. "Come on," he said, "let's get you back to your mother's."

She glanced away, looked around as if trying to figure what to do. "No, I—"

"Rachel," he said quietly but firmly, "you know you absolutely cannot stay here tonight."

Again she looked away and then back. Finally, she gave a small nod. "*Ja.* You're right." She stopped. "But the house...anyone could come in—"

"The house will be all right. This is over now."

Over for tonight maybe, but not over.

"I told you...I'll come out tomorrow and fix the door. For the next few days you can stay at your mother's, or I'll give Gideon the time off so he can stay here with you."

The tight set of the mouth he'd come to recognize as her signature of stubbornness appeared. "No, there's no need for that—"

"Rachel," he said, his tone harder as he took her arm, "it's getting late. Let's go before we have to wake up Doc and your mother."

For just an instant it seemed that she would argue, but Gant arched a brow, waiting. After another moment she silently gave in and started for the door.

Rachel carried the lantern to the buggy. Gant kept the gun drawn with one hand and a firm grip on her arm with the other. Once, a feeling of being watched snaked through him, a feeling of someone possibly standing offside, enjoying what he had just put them through. He increased his pressure on her arm, propelling her to the buggy. After what he had just seen in the house, he felt a weight of genuine fear for her.

The Amish represented easy prey for vandals. They seldom locked their doors and were known pacifists, not given to returning the wrongs inflicted on them with violence of their own. Still, he couldn't shake the feeling that what had happened here tonight was more than the random work of an ordinary vandal. He was convinced it was personal, an ugly act perpetrated against Rachel herself for some reason.

For now though, he wouldn't think about that. Later, when he was alone and Rachel couldn't see how troubled he actually was, he would give it more thought. The only thing that mattered at this moment was getting her out of harm's way and keeping her safe.

A Cry on the Mountain

...and the dark wind brings
his lonely human cry.

Thomas Boyd

After taking Rachel back to Doc and Susan's place, Gant returned to the woods across from Rachel's house.

He found a small clearing nestled in the midst of a thick grove of pine trees and parked the buggy where he would be well-hidden and yet able to watch the house. He didn't really expect the night's intruder to come back, but in case he did, he intended to be ready for him.

The few stars that had brightened the sky earlier in the evening were gone now, obscured by a range of clouds that pressed low. It would rain soon. Gant was glad for the heavy blanket he carried in the buggy and the oilcloth he'd tossed in just before leaving town.

He had said nothing to Rachel about what he planned to do the rest of the night. She would have made a fuss had she known. At least he thought she'd fuss.

Or was he being too optimistic or unjustifiably smug that she cared enough to worry about him?

Again he wished he had brought Mac along. The big hound was surprisingly good company and intimidating in his own right. One encounter with that fierce, strong-jawed head and the low, menacing growl could put a healthy dose of fear into even the nastiest no-good out there.

He jumped when scattered pine needles behind him crunched, but he settled when he realized the sound was too subdued to belong to anything bigger than a 'coon or a stray dog. And when the distant cry of one of the big cats on the mountain broke the night stillness, he shrugged it off. Couldn't be *his* cat, not this far out.

Finally, with a heavy sigh, he retrieved the blanket from the floor and hunkered down for the duration.

"*Kumm rei*," Rachel said, her voice soft.

Her mother opened the door, waiting a moment before stepping inside. "Rachel? I just wanted to make sure you're all right before I go to bed."

"I am, Mamma. I'm fine."

In truth, she wasn't, but Rachel didn't want her mother to know how upset she still was. Her own night would almost certainly be sleepless, but her mother's didn't need to be.

"It's *gut* Captain Gant was with you tonight," Mamma said, coming to sit beside her on the bed and taking her hand.

Rachel hesitated and then nodded. "*Ja*, I was grateful for his help."

"He's a kind man."

It was one of her mother's most often repeated comments about Jeremiah. In truth, it was a remark frequently applied to him by many of the People. Outsider though he was, he had come to be liked and respected by those who knew him. Had he not been an *Englischer*, no one in their Amish community would have been likely to frown on her marriage to Jeremiah.

But he was *Englisch* and therefore *verboten*.

They could be friends only. Even then they weren't supposed to be alone together. But if they hadn't been together tonight, how would she have dealt with the ugly scene that had awaited her at her house? To have faced it by herself…

She shuddered. Her mother, obviously sensing her distress, clasped her hand more tightly. "Oh, daughter, I'm sorry this happened to you! But I'm so grateful to Captain Gant for bringing you here. You mustn't stay alone anymore, Rachel—not until all this trouble is finally over. You will stay with David and me until then."

"I can't do that, Mamma. I have to take care of my house and my animals. I have things that need doing every day, and with Christmas coming I have pending orders for my birdhouses—"

"David and I will help you see to your work," her mother broke in. "But I won't hear of you staying alone at night, Rachel. Not after what just happened."

As much as Rachel dreaded even the idea of being alone right now, she knew she couldn't do what her mother was asking. Mamma and Dr. David were just beginning their new life together as husband and wife. They had their own home to maintain, their own lives to live. No, she couldn't, she wouldn't intrude on their marriage. They were so happy together. She would do nothing to interfere with that happiness.

She covered Mamma's hand with her own. "Let's not worry about that tonight. We both need to get some sleep. I'll be all right, Mamma. Really, I will."

Her mother searched her eyes, finally releasing her hand and getting to her feet. "You're right, of course. But first thing tomorrow we'll talk with David—and Gideon, if he's here—and work things out so you won't be alone, at least until all this trouble is finally over. Are you sure you'll be able to rest now?"

Rachel stood, taking her mother by the shoulders. "I'm sure. I'm really tired, and I know you are too. You go on to bed. I'll be just fine."

She watched as Mamma closed the bedroom door, listening until the sound of her footsteps died away at the end of the hall before sitting down again on the bed.

"Until all this trouble is finally over..."

Would it ever be over? What was it going to take for the People to finally be free of the harassment, the malice, the evil that seemed to be creeping in on them more and more, like a poisonous mist, threatening their community, their peace, their very lives?

Who was responsible for the other cruel acts that had occurred long before the breaking and entering of her house tonight—the barn fires, the theft of Mamma's horses, and all the other hateful deeds, including the attack on Fannie and Phoebe Esch's death?

True, Dr. David said Phoebe had most likely died of a heart attack and that her death might have been accidental. But he made no secret of the fact that he believed it had been brought on by fear, given Phoebe's disappearance and the condition in which they'd found her that awful night.

Rachel thought she could understand that kind of fear. She remembered all too vividly how frightened she'd been the night she and Eli were attacked, the night he was beaten to death.

And tonight...what if she had been at home when the intruder broke in? She hated to think about how terrified she surely would have been. The very thought made her cringe.

Was all this the work of one person? Her memory flashed back to the day Fannie had been attacked by a group of *Englischer* boys on the road not far from home. In the middle of the day, that was! They had always believed what happened to her younger sister to be the work of a rowdy group of boys, just a prank gone bad that could have ended up as a terrible tragedy if Jeremiah hadn't come upon the scene to rescue her.

Jeremiah. How often he appeared when help was needed. Rachel had heard the rumors that perhaps the *auslander* appeared *too* conveniently, that perhaps he was the one behind the trouble.

She didn't believe that for a minute. True, Jeremiah was a big man with a powerful way and an air of authority about him, but she knew in her deepest heart that he was also a kind and gentle man who would never hurt anyone or anything if he could help it.

She was thankful that those rumors finally seemed to have died. Even the few among the People who might have kept the vicious tales alive had apparently grown tired of the gossip and gone on to other murmurings and far-fetched ideas.

She sighed and with an effort got to her feet. A few minutes later, while she was changing for bed, she heard the soft splashing of rain against the windows and on the roof. Somehow the sound intensified the lonely ache stirring deep within her.

It was the same feeling she experienced each time she had to part from Jeremiah.

❖

Gant grumbled under his breath at the rain just beginning to fall. Of course, it might not be such a bad night so long as the wind didn't turn wild. On the other hand, on this kind of November night in Ohio, the wind most likely would rise. In preparation, he closed the flaps on the buggy. He reached down and touched the oilcloth. He'd want it handy if he had to get out in the rain.

Given the weather, it wasn't likely that Rachel's intruder or intruders would come back yet tonight. Even so, he intended to stay put.

Who was the intruder? Or who were *they*?

It occurred to him that he'd seldom been inclined to think in terms of "they." His mind had latched onto the likelihood that one person was behind the harassment of the Amish, and he couldn't seem to shake loose of his original conviction. Yet wasn't it likely that more than one was responsible, especially when it came to the death of Phoebe Esch? Could one person have managed to terrorize the poor woman into a heart attack? That was what Doc was convinced had happened.

Well, he supposed anything was possible. But likely?

He shook his head to clear it and rubbed a hand down his neck. In spite of being strung tight by Rachel's bad business earlier, he was tired. He didn't want to doze off.

Somewhere on the mountain behind him a cat screeched again. Closer this time. Strange. It almost sounded like *his* cat—the bobcat.

He *was* tired. Bobcats might be nocturnal, but he seriously doubted one would travel so far out in this kind of weather. Still, they did like to wander...

After a moment, he caught himself nodding off. He jolted awake, straightened, eased his shoulders, and yawned.

The cat screamed again, and a chill crept down his spine.

Sure, and it sounded like his cat.

Suddenly he caught a faint glimmer of light. Off to the side of Rachel's house, toward the back of her property, it flickered and then disappeared.

He watched, his eyes trained on the spot where he'd seen it.

Nothing.

The stand of oaks near her house could barely be seen. The night was one vast sheet of veiled darkness, a barren land braced for the first cold grip of winter.

His hand covering the gun on the seat beside him, Gant continued to keep watch as best he could through the pelting rain, but whatever he'd seen never reappeared.

He drew a deep breath and suppressed a cough, clearing his throat against the cold dampness.

It was going to be a long night.

A NEW STRATEGY

"Good-bye," I said to my conscience—
"Good-bye for aye and aye,"
And I put her hands off harshly,
And turned my face away.

PAUL LAURENCE DUNBAR

The watcher doused his lantern, peering from beneath his hat into the woods across from Rachel Brenneman's house, but what with the darkness and the rain splashing off his hat, he could see nothing.

Had Gant seen him? Of course not. Not with the rain. And it was too dark. But what about the light from the lantern?

The minute he saw Gant pull into the woods, he cursed his own lack of foresight. He hadn't expected the man to return after taking Rachel to her mother's house. Instead he'd thought to have the rest of the night to complete what he'd begun.

Twice in the same night now, the outsider had thrown a halt into his plans. He had barely had time to get out of the house and run for cover when Gant and Rachel pulled up front. Another minute or two and they would have caught him. And now, instead of going back to town after setting Rachel off, here Gant was again, this time by himself.

Fine pot of stew this was.

Might have known. Even if nothing much was said about it, everybody knew Gant was still sweet on Rachel. If the man caught anyone poking around her house, much less making a mess of things, there was no telling what he'd do. He was a big, strong type, and even though he apparently had Rachel and a few others fooled into thinking he was a good enough sort, he had a look about him that bespoke a mean streak if he should be riled.

Well, he hadn't been caught, and that was all that mattered. Not that it had ever been that much of a possibility. A big fellow like Gant wouldn't be fast enough on his feet to run him down. Besides, this wasn't about any face-to-face dealings with Gant, but about showing the People that the outsider had brought trouble upon them all when he arrived in Riverhaven and that he would bring even more if he stayed around.

Gant had to go. Unfortunately, from the looks of things, he had no intention of leaving. He was of no mind to leave Rachel. For sure, he wasn't the type to be scared off. No, the People needed to realize that having him around was only making their problems worse, that he was unable or unwilling to help them.

It was taking longer than he'd expected though. He hadn't counted on the People taking up with the man. He had thought that because Gant was a stranger from the outside world, they would distrust him and keep him a good distance away. Instead, some seemed to have taken a liking to him, even to the point of making friends with him.

Including Rachel and her family.

For the second time he heard a wildcat cry from somewhere on the mountain. He shuddered at the sound. He hated those creatures and their sly, sneaky ways.

There had been no movement from the other side of the road for several minutes now, no sign that Gant had seen him. He decided he'd waited long enough.

Clutching his coat more tightly around him against the rain, he started off for home, moving quietly and slowly until he had passed far enough away from the house that Gant couldn't spot him. As he slogged through the wet leaves, he began to recognize some of the mistakes he had made. At the same time, a solution gradually began to unravel.

What he needed now was a whole new strategy.

That was it—a new *strategy*. He liked that word. It meant he had a smart and well-thought-out plan to accomplish his goal. Maybe he had taken a few wrong turns, but that didn't mean he ought to give up. There were other ways. Already, ideas were beginning to form.

After all, the goal all along had been to get rid of Gant. With him gone, Rachel would be free. Her mind would no longer be clouded by confusion and wrong choices. She would be able to make the decisions that were best for her.

And eventually that would make things a whole lot better for *him*.

NEW ARRIVALS

Nobody else can do the work
That God marked out for you.

PAUL LAURENCE DUNBAR

The next Monday Gant reluctantly admitted to himself that he wasn't as young as he liked to think he was.

After putting in several hours at the shop each day during the past week, except for Sunday, he'd spent almost as much time working at Rachel's house alongside Gideon and Doc. By bedtime every night he was more tired than he should have been and newly convicted that he needed to get more exercise from now on. Or at least not to spend so much time sitting on the shop bench while he worked.

The bright side was that he slept so deeply each night that a buffalo stampede wouldn't have roused him. The not-so-bright side had to do with the spasms that seized his bad leg when he least expected them. Like well-placed hammer blows, the pain ricocheted from his hip down to his ankle, threatening to take him to his knees.

Tonight he was working late again, but he'd finished up what needed doing at Rachel's that morning, so maybe from now on his days would be a little shorter and less tiring.

Besides cleaning up the workroom and repairing the damage, he'd replaced the glass in the broken window and repaired the frame. He also installed a new, sturdier lock and a sliding metal bar to the front and back doors and repainted them. Some of the shelves that held supplies for the birdhouses had never been properly sanded or painted, so he took time to finish them and set everything back in place after they dried.

He was bent over the lathe, plying the treadle as he finished the last leg for Mylon Baker's dining room table when someone knocked at the back door. Mac, dozing nearby, shot to his feet and gave a short bark.

Gant stopped and listened. When the knock came again, he wiped his hands and started for the rear of the shop with Mac following him.

"Who's there?"

There was a delay, then, "A friend of friends."

The voice was low and sounded hoarse.

Gant hesitated only a moment before opening the door, edging Mac a little to the side. The figure standing in front of him was slight as a boy, but the dark expression that held Gant's attention was that of a man—grim, weary, and skeptical. He had the kind of skin that looked to be stretched tight across his face, with cheekbones like knife blades and a mouth set in a hard line.

"What can I do for you?" said Gant, caught off guard by the other's appearance and demeanor. This one was a different sort of runaway altogether. Moreover, for just a fleeting moment he looked vaguely familiar.

"I'm looking for Captain Gant."

Gant regarded him with interest. "You've found him."

The man—or was he a boy?—let his coat, a full two sizes too large, fall open a bit as he fumbled in his pocket and withdrew a piece of badly wrinkled paper. He thrust it at Gant, who didn't miss the hunting knife tucked behind the other's belt.

On the paper was a hastily scrawled note from Eldon Turner—cryptic, but words Gant understood: "Arrangements made for delivery. If practical, ship materials within the week. This being such a large order, could use some able-bodied help as we're shorthanded right now."

So Turner would be the next stop down the line, and he'd be expecting the runaways to leave Gant's within two days.

Gant met the boy's eyes. "How many are you?"

"Eleven, with myself."

Eleven. And all on foot, from what he could see. That's why Turner had suggested more than one conductor and hinted at the need for two wagons instead of one. He looked past the boy to the others huddled in the darkness a few feet behind him, looking around as if they expected to be ambushed at any minute.

He could only pray Asa would be back in time with the extra wagon and team. Gideon could drive one wagon, if he were willing, and Asa the other. Of course, with both Gideon and Asa gone, he'd be alone in the shop again, but there was nothing else for it. He wanted no more overcrowding in one wagon, the way things had been until recently. It was just too hard on the people, cramped together like that. There'd even been talk of some runaways dying due to such wretched transportation conditions.

But if Asa didn't get back in time—well, there was nothing to do but wait. It wouldn't be the first time. He wasn't about to send this boy off on his own with that many fugitives.

"All right, then," he said. "I'll take you out to the barn. Everything you need is out there. You'll have to stay below ground in the daytime. You can be up on the ground floor at night, at least for a short time. It's best to take turns. We can't risk someone coming by and seeing you or hearing you. I'll bring you some food as soon as I get it together."

He stopped, looking at the boy, who had moved slightly to one side. The light from inside revealed a faint scar running down the side of one cheekbone to the corner of his mouth.

"And if I were you, son, I'd keep that knife well-hidden. If a slave catcher should run you down and spot a knife like that, he might just use it on you."

The other visibly bristled.

"What's your name?" Gant asked.

"I'm called Silas," the boy said, his tone grudging.

Strange. He didn't even talk like most of the other runaways. His speech was like that of a white man, even a somewhat educated white man. "Well, Silas, I'll get a lantern and take you and your people to the barn. You'll need to keep everyone as close together as possible and warn them not to make a sound. No talking, no whispering." He paused. "Any children with you?"

The other nodded. "Two, a girl and a boy. Both of them are under ten years."

"Well, keep them quiet."

The boy-man leveled a look of impatience on him. "We know what to do. We've done it before."

Gant gave a slow nod. "Aye," he said, "I expect you have."

With his new visitors finally settled in and fed and Mac padding along beside him, Gant made his last trip from the barn back to the house. He was more than a little weary and ready to turn in after all the commotion of the night.

"What do you say we share the last piece of that cornbread from supper and then call it a day?"

Mac chuffed in agreement, picking up his pace.

They were about to step inside when the bobcat gave a screech from the hill in back. This had become the creature's way of letting them know he was watching them. Especially when they had been away from the house for a while and then returned, the cat had taken to giving them that short, piercing cry.

Was this its way of telling them it was about time they got back?

In any event, the call of their nightly watcher no longer sounded quite so intimidating but more like a greeting.

On the heels of that thought, Gant decided he was more tired than he'd realized.

⇥ 13 ⇤

WHAT A MORNING

God strengthen me to bear myself.
CHRISTINA G. ROSSETTI

Nothing could have prepared Gant for the events of the next morning. The day started out typically enough. After getting breakfast for himself and the folks in the barn, he made his way to the shop. By eight thirty he had glanced through his most pressing orders and helped Lon Pierce unload the lumber from the mill, and now he stood staring with distaste at the wood he intended to use for the sideboard Samuel Beiler had commissioned him to make for Rachel's birthday.

Not that there was anything wrong with the wood. To the contrary, it was excellent, a fine walnut for which he'd paid a handsome price. Despite his resentment of Beiler being the one to present her with such a special gift, he wasn't about to build anything of inferior quality for Rachel.

It wasn't his nature to procrastinate, but he'd been doing just that for far too long now. Every time he thought of making the first cut, a twist of his emotions stayed his hand.

Gant still had a bitter taste in his mouth when he thought of Beiler's insolence the day he walked into the shop and ordered the sideboard. The man had clearly enjoyed himself. His intention to rile Gant could not have been more evident, given the way he'd watched Gant's reaction to every word he spoke.

The most infuriating thing about the entire encounter was that Beiler obviously thought Gant would refuse to fill the order. He simply meant to mark his territory, to leave no doubt in Gant's mind that he and Rachel were a couple. After all, no Amish man would present such a personal and expensive gift to a woman unless they were married or at least promised to each other. According to Doc, for an Amish man to give a woman anything but the most impersonal of gifts before they entered a committed relationship bordered on an embarrassment or even an insult.

Beiler had to know that by placing such an order with Gant, he was all but declaring his and Rachel's engagement. Had Gant not been so irritated by the other's impudence and so stunned by the significance of the man's act, Beiler's surprise at his acceptance of the order would have been almost comical. Somehow, Gant had managed to check his anger until after Beiler left the shop, but even now it threatened to surface when he thought about the other's motives.

But he'd made an agreement, and he would keep it.

He was still inspecting the wood when the shop bell rang and Doc Sebastian walked in. One look at his friend's usually pleasant, serene features, now flushed with what appeared to be either excitement or agitation, told Gant something was up.

David Sebastian knew he needed to be careful how he broke the news to Gant. He'd been taking deep breaths in an attempt to calm himself ever since stepping out of the buggy. In truth, his hands were shaking enough to endanger the pie he carried. He had slept little the past night and hadn't eaten much breakfast. Too much going on to relax.

"I hope that's for me," Gant said, his gaze going to the pie.

"It is indeed," David replied, setting it on the counter. "From Rachel, with thanks for all your help with the house."

"She didn't have to do that."

"She wanted to. And Susan sends her gratitude too. For everything you did at the house, of course, but especially for being with Rachel the night of the vandalism. We're all indebted to you."

Gant was still eyeing the pie. "Apple?"

David nodded. "I believe that's your favorite?"

"Tops on the list."

After a moment, Gant said, "You look like a man with something on his mind."

"I'm that transparent?"

"Not often. But right now, yes."

David took his time replying. Finally, he drew a long breath and, worrying his hat between both hands, said, "Well, you're right. There's news."

"Bad or good?"

David hesitated. "Depends on how you look at it, I suppose." He paused. "Bishop Graber passed on last night. Hard on his family and the People, but he died peacefully in his sleep." He paused, not missing Gant's quick intake of breath.

"It wasn't entirely unexpected you know," David added. "The diabetes had been taking its toll on him for some time. He had a number of problems that weren't likely to get any better. And the dementia didn't help."

Gant nodded slowly, obviously distracted. "Will they be needing a coffin?"

David shook his head. "No, the men will take care of that themselves. It's their way—our way," he amended.

Again Gant nodded and turned his gaze toward the front door. "Well then, let me know if there's anything else I can do for the family."

Silence hung between them for a few seconds before David voiced what had been on his mind earlier. "You know what this means."

Gant turned to look at him.

"A new bishop will be chosen. It's not...seemly for us to talk about it right now, of course, but all of us will be praying. For the right man. For God's choice."

He felt the intensity of Gant's searching gaze. Neither spoke.

"Well then," David finally said, "I'd let you get back to your work, but I told Susan and Rachel I'd wait here for them. They wanted to say hello."

He saw Gant's expression quicken. "They're with you?"

"Why, yes. I took the pie off their hands so they could finish their shopping without having to carry it around with them." He glanced toward the door and then back. "Something I've been meaning to ask you when Rachel isn't nearby. What do you think the break-in was all about?"

Gant's features tightened. "I think it was meant to frighten her."

David frowned. "But why? Who would want to frighten Rachel?"

Gant backed up a little to lean against the counter. "I don't know."

"You don't even have an opinion?"

"Why? Do you?"

David shook his head. "Nothing was taken. And nothing in the house was actually disturbed—except in the workroom. It makes no sense."

"Not to us, maybe. But you can bet whoever did it had a reason."

"You don't think he meant to hurt her?"

Gant's eyes went cold. "Not physically. Otherwise he would have waited until she was there alone."

"Yes, well, we can be thankful she wasn't. I still don't see—"

David broke off at the sound of the shop bell as Susan and Rachel stepped inside.

Gant started toward the two women as they entered but then stopped, suddenly awkward in front of the others. As always, Rachel looked wonderful, her cream-smooth skin faintly flushed by the cold morning, the hair framed by her Plain bonnet shining like polished wood.

The faint light in her eyes asked, "You heard?" and his silent acknowledgment carried the tenuous reply that he had but was afraid to think about it. They might just as well have spoken aloud, for there was no denying the thoughts arcing between them.

He realized he was staring when a deep blush stained her face and she glanced down. In an attempt to relieve the tension, Gant inclined his head toward the counter. "I appreciate the pie, Rachel. But you didn't need to do that."

"Oh, no, I wanted to…to thank you somehow for…well, for everything. The workroom. Everything."

"I didn't do that much. But you can be sure I'll enjoy the pie."

Again they stood looking at each other. Doc finally cleared his throat, saying, "Well, ladies, if you've finished your shopping, we'd best be getting along. You wanted to visit with your cousin Sara Ann a few minutes, Susan."

Susan nodded but took a moment to thank Gant before leaving. "We're grateful for all your help, Captain Gant. You've been a *gut* friend to us."

Always uncomfortable with another's thanks, Gant merely nodded and watched them go. Rachel glanced back over her shoulder before reaching the door.

As soon as she left the shop, he felt the same cold emptiness he always felt when they parted, even when they'd been together only a brief time.

For the rest of the morning, he tried not to think about the death of Isaac Graber. As Doc had pointed out, this wasn't the time to consider any personal consequences of the bishop's passing. What kind of a man would stoop to wondering what another's death might mean to his own hopes? The question made Gant so uncomfortable that he launched into a fury of work that freed his mind of speculation and its accompanying guilt.

When the shop bell rang again almost an hour later, he looked up with impatience. He had been so immersed in the tedious process of carving an ivy motif on the back of a chair that he very nearly gouged his finger.

At the sight of Ellie Sawyer with wee Naomi Fay, he quickly straightened, wiped his hands, and crossed the room to greet them.

"Good morning, Captain. We were out for our walk and thought we'd stop in to say hello."

The fair-haired, attractive Ellie Sawyer always reminded Gant of a flower. A daffodil or maybe a lily. With her sunny appearance and bright disposition, the pretty young widow had a way of brightening her surroundings wherever she happened to be. She invited a smile simply by walking into a room. And although Gant had never been one to make a fool of himself over a baby, he found it impossible to resist the tiny girl in her mother's arms.

"I'm glad you did," he said. He nudged the blanket back from the sleeping baby's face. Mindful of the paint and dust that almost certainly lingered on his hands from the morning's work, he was careful not to touch her.

"She gets prettier all the time, Mrs. Sawyer."

"I thought you were going to call me Ellie."

"Things slip my mind these days, Ellie. I'm getting older."

She made a sound of derision. "Hardly."

They made small talk for another few minutes while the baby went on sleeping.

"I should let you get on with your work, Captain. But I actually had another reason for stopping. I was wondering if you'd like to accompany Naomi Fay and me to the monthly supper at the church this Friday evening."

Caught off guard, Gant fumbled for an answer. "Well…"

"Now before you say no, let me just tell you that it's a small group that attends these suppers. I'm sure you would know everyone there." She hurried to add, "And the food will be wonderful. We attended last month, and the tables were almost buckling from all the different dishes."

"I don't think I can make it this week, Ellie. Maybe another time," Gant managed to say, suddenly uncomfortable.

"You can't make it, or you don't want to?" she said, her smile faltering a little.

"To be honest? I'm not much on…social affairs."

She regarded him with a studying look. "I might have guessed that, Captain. You *do* strike me as a solitary kind of person. But don't you ever get tired of being alone? I know I do."

Gant spoke before he thought. "But you're not alone. You have Naomi Fay."

The liveliness left her face. Surprised, Gant saw an almost petulant expression come over her features.

"Yes," she said. "And I'm exceedingly thankful for her. But that doesn't mean I don't need the company of an adult every now and then."

"I suppose we all do," Gant said quietly. "I just don't like my company in the form of a crowd."

He cringed the instant the words were out, thinking he sounded harsh when he didn't mean to at all. Ellie Sawyer was young, newly widowed, and living a kind of life that was no doubt far different from anything she might have imagined. She probably *was* lonely. But he sensed that in trying to be tactful in his refusal, he'd managed to hurt her feelings.

He had never been any good with the social niceties. And not much good with women either, when it came down to it.

"Ellie…"

Her smile quickly returned, or at least a semblance of it. "It's all right, Captain. I think I understand. It seems if I'm going to have supper with you some night, it will have to be a quiet affair, just the two of us. I'll work on that. For now, I need to go and get Naomi Fay settled in so I can get back to work. It's almost lunchtime. Marabeth will be wondering where I've gone off to."

She left in a bit of a sweep. Gant stood staring out the door after her, wondering what had just happened.

Surely he'd misread her. Ellie Sawyer was little more than a girl. Well, all right—she was a widow with a baby. But she seemed like a girl. She'd always struck him as young and a little naive. And yet there probably weren't all that many years between her and Rachel. Unlike Rachel, however, Ellie always made him feel…well, if not old, at least older. Brotherly. Even paternal.

That stung.

Not that it mattered. At least it shouldn't matter. She couldn't be interested in him, not that way.

But what if she was? What kind of big *amadan* wouldn't return the interest of a pretty young thing like Ellie Sawyer?

An *amadan* indeed. A fool. The kind of fool who was getting older all the time while he waited for a miracle to happen. A fool who continued to hope when no reason for hope seemed to exist. A fool who sat waiting for a locked door to open. A door without a key.

Waiting for Rachel. Was that to be his life then? A hopeless waiting that might never know an end?

But was the waiting entirely without hope? After all, the new bishop, whoever he turned out to be, could make a difference.

Couldn't he?

No. Gant couldn't…wouldn't go down that path. Not yet, not when Isaac Graber wasn't even in his grave. Besides, Rachel had said they must pray only for God's will for them, and he had promised her he would. So far, he had kept his word.

But it was hard. So hard…to pray with no real hope. Was that even praying?

He shook his head as if to shake off his own impatience with himself. Finally, he pulled a long breath, turned away from the door, and went back to work.

14

SECRETS

Before I built a wall I'd ask to know
What I was walling in or walling out.

ROBERT FROST

Gant could have shouted for joy when both Asa and Gideon showed up at the shop three days later.

Gideon came through the back door bright and early, grinning as if he knew something Gant would like to know. But if that was the case, the boy was keeping it to himself. He offered nothing except a greeting and his thanks to Gant for giving him an extra few days off in addition to what he'd requested.

Gant had a hunch the boy's good mood might have something to do with Emma Knepp. He'd noticed his young apprentice tended to wear that same smitten smile after even the briefest encounter with Levi Knepp's only daughter.

By the time Asa arrived, Gant had already sent Gideon off with a few deliveries and was checking his measurements for a cupboard John Coblentz had ordered. The Amish dairy farmer had been a good customer and always an appreciative one. He also paid on time. For all those reasons, Gant liked working for him.

Asa came in through the front door for a change. Gant noted the fatigue lining his strong features and the dust embedded in his hat and coat. As always, he took off his hat as he entered and rubbed a hand over it.

"So you're back." It was an inane thing to say, but Asa didn't like a fuss. If Gant had told him how happy he really was to see him, his friend would have ignored it anyway. Still, he couldn't resist adding, "I'm glad."

Asa's face creased into a wry expression. "Does that mean you've been busy?"

"No, it means I'm glad to see your cynical self back in town. But I have been busy." He studied the other for a second or two. "You look tired."

"I stayed on the road last night. Didn't stop."

"So you got no sleep?"

"Felt no need for sleep until later this morning. I'm all right."

"Go get yourself some breakfast and take a nap. Gideon's back too, so I'll have help this afternoon."

"Where's he been?"

"Off for a few days helping out at his mother's place."

"Don't you want to know how the trip went?"

"You'd have told me by now if there'd been trouble. We can talk later."

Asa gave a nod, wasting no time before heading out again. "I'll pull the wagon in back first."

Gant turned back to his papers and then remembered. "There's some cornbread and bacon left over from supper last night," he said. "Help yourself."

"Now that sounds good, Captain. I'm ready for a decent meal."

With a close look at his friend's tall frame, Gant saw that he looked leaner than usual, and Asa had no extra flesh to begin with.

"Some fresh eggs in the icebox too," he added.

Gideon Kanagy drove the wagon back toward town after his last delivery to Aaron Lapp's farm. Halfway down the road, he caught himself grinning again.

He'd been doing that all morning, ever since meeting up with Emma and her *dat* going in the opposite direction as he left Mose Bender's place. Levi Knepp hadn't stopped the buggy, of course. Not even for a minute. To the contrary, Gideon thought the man had actually urged his team faster just to make sure he and Emma would have no time for even a civil hello.

Even so, Emma had managed a brief but warm smile for Gideon, which he returned.

What Levi didn't know was that his daughter had favored Gideon with more than one smile lately. While helping out at his mother's farm, Gideon had taken to riding past the Knepp place in the afternoon, hoping to catch Emma outside. He knew it wasn't likely, given the miserable weather they'd been having, but he'd made a daily attempt anyway. And twice his effort had been rewarded.

Yesterday had been one of those times. Emma was coming out the gate with some kind of a covered dish in her hands when he pulled up beside her. He wasn't surprised that she glanced back at the house as if to see if anyone was watching before turning to him. It seemed that she was taking a dish of chicken and noodles across the road to the Mast farm. "Lovina sprained her ankle last week, so Mamm and I have been helping with extra food," she told Gideon.

She gave him her usual small smile, though he noted it no longer seemed quite as shy as it once had. Ever since the day he'd taken her home in his wagon after finding her stranded alongside the road with a broken wheel, she had seemed a little more comfortable with him, a little more open in her speech and actions.

Gideon was glad for the difference. There was something about Emma Knepp that drew him. Something more than her pretty face, although she was an extremely pretty girl. Maybe it was a lot of things. Out-of-the-ordinary things, such as the fact that she seemed so...untainted. Pure. But not in a prudish, stuffy way. No, it was more a clean freshness about her that set her apart from most girls he'd gone out with.

It was more than her appearance, though. Somehow Gideon knew that Emma was unusual. Different. He could tell she was a good, gentle person but with a strength and kindness that made folks naturally respect and like her.

Young as she was, she was already someone special. At least she was becoming special to Gideon. And he found that surprising. Even a little scary.

For example, yesterday he'd actually asked her if she went to the singings—the Sunday evening gatherings for the Amish young people, where couples often started courting. A good number of those couples eventually married.

The look she'd given him had been one of obvious surprise and puzzlement. "Oh…well, sometimes I do. When one of my brothers is free to take me and bring me home."

So she wasn't seeing anyone in particular. At least not yet.

Then she'd added, "I've…I've never seen you there though."

Gideon had almost choked on his reply. "Well, you just might soon."

At first he'd thought she wasn't going to say anything. But after a few seconds, she looked directly at him with a long, searching look that was unusual for Emma and said in a quiet but steady voice, "That would be nice, Gideon."

She paused, and a faint blush stained her face as she added, "The next singing is this Sunday at the Springers'." Again she hesitated. "In case you wanted to know."

Gideon had gone on his way feeling a little light-headed and with his mind already set to show up at the Sunday night singing. He wondered only briefly if he would be welcome, absent as he'd been from the church services and the singings for months now. But he didn't fret about it long. It wasn't as if he were under the *Bann*, after all. He was still Amish, even if he hadn't joined the church. He was still in his *rumspringa* and was allowed to have his running-around time before joining the church—if he ever did join.

Welcome or not, he was going to that singing.

Gant waited until late that night before taking Asa to the barn to meet the newest runaways. The children were already asleep, as were a couple of the women, but the men were wide awake. So alert and restless did they appear, they might as well have been keeping watch.

And maybe they were.

Silas, the youth who seemed more man than a boy, didn't budge from his place at the far end of the barn, where he could look out through a wide crack between the boards. He didn't even turn around until Gant and Asa were almost up to him.

Once introduced, he greeted Asa with an impassive, even cold expression. But then his interest seemed to quicken. In fact, the stare he fixed on the older man almost bordered on rudeness. It was as if he were taking Asa's measure.

If Asa took exception to the boy's scrutiny, he didn't show it but simply stood regarding him with a faint smile that held a hint of curiosity. "So is your family with you, son?"

Gant had already told Asa about Silas, but Asa liked to ask his own questions and gather his own information.

"No family," Silas said.

Asa crossed his arms over his chest, a sign that he was going to take his time sizing up the boy. "Where you from?"

"We come from more than one place."

"Uh-huh." Asa waited, as if expecting more than a short reply that hinted of insolence. When the boy offered nothing more, he tried a different tack. "You're all traveling together though," he said, glancing around at the people scattered about. "So you're their guide?"

Silas nodded.

"You're young to be taking on that kind of responsibility."

"I'm old enough," Silas said, his gaze holding steady. "Besides, there wasn't anybody else."

"I see. Well then, in that case I expect they're lucky to have you. All the same, you've undertaken a heavy load for one so young."

The other's expression didn't change, nor did he make any reply.

What kind of youngster was this anyway, when a man like Asa couldn't crack his shell?

A similar thought had occurred to Gant when Silas and Gideon had first met. Gideon was obviously older and considerably bigger, and he had a maturity about him beyond his years. All that and the fact that he was white might have intimidated a Southern black, especially one who looked to be still in his teens.

But Silas had shown no sign of being unsettled by Gideon, no hint of being put off by him. So maybe it should have come as no surprise that he wasn't cowed by Asa either.

Still, the more Gant came into contact with the unusual youth, the more his curiosity about him grew. Time would no doubt give up some of the mystery that hung over the boy like a cloud. Especially time spent with Asa, who had an uncanny way of peeling back the layers of another's secrets and bringing them into the open without the slightest discernible effort.

He should know. Over the years, his good-natured friend had managed to unearth all manner of his secrets—even a few that Gant himself hadn't been aware of.

15

THE WARNING

Be wary of a caution spoken by a friend
when the words seem more to wound than to warn.

ANONYMOUS

F annie left at a run, her lessons completed for the day.
Rachel was standing at the front window, watching her little sister bolt
across the field for home, when she spied Samuel Beiler coming down the
road. There was no mistaking Samuel's buggy, even at a distance. His
fancy, high-trotter of a horse made him hard to miss.

Samuel Beiler's liking for rich-blooded, fine horses was no secret among
the People. Gossip had it that he paid a pretty penny for this latest one.
Of course, an Amish man's liking for good horses wasn't unusual. Not
a bit. But it had always struck Rachel as somewhat odd that for a man
known to be exceedingly tight with his money, Samuel traded or bought
and sold his horses mighty often.

Hard on the heels of her thoughts came a sting of guilt. She was being
unfair. She had no way of knowing if Samuel was extravagant with his
money in any area, and even if he was, it was certainly none of her business.

She sighed when he slowed the buggy and pulled off the road in front
of the house. What was it this time? She had so hoped he'd finally given
up on any idea of courting her. By now her resistance to his numerous
proposals of marriage should have quashed his interest. Yet he seemed
intent on drawing her into a relationship she couldn't even bear to consider.

Apparently he continued to believe that if he was patient and exerted enough pressure, she would eventually give in and become his wife. Rachel knew that many among the People believed she was foolish to reject Samuel. Some had even spoken to her about her unwise discouragement of his affection.

She couldn't help it. Although he had been a friend of her family and a deacon and a preacher in the church for years, something about Samuel kindled an uneasy sense of distrust in Rachel. She simply could not imagine living under the same roof with him, much less tolerating the intimacies of marriage with him.

Not that he'd ever made any sort of improper advances. But there were times when he looked at her in a way that made her feel unaccountably...unclean. And there was something else, something that hinted of a current of anger continually churning just beneath the surface of his seemingly impeccable behavior.

Anger always put Rachel on edge. It was something she'd never had to live with. Her parents had both been even-tempered, and Eli, even when distressed or exhausted, never said a harsh word to her. His disposition had been unfailingly gentle and good-natured.

Truth was, she was never completely comfortable around Samuel or entirely trusting of him despite his declarations of high regard and affection for her. Yet most of the time she managed to treat him with the respect due to a leader in the church and to a family friend, which he claimed to be.

Even so, because any esteem or show of genuine warmth for him required real effort on her part, she had come to dread his visits. Although he usually called as a leader in the church, supposedly to see to the welfare and needs of a widow in the community, too often his calls turned personal. It was as if Samuel had made it his mission to rescue her from widowhood and bring her under his protection.

And his control.

Rachel, however, felt no need to be rescued or protected, and she certainly had no desire to be controlled.

➔❖

For once, Samuel actually seemed to have come with the legitimate purpose of checking on a parishioner's well-being. He spent only a few minutes in impersonal conversation before carrying in a hickory smoked ham sent by his sister, accompanied by an applesauce coffee cake large enough to feed half a dozen people. A wonderful cook who enjoyed sharing the fruits of her labor, Rebekah was forever favoring Rachel with delights from her kitchen and smokehouse.

Rachel appreciated the wonderfully *gut* fare, but she sometimes thought Rebekah must consider all widows to be poor starving souls dependent on the kitchens of others to keep them from wasting away. But with Samuel's impersonal behavior and his sister's generosity, she felt some of her earlier antagonism drain away.

He insisted on filling her wood box, and when he finished, Rachel felt the least she could do was offer him a hot cup of tea.

"If it's no trouble," he said, warming his hands at the stove.

"No, of course not. It will take only a moment."

They drank their tea in relative silence until Samuel said, with his usual bluntness, "I hope you're being more careful these days, Rachel."

Rachel looked at him. "Careful?"

"Since your house was broken into. Surely you lock your doors now, even though it's a bitter thing that we need to do so."

"My doors were locked the night of the break-in, Samuel," Rachel said quietly. "And yes, I always make sure they're locked."

He nodded. "A woman alone can't be too careful in these times." He paused. "So the intruder forced your doors, then?"

"The side door. He broke the glass and reached in to unlock the door from inside."

"I came by when I heard to see if I could help with repairs, but you weren't here. Only Dr. Sebastian and that Gant fellow working inside. The doctor said you were staying with him and your mother at the time."

Now he was watching her closely, with that intense, disapproving stare he sometimes adopted with her. She felt as if she were a child caught in a questionable act and he a reproving elder.

Rachel chose not to reply but simply glanced away. His reference to "that Gant fellow" had stirred her irritation with him again.

"Why didn't you let the People know you needed help, Rachel? You would have had friends at your door the moment they heard."

"Doc *is* one of the People, remember? And Captain Gant knew about it as soon as it happened, because we were together—"

She nearly groaned the instant the words escaped her. Her impatience with what she viewed as Samuel's interference had made her careless.

He looked at her, frowning as if she'd just confessed a terrible sin. "You were with Gant?"

His tone made it sound as if he'd just tasted something vile. "Didn't Bishop Graber warn you that you weren't to be with the outsider?"

"He said we weren't to be alone together. The night of the break-in we were at my mother's house having supper."

Please, don't let him press for more...

She saw his quick intake of breath, his look of surprise as he stood. "What is this? Your mother is entertaining the two of you as a couple?"

Rachel clenched her hands. "It wasn't like that."

There was no mistaking the anger that glazed his expression as he stood glaring down at her "Then how *was* it, Rachel?" He paused. "And how did Gant find out about the break-in if the two of you were at your mother's?"

An unreasonable wave of guilt slammed into Rachel, a feeling that only renewed her resentment toward Samuel. This was none of his business, after all. Why should his remarks make her feel guilty?

But it was *his business if he chose to make it so. He was a leader in the church, and therefore she was answerable to him for any behavior outside the* Ordnung—*the rules, unwritten as they were, that regulated the Amish way of life.*

"Rachel, didn't the bishop instruct you and Gant not to be together?"

"Bishop Graber said we weren't to be alone together, that's true. But after supper, because of all the bad things that have been happening, Jeremiah—Captain Gant—insisted on seeing me safely home." She cringed at the note of defensiveness in her voice.

Samuel shook his head, his expression one of disbelief. "You have always had a bent toward rebellion, Rachel, but this is too much." He stopped, and his expression turned hard. "What were you thinking, deliberately disobeying your bishop?"

Rachel couldn't stop herself. "Bishop Graber is dead, Samuel."

His mouth thinned. "You would do well to remember that there will be a new bishop, and he must be told of your disobedience. Your behavior cannot be ignored."

A cold twist of unease coiled through Rachel as she was reminded that Samuel himself might be the next bishop. She knew as a certainty that if that should come about, her "behavior" would most definitely not be ignored. And in that jarring, unguarded moment, she finally put a name to the feeling Samuel Beiler had long evoked in her.

Dread.

She dreaded this man who for years had called himself a friend to her and her family, who had made numerous pronouncements of affection for her, even proposed marriage.

Her chair scraped against the floor as she shot to her feet. "I think you should leave now, Samuel."

"Rachel—"

"I mean it. I want you to leave."

He continued to study her, his stony silence oddly threatening. Rachel could almost sense him struggling to control his temper.

Finally, he released a long breath. "Your foolishness demeans you, Rachel. But I can see there's no reasoning with you right now, so I'll go."

He started to turn but then hesitated. "It's my responsibility as one of the leaders in the church to remind you that there's always a penalty for disobedience to the *Ordnung*. Oftentimes a severe one. I hope you'll give some serious thought to what you may bring upon yourself if you continue on this course."

Rachel didn't trust herself to respond, but merely stood waiting until he left, her hands clenched so painfully at her sides that her nails felt as if they would pierce her skin. The moment he stepped outside, she fairly threw herself at the door and locked it.

16

An Enemy Within

Deliver us from the evil one.

Matthew 6:13 nkjv

David Sebastian took a break from restocking his medical case to stand at the kitchen window and gaze out at the storm battering the house. The temperature was dropping, turning the rain that had begun earlier to snow and icy pellets that slashed the windowpanes like shards of broken glass driven by the wind.

Susan and Fannie were upstairs, ensconced in the cozy sewing room, where they would no doubt stay until they completed the infant items they'd been creating for Waneta Fisher's new baby girl. Feeling somewhat at loose ends, David had spent much of the morning doing things that didn't really need to be done in an attempt to keep his mind off other matters that had been troubling him lately. Matters that had to do mostly with the winds of change he sensed stirring in the Riverhaven community.

There had been a time when few things seemed to change for the Plain People. From what he'd observed over the years, life among the Amish stayed fairly predictable and routine with little happening to interrupt or disturb their lifestyle.

Not so these days. A number of things seemed to be changing, and

David harbored a measure of concern that at least some of the change wasn't for the better. Of course, his conversion to the Amish church and his marriage to Susan were recent enough that he could be mistaken, but he didn't believe that was the case. He'd been a physician and a friend to most of the Plain families for many years, so even though living Amish was fairly new to him, the people weren't.

Nor did he think he was mistaken about the source of at least some of the changes. David was convinced that much of what had transpired over the past few weeks could be traced to Samuel Beiler.

Perhaps that was to be expected. After the death of Bishop Graber, the People had naturally begun to seek out a leader within the community, albeit a temporary one, until a new bishop could be chosen.

The People had always looked after one another, but there were also those among them who required more than material necessities—folks who needed spiritual direction or advice in family problems or disciplinary matters. There were also the usual disputes and grievances to be settled. When it came to the young people, strong guidance from someone other than a parent was occasionally deemed necessary.

Sometimes, though rarely, a member deliberately disobeyed the *Ordnung*, evoking the *Bann*. Although shunning was applied to help the offending person see his sin for what it was and take the required steps to repent and be accepted back into the church, it could cause problems among family members and friends. It took a strong leader to deal with such situations.

With their former bishop of many years now gone, the People would naturally be feeling the absence of a spiritual leader. Both Malachi Esch and Abe Gingerich were growing more advanced in years, and Malachi was still grieving the death of his wife, so it was probably to be expected that some of the People would turn to their other preacher, Samuel Beiler, to be that leader.

Beiler was considerably younger than the other two preachers, physically strong and fit, and well experienced in matters of the church. David couldn't stop the somewhat cynical thought that the man also had a way of conveniently insinuating himself into a leadership position. It was almost as if he *wanted* to be recognized as the People's authority, although such a desire would defy the typical Amish man's nature. An Amish leader would never actually seek authority or power, although a bishop needed to exercise both.

More common by far was a feeling of dread when a man received the call to serve as bishop. The duties and responsibilities that accompanied the position—a lifetime appointment, entirely without pay or any other form of compensation—could become burdensome and nearly over-whelming for most ordinary men.

However, once struck by the lot, a man was expected to serve regard-less of how he might feel about it. David knew from his long friendships among the People that many Amish men held serious doubts about their capability to serve as bishop, but none would shy away from what they considered a genuine call from God.

In Samuel Beiler's case though, David's instincts told him that this was a man who would not be reluctant to assume the role of bishop and might even be eager to do so. David admitted to himself that his thoughts bordered on cynicism—not a fitting emotion and certainly not a common one for an Amish man to harbor. But if truth be told, he had never trusted Beiler. He had long sensed that the man's disposition was prideful, his ambition probable, his character questionable and possibly bent.

At one time, Beiler had served as a deacon— a position that was often carried out less noticeably than that of a preacher. A deacon looked after the poor, saw to various needs of the community, assisted in baptisms and weddings, and sometimes investigated reports of transgressions, even carrying word about excommunication.

However, due to the departure from the community of another ordained deacon and a somewhat dubious transfer of duties by Bishop Graber, Beiler had quietly assumed many of the responsibilities of a preacher. When the time came to choose a man for the actual position, Beiler's name was somehow submitted for consideration, despite the fact that things had never been done quite that way before. As it turned out, he was chosen for the position—a position he seemed to revel in.

Isaac Graber had always seemed partial to Beiler, for reasons David had never quite understood. The two men couldn't have been more dif-ferent in disposition. But he'd observed that Samuel Beiler had gradually

made himself all but indispensable to the aging bishop, so perhaps that
accounted for the way things turned out.

In any event, though David couldn't prove that the changes he found
so unsettling could be traced back to Beiler, neither could he help but be
troubled. He also knew that to some extent the recent changes bothered
Susan as well, so at least his distrust of the man wasn't altogether personal.
In fact, they had discussed their mutual concern only the night before.

Apparently, unlike some Amish communities David had heard of, the
Riverhaven settlement had never been unreasonably strict in their rules
and practices. At least not until recently. These days, however, there were
rumors of more stringent regulations being enacted and less tolerance
for those who broke those regulations either knowingly or unwittingly.

Not for the first time, one particular incident filtered its way into
David's thoughts. Three weeks ago on Sunday, he and Susan had hosted
the church service at their house and, later that evening, the young people's
singing fest. When things were about to come to a close that night, Reuben
Miller and Mary Yoder had been "caught" on their way to Reuben's
buggy by Samuel Beiler.

According to Barbara Short, a friend of Susan's, Beiler had openly
rebuked the two for "hanging around together" out of public view for
quite some time. From what Barbara told Susan, Beiler had approached
the couple as they were preparing to climb into Reuben's buggy and
leave for home.

Just how long they had been out of view was uncertain, but the two
young people had been seeing each other for months now, so it wasn't
all that odd that they might have sought a few minutes of privacy when
they could. Still, David acknowledged they probably should have reserved
their time alone for the ride home.

He had to wonder, though, if Beiler must have kept an unreasonably
close watch to have known about their movements and apprehended them
as quickly as he had. In any event, from what Susan had been told, even
though the two young people had admitted their indiscretion, Samuel
Beiler had gone on to issue a harsh scolding in a loud enough voice that
he could be heard at some distance.

David had known Mary and Reuben most of their lives. They were a fine young Amish couple, both of them trustworthy and obedient to the church. David seriously doubted that they'd been up to anything objectionable. They would have been humiliated by the experience.

He thought about how their former bishop, Isaac Graber, might have handled the situation and was pretty much convinced the older man would probably have rebuked the couple quietly and privately. Bishop Graber had never been one to make a scene or deliberately embarrass members of the church.

More than likely, he would have reminded the young people to live in such a way that would be pleasing to the Lord and in a manner that wouldn't make another stumble, and that would have been the end of it. Beiler, however, had not only embarrassed the couple but imposed a punishment on them, ordering them to confess their transgression to the entire congregation during the next church service. They were also to avoid each other for the next month. Even Susan, a staunch believer in discretion and wholesomeness among courting couples, thought the preacher's handling of the situation unnecessarily harsh and unreasonable.

There had been other changes as well. Rules had been tightened on how often courting couples could see each other, the time between dates being lengthened to three weeks instead of two.

Then there was the dress code, which, at least for women, was more rigid than it had ever been, allowing for no colors to be used in dress material—not even brown, but only black. Nor could the length of dresses reveal anything more than the tips of their shoes.

There was also a rumor circulating about a new rule being discussed that would dictate the conduct of a man and wife in their own home — that would, in fact, regulate the frequency of their most intimate relations. Such a rule was sure to be highly controversial in an Amish community.

The Plain People valued children as gifts from God, true blessings to be welcomed with joy and thankfulness. Any practice that would seem to limit the number of children a family might have would almost certainly be looked upon with indignation and resentment if not outright defiance.

It was only a rumor, to be sure, but David worried that if an issue that sensitive had indeed been raised, the church leadership was close to crossing the boundary of guidance and influence over the People's private lives and venturing into an area that was nothing short of invasion.

He knew he wasn't the only one questioning these new conventions. A few of the men he'd recently seen as patients—men he'd known for years—had guardedly broached their concerns, but David knew no more than anyone else about who or what was behind the recent changes.

His suspicions were just that—suspicions. He had no right to discuss his thoughts about such matters with anyone other than Susan, and even with her he had to tread cautiously—not because he didn't trust her to keep his confidence, but because he didn't want to cause even the slightest tear at the hem of her trust in the church and its leadership. Susan had been devout all her life. He wouldn't be comfortable foisting his own doubts or suspicions onto her and had tried for the most part to keep his silence.

In spite of his caution, however, she was too sensitive by far not to know that something was bothering him. For a time he had been deliberately vague in his replies to her questions. Still, he should have known that she would eventually have her own concerns, and to be sure, only last night she had raised those concerns and her uneasiness.

It had been something of a relief to learn that she not only shared his concern about the changes taking place but also suspected that Beiler was the likely instigator of those changes. David had learned to trust his wife's judgment. Where his own imagination tended to take flight all too easily, Susan was more practical and levelheaded. Before she formed an opinion or drew any conclusions, she had a way of gathering her instincts and examining them in light of any other evidence. Only then would she share her thoughts with him.

Last night she'd surprised him by raising the subject of the recent happenings in the community and admitting that, like David, she thought Samuel Beiler might be involved, at least to some extent. Hearing Susan echo his concerns in her usual direct way, David had realized with a new twist of dread that the trouble he had only sensed to be creeping in among the People was more than likely all too real.

Now, watching the storm hammer the usually serene landscape he so dearly loved, a chill gripped his spine. He knew that evil didn't always entrench itself from the outside and that it could just as easily take an entire community captive from within.

Please, Lord God, don't let that happen here. Place a wall of Your protection around these people, around all of us, that no evil can penetrate...

He was still praying when Susan quietly walked into the kitchen and took his hand.

17

A CHANGE OF PLANS

The hounds are baying on my track, my Master's just behind,
Resolv'd that he will bring me back and fast his fetters bind.

GEORGE N. ALLEN, FROM *The Underground Railcar*

G ant was unprepared entirely for the message delivered to his door in the middle of the night.

Word came down the line from Keller's station well after midnight, delivered by one of Tom Keller's sons. So rushed was the warning that apparently no thought had been given to sending a note. Instead, young Merle Keller gasped it out in a harsh whisper. The boy quickly agreed to take the same message to Turner's station, and then he bolted back to his horse and rode off.

Gant's mind raced as he watched him ride away. So the runaways would not be leaving as planned. At least three teams of slave catchers had been spotted in Washington and Noble counties over the past few days. No fugitives or conductors would be safe on the roads regardless of how well traveled they might be.

Gant wasn't a worrier by nature. He had long ago learned that prayer was the underground operation's most dependable defense. Over the years he had taken to heart the apostle Paul's advice to pray without ceasing, so he often prayed for the refugees' protection while they were sheltered in his barn and during a move. But this sudden and wholly unexpected change of plans spooked him a little.

He simply had too many people on the premises to hide safely. Concealing two or three runaways was risky enough, but eleven men, women, and children were currently counting on his protection. How in the world was he to shelter so many indefinitely?

He bolted the door and decided against going back to bed. Sleep was the furthest thing from his mind now. Too much to think about, too much to figure out. And some of that unceasing prayer would seem to be in order as well.

From his place by the stove, Mac growled. Gant looked at him, but an instant later a low rumble made him turn toward the window. Again, Mac gave a chuff, but he too had grown accustomed to the sound the bobcat made when he was close by and paid the animal little heed these days. The cat would remain well hidden. That halfhearted snarl he'd just offered was simply his way of making his presence known.

As if Gant needed a reminder. He was beginning to feel as though the creature had taken to tracking his every move.

Finally he went to the window and looked out, but as he'd expected, he could see nothing but darkness. But the cat was out there all right, slinking around in the trees and behind the bushes, watching the house and waiting.

Waiting for what? Gant wasn't sure he wanted to know.

Asa was just as reluctant as Gant to break the news to the people the next morning.

They went to the barn early, before dawn, to get it over with before taking them their morning meal. Just as they expected, when the refugees heard about the delay, the weight of disappointment was heavy. Gant's attempts to brighten the situation fell flat for the most part, although he could sense some of the folks making an effort to stay positive.

"It may not be all that long," he said, watching their faces after he explained the problem. He couldn't blame them for feeling discouraged and apprehensive. Even to him, his words sounded unconvincing.

The boy Silas made no attempt to hide his frustration. "How long will we have to wait?"

"There will be people keeping watch day and night, passing the word down the line," Gant said. "As soon as the slave catchers are out of the area, we'll know."

"Are you talking about hours or days or what?"

Gant shrugged. "There's no telling. All we can do is stay put until word comes that it's safe to move."

"So in the meantime we just sit here and wait to get caught," the boy shot back.

Asa was clearly growing impatient. "There won't be any getting caught so long as you do as Captain Gant says. You just have to stay out of sight and keep quiet."

"That's easier said than done," Silas muttered. "Folks are already getting restless. They want to be on their way."

Gant knew the boy was right, and impatience bred carelessness. But with everyone around them looking on and hearing their exchange, he held his own concerns in check. "No doubt. And I'm not saying it will be easy, but we don't have a choice. We just have to wait it out."

The boy's mouth pulled down. "Oh, there's a choice. I've outsmarted slave catchers before. I can do it again."

"Boy, don't go talkin' foolishness!" Asa shot back. "Just because you're willing to risk your own neck doesn't give you the right to put other folks in harm's way. You need to settle down and use whatever common sense the good Lord gave you."

Asa's outburst surprised Gant. He'd never known a man with a cooler head or one slower to rile. Something about the boy seemed to set Asa's teeth to grinding.

Silas stood glaring at Asa but said nothing more.

The youth's reckless air and apparent hotheadedness troubled Gant too. Before leaving the barn, he took the boy's arm and led him aside. "Take care you don't get your people stirred up. They're counting on you. There's always danger when you're on the move, but there's no need to go looking for more trouble. You'll be safe here for now, so don't get in a hurry and do anything foolish."

"I don't need you to tell me that," the boy said, yanking his arm away from Gant's grip. "I've done this enough times to know what's safe and what's not."

Gant studied him for a moment. "Then you're smart enough to know not to light out when there's a gaggle of riffraff prowling about just waiting to turn a profit off someone's lack of caution."

For an instant, the youth's eyes flashed defiance and a hint of deep-seated anger. But the fire banked as quickly as it flared. "I'm not stupid," he said. "Don't concern yourself about me."

"See that I don't need to," Gant grumbled, following Asa out the barn door.

❖

Outside, Mac trotted ahead of them, but Gant slowed. "That boy's too young and too feisty to be in charge of all those people. Once you get on the road, you'll have to cool him down more than once, I expect."

Asa nodded. "He's some too big for his britches, that's for sure."

They took up a faster pace again. "Comes with being young, I suppose," Gant said. "He gets to you, doesn't he?" he added, grinning.

"He's a little impudent, all right." Asa hesitated. "I can't place exactly what it is about him, but he reminds me of someone."

"Who's that?"

"I don't know. Just something about him…"

"Well, I can't blame him for being jumpy. The longer we have those runaways under roof, the more risk for them all." Gant paused. "For that matter, I'm worried just as much about you."

Asa looked at him. "Me? Why?"

"You know why. You're a free man, but a lot of people aren't aware of that. And some who do know might not care."

"Ohio's a free state."

They stopped walking. "You're too smart to think that guarantees you a pass from trouble. There are just as many folks eager to help the bounty hunters as those trying to help the slaves."

"You'd best worry about yourself instead of me. I'd say a white man with eleven runaway slaves in his barn is living way too close to the local jail."

"Even so, you'd do well not to be too visible while we're waiting on word to move. Most folks in town know you're free and just think you work for me. But outsiders that stick around any length of time are going to question why you come and go as you do."

"Don't you worry none, Captain. I can do a pretty good job of pretending to be your 'boy.'"

"Hang it all, Asa, that's exactly what you *can't* do! If they assume you're not free but working for wages, they'll haul us both to jail. You know it's illegal for a white man to hire a slave."

Asa shrugged. "All right. I'll stay in the barn with the others for now."

"You will not!"

The dark, steady gaze Asa leveled on him made Gant flinch. "Captain, we've always known there would be things about this work we wouldn't like. But we both agreed we'd do whatever needed to be done." He paused. "Sleeping in a barn a few nights doesn't seem like much of a sacrifice to me when some of those folks have probably never slept even a single night by a warm stove."

They started walking again. "Best we get some food out to them now," Asa said mildly. "It'll be daylight soon, and they'll need to go below."

Gant nodded, still not liking the idea of his friend sleeping in the barn. But when Asa took that tone with him, he knew better than to argue any further.

"So where has young Gideon been keeping himself lately?" Asa said. "I know he's working in the shop, but I never see him anymore in the evening. He hasn't had supper with us for days now."

"Doc and Susan have needed help out at the farm lately," Gant said. "There's a lot to be done out there. Gideon leaves right after he finishes up in the shop and goes out to lend them a hand." He smiled a little. "I believe he also spends some of his time driving by a certain young Amish girl's place. That's just an assumption on my part, but Emma Knepp lives close to Gideon's family, you know."

"Ah. So he's gone sweet on a girl."

"I'd say so. But she's Amish."

"Well, he is too."

"But he's living *Englisch*, and that will be a problem if he tries to court an Amish girl."

"Well, love has a way of overcoming problems sometimes."

"Always the philosopher, eh?"

Asa shrugged. "You don't agree?"

Gant shoved his hands in his pockets and kept walking. "All I know is, even love isn't enough to bridge the divide between Amish and *Englisch*."

Asa looked at him but said nothing.

18

TROUBLE DESCENDING

In dark days of bondage to Jesus I prayed
To help me to bear it, and He gave me His aid.

FROM THE SPIRITUAL "I'M TROUBLED IN MIND"

G ant woke up before dawn, disoriented, his eyes still heavy with sleep. Someone was pounding full force on the back door. He sat up, waiting for his eyes to focus before swinging his legs over the bed and pulling on his clothes.

The pounding continued, so fierce it seemed to be hammering inside his head. He stumbled to the door, but before he could throw the bolt, someone called out, "Captain Gant!"

Mac had already lunged ahead and stood waiting for Gant in the kitchen, uttering a low but constant growl. When Gant opened the door he found the boy, Silas, his face a tight mask. "We got a girl taken sick," he said, his words spilling out in a hard rush.

Apparently Gideon had heard the commotion from his room over the shop. No more had Silas got the words out of his mouth than Gideon, still clad in his nightclothes, rushed up behind him. "What's going on?"

Gant swung the door wider. "Get in here, both of you. And keep your voices down! There's no need to wake up the whole town."

Both youths stepped just inside the kitchen. "Asa said I should come get you," Silas said, his voice low.

Finally, Gant's head began to clear. *Asa...Asa had slept in the barn overnight.*

He closed the door. "So...who's sick?"

"Tabitha. Jalee's girl. She's been sick most all night."

"Sick how?" Gant stared at him. "Throwing up sick? Fever sick? What?"

Silas rubbed his eyes. It looked to Gant as if the boy hadn't slept much, if at all.

"The fever. But Asa said she's hurting too."

"Hurting?"

The other nodded. "Her hands and her legs."

"How old is this girl?"

"About five or six, I reckon."

"Sounds as if she needs a doctor," Gideon put in.

Silas gave an angry shake of his head. "We can't do that! No way we can chance some white doctor seeing us here!"

"Well, the only doctor you're going to find around here is white, son," Gant said, his tone dry. "But he just happens to be someone we can trust."

After only a quick look at the child in the barn, Gant knew she was seriously ill and immediately turned to Gideon. "You'd best ride out and get Doc."

Gideon looked at him. "You know he's not supposed to be treating anyone except the Amish."

Gant leveled a long look on him. "We need him here. He'll come."

Gideon waited but then gave a nod. He started for the barn door, stopping when Silas snapped, "Wait!"

The boy whipped around to face Gant. "This doctor—what makes you so sure you can trust him?"

Sullenness laced the boy's tone, and Gant had to wonder if the youth had ever trusted another human being.

"I'd stake my life on this man's honor," Gant said. "And you can do the same. For now, you and the others stay out of sight. It'll be daylight soon."

Silas shot him a dubious look but said nothing more.

❖❖

Gant had taken care to move the fevered little girl away from the other runaways before Doc arrived. For more than a quarter of an hour now he'd stood watching Doc examine her, trying to assess the seriousness of the girl's condition by his friend's facial expressions.

A futile pursuit, as he should have known. David Sebastian was a master at concealing his thoughts.

Finally, Doc closed his medical case and walked over to where Gant was standing. Silas, who had stayed as close as Doc would allow during the examination, followed him.

Gant waited for Doc to fill them in, but Silas, who seemed to have no sense of the word *patience*, blurted out, "So what is it? What's wrong with her? Is it catching?"

Doc regarded the boy with a somewhat annoyed look. "I can't be sure."

"What, then?" said Gant.

Doc looked at him with weary eyes. "Sorry to say, the child most likely has a serious form of rheumatism. She's a very sick little girl."

"Isn't there something you can do?" Gant asked. "Some kind of medicine?"

Doc expelled a long breath. "Any number of treatments have been tried—quinine, different metals and medications—but none of them seem to help." He gave a shrug of frustration. "I've seen some relief using salicylic acid, but there's no cure. And it seems particularly vicious when it strikes the young. I'll do what I can, but it's never enough."

"Can she travel?" As soon as the words were out, Gant realized how callous he must have sounded. But he had to know. When the time came to move the runaways, they'd have little warning and would have to work fast.

Doc seemed to understand. "She can, yes, but she's going to be miserable whether she stays here or moves on. This is a disease that often comes in waves. An attack can last a few days or much longer. Sometimes weeks or months. And sometimes...well, sometimes it doesn't go away at all."

He went on to explain. "The pain and fever are caused by inflammation of the joints. If the inflammation can be decreased, so can the pain. I want to talk to the child's mother. There are a few things she can do that will help or at least give the girl some relief. Hot packs, warm baths...although sometimes cold seems to help more. Unfortunately, it takes some experimenting to find out what's most effective. What works for one doesn't necessarily work for another."

He paused, straightening a little before going on. "I'm concerned that there might be something else going on here as well."

"Something else? What?" said Gant.

Doc hesitated and drew a long breath. "I think she may have some sort of an ague. I'm not sure the fever is altogether due to the rheumatism. She's showing signs of something like a bad cold—perhaps even influenza."

Feeling a bit sick himself by now, Gant shook his head to clear his mind. "I don't know what we can do for her, things being what they are. She'll have to stay underground with the others through the day, and if anyone sees us going back and forth to the barn at night, it can raise questions. It sounds as though she's going to need more care than we can give her."

"You said you want to talk with her mother?" Silas asked Doc. "But Jalee, she doesn't speak much English. Not much at all. She's from one of those places in Africa. Hasn't been here long. Your man—Asa—he better go with you. He seems to understand Jalee pretty good." He darted a look at Gant as if seeking an explanation.

"Asa is originally from a village in Africa," Gant said. "He came here when he was a young man."

Asa had come to the States on a slave ship, but Gant didn't volunteer any more information. The thought of his friend's background never failed to bring a sour taste to Gant's mouth. He had heard more than he cared to know about the slave ships. The thought of Asa chained below decks in one of those floating coffins was intolerable.

But Silas clearly was reluctant to let the subject go. "Asa is a slave?"

"No, Asa is *not* a slave," Gant shot back. "He's been a free man for years."

"But he *was* a slave," the boy pressed.

Gant merely looked at him, saying nothing.

As if Doc sensed the tension between Gant and the boy, He broke in. "I'll get Asa to help me explain things to the mother. In the meantime," he said to Gant, "it would be good to collect some towels or cloths that can be used to apply heat. Moist heat is best. Perhaps you can heat a few at a time on the stove in hot water. Just...do what you can."

Gant nodded and went to hurry the few people who were still above ground down the ladder below before heading back to the house.

Uneasiness clawed at him like a buzzard on his back all along the path leading away from the barn. All this coming and going back and forth from the house to the barn, the need for Doc at the crack of dawn...it just made it that much easier for trouble to come down on them.

Finally, when he felt as if he was about to choke on the knot in his throat, he muttered a hurried prayer. *"Lord, the last thing we need right now is another complication...another burden to hinder us from getting these people out of here and back on their way to freedom. If You intend to get us out of this fix, it seems like now would be a good time to start."*

19

BECAUSE OF RACHEL

Why do we say love hurts?
It's the absence of love that hurts.

ANONYMOUS

From his workplace near the front window, Gideon Kanagy watched his boss, Captain Gant, talking with Ellie Sawyer in front of the shop. The Captain was sporting a wide smile while holding the woman's baby. At the same time, he looked a little tense, as if he might split and run any second.

This wasn't the first time Gideon had seen the two together, and as before, he couldn't quite stop a grin at the Captain's behavior around the pretty blonde widow. He always looked a bit *ferhoodled* in her presence. He laughed a lot, but it seemed forced, not his usual way of tossing back his head and laughing for real. Sometimes he pinched his face in an odd kind of frown, as if she'd said something he didn't quite get.

It seemed to Gideon that his employer didn't realize the woman was sweet on him. The Captain was no *dummkopf*, that was for sure, so why did he seem to go all mushy brained around the widow Sawyer?

Not that it mattered. True, if one didn't know better, it might seem that the Captain was taken with the woman. But Gideon *did* know better. His employer was taken with a woman all right, but not Ellie Sawyer. The woman who had captured Captain Gant's affections was Gideon's own sister, Rachel.

Of course, the Captain probably didn't realize that he knew. But he'd seen the way his boss's eyes followed every move Rachel made when he thought no one was looking. For that matter, he'd seen the way Rachel couldn't take her eyes off the Captain.

But there was also the crack Samuel Beiler's oldest boy had made, back when Gideon had still hung around with Aaron and some of the other Amish fellows. That night, some of them had been in town at Carroll's candy store, just horsing around and buying nothing while Ted Carroll kept a sharp eye on them.

Gideon had often had the feeling that Aaron had it in for him, although he couldn't think why. Maybe because he wasn't living Amish like the rest of them. Most of the fellows knew Aaron resented much of the *Ordnung* and having to live under all its rules. That night Aaron had made some crack that his *dat* would probably be courting Gideon's sister, Rachel, if only the *auslander* Captain Gant hadn't arrived in town. He made it sound as if he knew for certain that the Captain was sweet on Rachel and that some among the People were beginning to spread rumors that maybe the feeling ran both ways.

Gideon had been tempted to call Aaron to account for his gossip, but he held his silence. He hadn't known but what the younger boy's hints might contain some truth, so he'd decided to ignore the loose talk. Truth be told, by then he'd begun to have his own suspicions about Gant and his sister.

By now, however, he was convinced they were more than mere suspicions—not that he thought either of them was guilty of deception. He was pretty sure neither Rachel nor his employer would indulge in anything immoral. But he was almost just as certain that strong feelings were running between them.

Things were difficult when that happened between one who was Amish and another who wasn't. There was no bending the rules about courtship between the Amish and the *Englisch.*

The thought brought to mind his own situation with Emma Knepp. Of course, he was still Amish. But he couldn't openly court Emma—not that she would even consider the idea—because he wasn't *living* Amish. He knew that sooner or later he ought to give the matter some thought, yet every time he even started to dwell on the situation, he backed off. He wasn't ready to confront just how serious his feelings were or to choose the direction he wanted his life to take. Sometimes he genuinely missed the Amish life. But at other times he felt as if he were a stranger to both worlds, and he wondered if he really belonged in either. Lately he'd caught himself wishing that if one way of life were right for him and the other wrong, he could figure out which was which.

Standing on the boardwalk in front of the shop, Gant was trying to think of a way to take his leave of Ellie Sawyer without being rude. At the same time, he wondered what kind of an *amadon*—a fool—he was for wanting to escape a pretty young widow who, for some unaccountable reason, seemed to like his company.

Thing was, he always felt awkward around Ellie. Unless he was thickheaded entirely, she seemed interested in him. But why would she be? He was fairly certain he'd never given her any reason to think he returned her interest. To the contrary, he usually found it difficult just to be himself around her, much less strike the kind of pose some fellows might adopt when trying to attract a woman.

That wasn't Ellie's fault. She seemed to be everything a man with even a scrap of common sense would be drawn to. In addition to being attractive, she was bright and amusing and lively. She had a way about her that would probably make most fellows feel pretty good about themselves.

But the reality was that he wasn't interested in keeping company with *any* woman anymore, not in a romantic way. Because of Rachel.

Because of Rachel.

Just about everything in his life these days seemed to revolve around those words. Because of Rachel, he had stayed in a community where he was an outsider. Because of Rachel, he had all he could do to keep his mind on his work instead of wandering down paths that held only roadblocks. And because of Rachel, he couldn't rid himself of a restlessness and a dissatisfaction with most anything he turned a hand to.

If he had his way, he'd be with her every minute—day and night. Once he'd come to love her, he never felt as if he belonged anywhere else. He never wanted her out of his sight, yet he saw her so rarely that he ached with her absence.

What a fix he was in. He was like a lovesick schoolboy and a dimwitted one at that.

"Captain Gant...Jeremiah? Would you like me to take Naomi now?"

Ellie's question yanked Gant back to his surroundings.

He blinked. "Oh...aye, I imagine she's ready to go back to her mama." Quickly he returned the baby to Ellie's arms. "And I expect I'd better get back to work." He paused and then added, "I enjoyed the walk though. Thanks for insisting I get out for a bit."

She lifted an eyebrow. "Honestly, Jeremiah, if I didn't insist, I wonder if you'd ever leave that shop. You surely do seem to love your work."

Gant eased his shoulders after freeing himself from the weight of the baby. Wee Naomi seemed to be growing. "Well, it's just that I always have a lot to do."

Her expression was dubious as she continued to study him while patting the baby's back. "Yes, I've noticed. And that being the case, I mustn't keep you any longer. Hopefully, we'll see you again soon."

Gant touched his cap and tried not to appear too anxious to get away.

Gant was aware of Gideon watching him discreetly as they worked. Impatient and a little touchy with the lad's scrutiny, he finally expelled a long breath and faced his assistant. "You might just as well say what's on your mind."

Gideon had the grace to look embarrassed. "I'm not...there's nothing on my mind, Captain."

"I'm thinking there's something," said Gant, "else you'd be paying more heed to your work and less to me."

"No, I...well, I was just thinking, I suppose. Sorry if I was staring." The boy's face was still flushed.

"That you were," Gant said. "Staring, that is."

Gideon said nothing else for a moment. "I suppose I was thinking about Mrs. Sawyer. She's a pretty lady. A nice one too."

Gant nodded but kept his eyes on his work. "She is that. But she has a few years on you, lad."

"But not on you."

Now Gant looked at him. "Meaning?"

"Well, anyone can see she's sweet on you, Captain!" The boy clamped his jaws shut, clearly regretting his outburst.

"You think so, eh?" Gant sighed. So maybe he hadn't imagined Ellie's interest after all. He didn't much care for the grin Gideon flashed.

"I'm pretty sure, Captain."

The boy was way too impudent sometimes. "Well, it's neither here nor there."

Without warning, the lad took another tack. "So, have you been out to the farm lately?"

His expression was innocence entirely, but Gant wasn't fooled for an instant. "I've not. Why do you ask?"

Gideon gave a seemingly indifferent shrug. "No reason. I know you and Doc are good friends, that's all."

"That's true."

"And Mamm's fond of you as well."

"I'm glad to hear that. Your mother's a grand woman. Naturally, I covet her good opinion of me."

"And of course Rachel considers you a good friend too."

"Is that so?" Gant's pique had dampened. Indeed, he was rather enjoying himself by now. "Well, I hold your sister in high regard as well."

Again the boy took to silence, but not for long. "So...you've probably heard that the new bishop is to be chosen soon?"

He met Gant's eyes straight on. He was no longer smiling but wore a look of utmost seriousness. Gant's mood had also sobered.

"When?" he asked.

"Two weeks is what I've heard."

Something in Gant's chest squeezed so tightly he almost lost his breath.

"There's a lot riding on the man who becomes bishop," Gideon went on. "Much can change...or not, depending on a new leader."

"So I've heard," Gant said, his reply deliberately short and noncommittal. If the boy was fishing, and Gant believed he was, he had no inclination to respond. Obviously, he was hinting at the fact that a new bishop could make a significant difference for his and Rachel's relationship—a positive difference or a negative one.

As if Gant didn't carry that awareness in his head and in his heart every single day.

He turned back to his work with an expression meant to convey an end to their conversation. After another moment, Gideon took up the plane he'd been using and also carried on with his efforts.

→ 20 ←

ADVICE FROM A FRIEND

We fear the things we think
Instead of the things that are.

JOHN BOYLE O'REILLY

You know you can't keep this up, man. You're going to end up in jail!"
Gant had ridden out to Doc and Susan's early in the evening to take
Fannie the new collar he'd made for her dog. Thunder's neck continued
to grow and thicken along with the rest of him, and Gant had fashioned
a leather collar that would give him some more growing space without
allowing him to slip free, as he was wont to do.

When Susan pressed him to stay for a light supper, Gant, always up
for her cooking, quickly agreed.

Almost as soon as Fannie and the dog went upstairs, Susan shooed
the men to the front room so she could clear the table and do the dishes.
Within minutes after settling in the other room, Doc launched into a
spiel about Gant's "risky undertakings." This wasn't the first time Doc
had vented his frustration about Gant's involvement with the refugee
slaves. Even though he was sympathetic to the plight of the runaways,
and although he was the only man besides Asa and Gideon whom Gant
trusted enough to confide in, he made no pretense of his concern about
the danger in which Gant had placed himself by harboring the slaves
in his barn.

"Someone is going to find out," he warned Gant, not for the first time.

Gant glanced up from his chair to where Doc was standing with his back to the fireplace. "And just who might that someone be? Nobody knows anything except you and Gideon. Are you saying I can't trust the two of you?"

"You're smart enough to know what I mean. The longer you do this, the more you increase your chances of getting caught." Doc was really steamed this time. He glanced at the door as if to make certain no one was nearby before going on. "You need to get them out of your barn, and the sooner the better."

Gant shot his friend a wry look. "And just how do you suggest I do that? I already told you we have to keep them where they are until word comes that it's safe for them to move. We can't chance running into slave catchers with that many people."

"That's exactly my point," Doc ground out. "You've got too many to hide with any degree of safety this time." He broke off, studying Gant with a quizzical expression. "Why are you doing this anyway? Why take such foolish chances? Isn't it about time you settled down and stopped risking your stubborn neck?"

He stopped, and Gant sensed he was close to spluttering with exasperation. "And don't give me your usual prattle about the British oppression of the Irish and its similarity to slavery in America. I've heard it all before. Besides, it seems to me you've already done more than your share for the cause of freedom."

Gant shook his head. "It's not just that."

"Then what?" Doc came to sit down across from him.

"I can't explain it. Once I got into it, I felt as though I needed to stay. It just doesn't feel right to get out of it. Not now. Not yet."

"That makes no sense. You do this of your own free will, so of course you have a right to stop...you can stop anytime you want."

Gant trained a look on him. "No. It's not that simple. The folks involved in this tend to stay involved. For a long time. It's not just something you do for a while and then quit. The runaways know from word of mouth who we are, who they can trust. Not by name, although some of them also know that. But they know there's a place, say, in Marietta, where they can get help. They've heard about a preacher there who shelters them in a safe house." He paused and then went on. "Or they know about a lame carpenter in Riverhaven who's willing to shelter them until a conductor is available to take them on up the line. Word gets out."

Gant struggled for words. "It's hard to explain," he said. "It's like a building. You take even a few stones away, and you weaken the entire structure. Or a railroad. If you unhitch a couple of cars from the others, or if you have a conductor who doesn't show up for work, or if there's a split rail, you'll have a breakdown. Trouble. It's not something you can simply walk away from. People might die if you do."

Doc regarded him with a measuring look. "So in other words, you'll never quit."

Gant shrugged. "I don't know about that. But I do know that now's not the time."

Doc drew a long breath and then gave a nod of resignation, so Gant moved to change the subject. "So…I hear the new bishop will be chosen soon. As soon as two weeks."

Doc frowned. "Where did you hear that?"

Gant ignored the question, instead asking another. "Did I hear right?"

"Most likely."

"And are you still of the opinion that a different bishop might make a difference for Rachel and me?"

Doc pressed his lips together. "Yes. But remember, I said *might*. There's no guarantee."

"I understand that," Gant said.

He tried to swallow down the surge of hope that invariably accompanied any thought of things working out so he and Rachel could be together. "What about you?" he said. "Is there any possibility a new bishop might have an effect on your doctoring?"

"You mean by denying me the right to practice medicine, even among the People? I hope not. But of course it could happen. I suppose it's only to be expected that the new bishop will make some changes. Only time will tell."

Gant drew a long breath. "Well, I hope it doesn't take too long before we find out what some of those changes are going to be. I expect you feel the same way."

Doc glanced away, his only reply a slight nod.

Gant's question had made David uneasy.

In fact, he was tempted to mention some of the changes he'd already been seeing, even though a bishop hadn't been chosen yet. Only the thought that his own concern might serve to increase that of his friend made him hesitate. Was there any point in letting Gant know that he, too, was wont to fret over what the upcoming selection of a new bishop might mean...to them both?

Especially if Samuel Beiler happened to be the one chosen.

They sat in silence for a time, the only sound the hiss and crackle of the fire and the soft clatter of dishes as Susan tidied the kitchen. Finally, on impulse, David ventured a question. "I'm curious—not that it's likely, since you live in town, but you do have contact with a number of the Amish—have you heard anything lately about any...changes...taking place among the People?"

Gant looked at him. "What kind of changes?"

David knew he should choose his words carefully lest he plant ideas. Still, he valued Gant's shrewd power of observation more than that of most any other man he'd ever known. He didn't want to say too much, yet he genuinely wanted the other's insight.

"I'm not sure I can explain. It's mostly little things that taken separately might mean nothing, but everything together—"

He had no chance to finish. A scream exploded from upstairs. Fannie and Thunder came barreling down the steps, Fannie still screaming and the dog roaring a vicious barking that David had never heard from him.

He stumbled in his haste to reach the stairway while Gant clambered to follow. Susan met them at the bottom of the steps while the dog barked and circled at the front door like a wild thing.

Wide-eyed, her face pale with panic, Fannie tugged at David's arm. "Fire! Papa David—the barn's on fire!"

21

FIRE IN THE NIGHT

He who has a thousand friends
Has not a friend to spare,
And he who has one enemy
Shall meet him everywhere.

TRANSLATED BY RALPH W. EMERSON FROM A SAYING DATED AD 660

At first, Gant saw nothing but an eddy of black smoke rolling over the treetops. It would have been scarcely noticeable if the night hadn't been so brightly studded with stars and a nearly full moon.

As soon as they cleared the dense grove of evergreens in back though, he saw the blaze that had already begun to light up the darkness. It was a good thing Fannie had been upstairs and able to see the flames in the distance.

The acrid smell of smoke was strong, and by the time they reached the crest of the yard, his eyes were burning, his throat stinging. The sounds coming from the barn were nightmarish, the horses screaming in terror, both cows bawling. Gant's blood thundered with the desperation to reach them before it was too late.

Fannie had shot out in front of them, running behind her dog, Thunder, but Susan called her back. At first the girl didn't seem to hear, but when Doc shouted out another warning, she stopped.

"The bell, Fannie!" Doc called out to her. "Go to the bell!"

Fannie's feet barely touched the ground as she turned and retreated to the house, the dog racing ahead of her. In seconds the clanging of the dinner bell in the backyard could be heard.

"*Ach! Mein Gott in Himmel!*" Susan cried. "David, the horses—the cows!"

Gant heard the panic in Susan's voice and felt the same urgency pressing at his mind and driving his body. Not for the first time, he silently raged at his own weakness, the ruined leg that held him back and slowed his every step. He pushed himself as hard as he could, but there was no way a man with a cane could keep up with the others.

The moment David threw the barn door open, he saw the angry flames breaking the shadows on the back wall and heard the hiss and pop of fire traveling among the hay bales. Thick, black fingers of smoke coiled upward, heading for the roof.

Stunned by the sight of the spreading blaze, he gasped but forced himself to move. He ran toward Cecil's stall first and yanked the door open. The big Percheron draft horse Amos Kanagy had valued so highly hesitated at first, but when David gave him a light slap on the flank he took off for the open door.

David glanced over to see Susan leading the elderly Rosie out of her stall, so he went to free Smoke. The feisty young buggy horse's eyes were wild. The moment David threw open the door of his stall, he whinnied and galloped out of the barn.

Gant was there by then, and David went to help him loose the cows from their posts and get both buggies outside. As they hurried from the barn, right behind Susan, they met Fannie, tears streaming down her face as she and Thunder ran toward them.

He caught her arm. "The animals are safe, Fannie. Go back to the bell. We need all the help we can get to keep the fire from spreading."

He checked to make sure Susan and Gant were all right before helping them herd the animals to the small pasture north of the house. By the time they turned back, Rachel and some of the neighbors had arrived and were forming a double line with buckets in hand.

When Gant saw Malachi Esch manning the pump, he relieved the aging Amish man with the excuse of needing him to oversee the efforts of the others, making sure no one got too close to the blaze. The pump, at least, was one thing he could handle. His leg might be a problem, but his arms were strong.

Only then did he see Rachel as she moved up to him and held out her bucket to be filled. He plied the pump, watching her at the same time. Her face was pale in the eerie light cast by the fire, but her mouth was set in the familiar, determined line he had come to recognize. The inferno before them had to strike fear and anguish in her, but she wouldn't fall apart. Not Rachel. At least not until she had done all she could do to help her family.

"You be careful, Rachel," he said, his voice low.

"The Amish know about putting out fires," she bit out. Her words were clipped, her voice hard, but there were tears in her eyes as she spoke. "I saw the animals. They're all right?"

"Aye. They're all safe."

"And Fannie—she's at the bell?"

"She is. Your sister has a pretty cool head, young as she is." He glanced in the direction of the house. "Doc told her to keep ringing it for now."

She looked at him. "I'm glad you're here, Jeremiah," she murmured just before stepping away with her bucket.

Gant continued to pump after Rachel left, watching her as she hurried off. The heat was intense as the flames blazed higher, and Gant struggled for air, feeling as if his lungs might explode from the weight of the heavy smoke.

Neighbors kept coming, some arriving by themselves, others with their families. Everyone seemed to know what to do and went right to work, wasting no time before joining the lines.

Rachel was right—the Amish knew all too well about putting out fires. The lines worked almost automatically as if driven by an unseen motor.

A sudden movement just across the road caught Gant's eye. A flash of white and something dark. A man slipping out from among the trees. Gant couldn't be sure, but he thought someone was watching the fire from the other side of the road.

Watching? Who would stand watching instead of joining the others to help put it out?

But sure enough, someone was simply standing there, taking in the scene. Gant rubbed his burning and grainy eyes with the knuckles of his free hand, but the figure was too well concealed by the trees.

Suddenly, as if he'd noticed Gant's gaze on him, the other began to move.

Gant glanced around, looking for someone to take his place at the pump. Toward the end of the line, he saw Gideon and caught his eye, motioning him forward.

Gant didn't take time to explain but just turned the pump over to him, grabbed his cane, and started down the path toward the road as fast as he could move. Just as he'd feared, though, by the time he was about to cross, the watcher had disappeared. He continued to the other side, but there was no one to be found.

The workers managed to extinguish the fire in little over an hour, but the barn was totally destroyed. Most of the neighbors who remained followed the family indoors for a few minutes. The night air carried the smell and taste of smoke inside. In fact, Gant thought he would be tasting the caustic bite of smoke for days.

Some of the women had made fresh coffee and tea, and Susan rushed around the kitchen to set out cream and sugar along with plenty of fresh-baked cookies. There was little in the way of conversation. The ordeal they'd just been through had left everyone exhausted and solemn.

Before anyone began leaving for home, Susan again thanked them for their help. "We're so grateful to all of you and to the Lord God for all He's done this night, for sparing our animals and for sending such *gut* friends to help put the fire out."

"We'll be over Saturday to raise a new barn," Malachi Esch said. "Can you get us enough lumber that soon?" he asked Gant.

"Consider it done."

"We'll hope for good weather," said Susan.

"God knows what we need," Malachi replied. "He'll see to it."

Gant was no longer amazed by this Amish way of giving thanks and trusting God in even the worst of situations. They were a people who lived in continual trust and constant gratitude to their Maker. He had learned much from them over the past year. Even though he still struggled with some of their ways, he respected those ways and attempted to emulate the ones he admired most.

After everyone had gone, and while Susan and Rachel cleaned up the kitchen, Gant explained to Doc and Gideon why he'd left the pump and gone across the road.

"You didn't get a good enough look to tell who it was?" asked Doc, clearly troubled by this disclosure.

Gant shook his head. "Could have been anyone. I saw something white, but I couldn't tell what. But whoever it was seemed awfully interested in what was going on."

"And not interested in helping to fight the fire," Gideon put in, a scowl darkening his face.

"So you think the person you saw might have set the fire?" Doc asked.

Gant shrugged. "You have to wonder. If not, why wouldn't he have come over and helped the rest of us? Obviously, he intended to stay out of sight."

"Well, I'm going over to the woods and look around," Gideon said, moving toward the door.

"That's probably not such a good idea," Gant said. "We don't know who's out there. There could have been more than one. Just because I didn't see anyone else doesn't necessarily mean he was alone."

Gideon whipped around with an impatient frown. "I'm not exactly helpless. I can take care of myself." His face flamed as if he thought that Gant might take his words as an insult. "I'm just going to look around. Somebody needs to do something."

Gant drew a long breath. He was already familiar with the youth's impetuous nature. But he could hardly fault him for his frustration. Gideon might not be living Amish, but these were his people, his family, and their troubles were mounting. It was only natural that he would want to find out who was responsible for those troubles. In the end it was Rachel who convinced Gideon to stay. Gant hadn't realized she'd come into the hallway and had heard at least part of their conversation.

"Don't, Gideon. Please." Her voice was low but firm. "You're not going to do any good by going out there tonight. Whoever was there is long gone by now. All you'll accomplish is to worry Mamma. At least wait until tomorrow."

She paused. "How did you get here so quickly, anyway? Mamma said you were staying in town tonight."

The instant change in Gideon's expression pricked Gant's curiosity.

"I changed my mind." Gideon's tone was unusually sullen, and he was clearly avoiding his sister's gaze. "I was already on the road home when I saw the smoke."

Gant couldn't help but wonder about the boy's reply and the furtive look on his face. He'd noticed that the pretty young Emma Knepp had showed up quite a while after her parents and brothers tonight, but not long after Gideon arrived. He hadn't thought much of it at the time because of all the commotion with the fire, but now he wondered if those two had possibly worked out a way to see each other on the sly.

If so, they'd better be prepared to put out another fire—one with Emma's father.

Doc spoke up then. "Rachel's right, Gideon. "Wait until morning, when we can see. I'll go with you, and we'll have a look around the barn as well. If you're staying here tonight, that is."

Gideon glanced from Doc to Gant and then to Rachel. Finally he gave a short nod.

Rachel followed Gant out when he prepared to leave, an act that pleased him no end. He wouldn't have put her on the spot by asking her, but the entire time they'd been in the house he was hoping for a way to see her alone, at least for a moment.

She said nothing to her family but simply pulled her coat from the hook by the door and threw it around her as they stepped out onto the porch. "Thank you for your help," she said as she shut the door behind them.

Gant smiled a little at the almost formal tone of her voice. "You don't have to thank me, Rachel. I'm just glad I was here." He waited. "Are you all right?"

She nodded. "I just...I hate all this." She made a gesture of frustration with her hands. "All this trouble. Someone wanting to hurt us. Never knowing what might come next or why it's happening. It's hard."

An old anger Gant had felt before again rose up in him. The injustice and trouble wreaked on such a gentle, pacifist people never failed to rile him. "Doc told me about the mistreatment the Amish have suffered in other places besides Riverhaven. He said it's been going on for generations."

"*Ja*," she said quietly. "This is nothing new. There has always been violence against us. Before our people ever came to America, there was trouble. They thought it would be different here. But it seems wherever we go there are always some who resent us...even hate us."

Gant studied her. Somehow the confusion and sadness in her face worked together to heighten her loveliness.

"There's no understanding it..."

He let his thought drift off, unfinished, but he couldn't stop the worrisome question that had plagued him before tonight. What was it about the Amish that evoked this desire, the need to hurt them, to attempt to drive them away? If indeed that's what all this was about—a hatred so intense that whoever harbored it was resolved to make life so miserable for an entire people that they would just up and leave.

Whoever it was—whoever *they* were—knew enough about the Plain People to feel secure that they wouldn't retaliate, wouldn't defend themselves regardless of the cruelty leveled at them.

He made an effort to shake himself out of the black mood that had earlier begun to settle over him. Reaching for Rachel's hand, he touched it only briefly before releasing her. "It's cold out here. You'd best go inside."

She nodded. "You'll be careful going back to town?"

"I'll be fine. There's not another creature in the county that can outrun Flann." He hesitated. "But Rachel, please don't stay alone tonight. Stay here, with your family."

He could sense that she was about to protest. But instead she searched his face for a long moment, finally giving a conciliatory nod. "If you think I should."

"I definitely do."

Relieved, he very nearly took her hand again but stopped. As much as he wanted to touch her, it was a hard, hurtful thing to let her go. He wanted...he needed more from Rachel than a touch.

He wanted her heart.

22

COUNTING THE COST

It's wiser being good than bad;
It's safer being meek than fierce.

ROBERT BROWNING

"Captain?"

Gant had just reached Flann, hitched in front of the house, and was about to mount the big red horse when Gideon stopped him.

"You could do with a coat, lad," Gant told him.

The youth glanced down over himself as if he'd only then realized he was still in his shirtsleeves. "I'm all right. I wanted to catch you before you left."

"Something wrong?"

"No. Well, I don't think so. It's just that—I saw the way you looked at me when Rachel asked how I got here so quick."

"What way was that?" Gant said, intrigued by the boy's apparent unease.

"I just wanted to make sure you didn't think I had anything to do with the fire."

Surprised, Gant stared at him. "Why would I think anything of the kind?"

"I don't know. I just…had the feeling you might not have believed me."

Gant studied him for a long moment. "You don't have to explain yourself to me, lad. But now I'm curious. Why would you ever think I'd suspect you of burning down your own family's barn?"

The boy seemed to loosen up a bit at that. "Well…I hoped you wouldn't." He dug the toe of his shoe in the dirt a couple of times. "All right, then. I just wanted to make sure."

"One thing though…"

Gideon visibly tensed again. "I don't know what's on your mind, but whatever it is, let me just suggest that you *do* want to be careful not to bring any trouble down on yourself or anyone else by some manner of foolishness. Speaking from experience, it's a good thing to count the cost of any behavior you're not quite comfortable with. Acting on impulse can be a treacherous thing."

Gideon glanced away, then back. "I'm…pretty careful about what I do."

"Good." Clearly, the boy still felt awkward. No doubt because he knew what—and whom—Gant was referring to. Emma Knepp.

He moved to change the subject. "By the way, there's something I was going to ask you earlier but didn't have a chance. Did you happen to notice anyone missing tonight? Someone you'd expect to show up where there's trouble?"

Gideon frowned, but his expression quickly cleared. "Samuel Beiler."

"So you didn't see him either."

Gideon shook his head. "No. But I know why. He was spending the day in Marietta."

"How do you know that?"

"I was talking to…I happened to meet up with Emma Knepp in town, and her *dat* was going too. And her brothers. They were all going to an auction."

Gant nodded, his curiosity satisfied for the moment, though he still felt strangely unsettled. He mounted Flann and would have left had Gideon's next words not stopped him.

"I don't blame you for wondering. I don't quite trust Samuel Beiler either."

"I don't recall saying anything about not trusting the man." Gant hesitated before adding, "But what accounts for your feelings?"

Clearly, the boy was now feeling the need of a coat as he hugged his arms around himself. Even so, he shrugged and made an effort to explain. "It might be because old Sam thinks he's so perfect nobody else can live up to his standards. I probably shouldn't say this, but I have a hard time believing anyone is that perfect." He paused. "Truth is, I've always been kind of sorry for his boys, being raised by that kind of father."

Gant waited. He didn't want to bait the boy, but his curiosity was growing.

"They haven't had it easy, it seems to me," Gideon went on. "I doubt if anyone could live up to that man's demands. I've been around them some over the years, and I don't believe I've ever heard him give one of his boys a kind word. Especially Aaron."

"Aaron?"

"He's the oldest son. And maybe *because* he's the oldest folks seem to think he's had things the hardest at home. I've heard tell his *dat* takes his temper out on Aaron on a regular basis. More than on the other boys."

"So Beiler has a temper?" Gant wasn't in the least surprised, although the comment might have surprised him had it been offered about most any other Amish man.

"A bad one, from what some folks say. I never actually saw it for myself, but Aaron has said things that would seem to point to it. And people talk."

Gideon seemed to think a moment. "Samuel fancied himself a friend of my *dat*, but I'm not so sure Dat counted him that good a friend. In truth, I never thought he liked the man all that well. I know he didn't care much for old Sam's puffed-up ways." He stopped, darting Gant a knowing look. "And I don't like how he won't leave Rachel alone."

He stopped. "I'd better not say anything more. Mamm would be all over me for gossiping."

"She's going to be out here giving both of us a piece of her mind if you don't go inside and get warmed up."

Gideon grinned. "No doubt you're right. I shouldn't be keeping you either. You've got a ways to ride yet."

Gant nodded. "You take care now. I'll see you tomorrow at the shop?"

"Oh, I'll be in at my usual time. And Captain, thanks for your help tonight."

Gant nodded and rode off, mulling over Gideon's remarks about Samuel Beiler all the way into town.

→ ←

In spite of the captain's advice about going inside to warm up, and despite the fact that he was shivering, Gideon delayed going back to the house. He felt as though he had guilt written all over him. His employer's warning about the treachery of foolish behavior had found its target, though he hoped the captain hadn't realized it.

In truth, he had been with Emma tonight. After much persuasion, he'd convinced her to meet him at the old mill bridge. No doubt the fact that her father and brothers were still down at Marietta accounted for her eventually giving in to his urging. Even so, once they were together he was pretty sure she was glad she'd come, even though he could tell she felt nervous about being alone with him in such a remote place after dark.

He was convinced she was as attracted to him as he was to her. The shine in her eyes when she allowed herself to look at him more than a second or two, the pretty shade of pink her face turned at the same time, and the way she seemed to hang on his every word...well, it was fairly obvious she liked him all right.

All they did was talk. He sensed that if he so much as touched her at this point, he'd spoil any chance he might have of courting her. Besides, something about Emma made him want to treat her as if she were made of glass. She was a special girl, a good Amish girl, and he meant to respect her just as any decent Amish man would. And he was still Amish, after all.

But the notion of actually courting her might be too far-fetched to even consider, other than seeing her in secret. But wasn't that pretty much how his people carried out their courting anyway?

Emma, however, would never go along with some kind of *verboten* relationship. Even if she wasn't afraid of her *dat*—and Gideon was fairly certain she was afraid of him—she wasn't the kind of girl to turn her back on the way she'd been raised.

No, Emma wasn't made for deceit. She would stay true to her family and her faith. She would marry a good Amish fellow and be a good Amish wife and mother. And even if she were tempted to stray from her beliefs and her heritage, her folks would find a way to stop her.

But they wouldn't need to stop her. Emma had said it herself, making her feelings very clear before they separated. "I can't meet you like this again, Gideon. It's not right. I like being with you, but I won't do this again, so please don't ask me to."

So, then, why was he even thinking *about courting her when he knew how impossible the whole idea was?*

Because he wanted her. Trouble was, he wanted her in the right way, not in some secret, tarnished relationship.

Foolish! He wasn't ready—he didn't know when or if he would ever be ready—to go back to the Plain life. Living Amish, leaving the *Englisch* world altogether, becoming boxed in again with all the confining rules and restrictions of the Plain ways…could he really see his future in that light?

He had promised himself he would live *Englisch* until he could find out who was causing all the trouble for the Amish. Otherwise, he could do nothing to stop the ones responsible. The Plain People didn't believe in revenge or even in defending themselves. If he went back to the community, he'd have to accept the beliefs in which he'd been raised. Those beliefs didn't include any kind of retaliation or physical threat. Even if he should happen to find out who was bringing down all the trouble on the Amish, he wouldn't be free to do anything about it.

Right now, with things as they were, his situation was entirely different from Emma's. He couldn't be shunned because he had never joined the church. He might rate the disapproval of the community, and some might even turn their backs on him, but by rights they couldn't shun him for the way he was living.

Emma's situation was different though. She had taken her church vows, so she could be shunned. Her life could be ruined by taking up with him.

The captain had even hinted at that very thing. Hadn't he just warned him to be careful not to bring trouble down on himself—or anyone else?

He would never want to be responsible for hurting Emma. Never. Better to stay away from her altogether. The very thought brought a hammer of pain to his heart, and in that instant, he knew he had allowed his feelings to overwhelm his good sense. He felt like a *dummkopf.* Like a foolish, lovesick schoolboy.

Worse still, he was starting to feel all the makings of a trap closing in on him.

23

FAILED PLANS

Black our fearful crime must be.
RICHARD D'ALTON WILLIAMS

He clenched his fists in frustration. Things couldn't have gone more wrong.

Nearing home, he tugged his coat more tightly around him, aggravated by the cold, the odor of smoke he could still smell on himself, and the memory of all the people crowding to help, with that Gant fellow in the midst of them as if he belonged.

Just his luck the outsider would be right there in the house when the fire started. He hadn't once thought of that. By the time he'd seen Gant's big red horse, it was too late. The fire was well under way.

His plan had depended on a serious loss and on suspicion falling on the outsider. Instead, Gant ended up looking the hero—manning the pump, helping out wherever he could, the others counting on him, looking up to him. Their faces, shining in the light of the fire, even seemed to show *respect* for him!

Another plan botched. Nothing was going as he'd intended. Somehow, Gant always spoiled everything.

What was it going to take to get rid of him? Obviously, more than he'd first thought. There had to be something that would force Gant to leave—or at least something that would finally press him to stay away from Rachel and the People.

He stopped at the lane leading up to his house, waiting for a fresh surge of strength and determination to well up inside him. Within minutes, he could feel himself growing stronger, more focused, more dedicated. The failed barn fire was just an obstacle on the path, after all, not a defeat.

Hadn't he known from the beginning it might not be easy, that most likely it would take more than one or two incidents to accomplish his goal? So he had more to do. He simply needed yet another plan. He was committed to doing whatever it might take to rid their lives of the menace among them—and at the same time make his own life considerably easier.

This much he now promised himself: Regardless of how difficult or how dangerous, he would do whatever it took to get rid of Gant. He wouldn't be hindered by what hadn't worked, but instead would look forward to the next event.

And now that he knew Gant's secret, the next challenge would almost certainly be the final one.

24

DAY OF BLESSING,
DAY OF TROUBLE

*Shall we indeed accept good from God,
and shall we not accept adversity?*

JOB 2:10 NKJV

Families began arriving early on the day of the barn raising. Although the weather had forced them to postpone the work a week, a number of men had come in the evenings to measure and sort the lumber in advance.

The women had also been working in advance, getting ready for Saturday as they cleaned and prepared the large quantity of food that would be needed for so many workers. Even before the frames were hammered in, everyone, including children who were old enough to work, had their own tasks assigned, their groups organized.

Although the work had already begun, the buggies kept coming, a steady stream of black rolling down the foggy lane, parking along the fence and across the road as their occupants emptied, supplies and tools in hand.

Gant and Gideon worked alongside Malachi Esch, whose skills were widely recognized. Malachi needed no instruction. Further, he was good with managing the older men, as he knew their strengths and weaknesses and could designate jobs accordingly.

Taking a moment to watch from the crest of the yard, Rachel noted that a number of the boys and younger men went to Jeremiah and Gideon for instruction while hammers and handsaws provided a steady rhythm to the quiet discussions taking place. She couldn't quite stop a tug of pride as she witnessed how her brother and the man she secretly loved commanded the respect of so many of the other men.

Even so, she didn't miss the dark, indignant glances Samuel Beiler often cast in Jeremiah's direction. To her surprise, even Samuel's sons wore expressions clearly resentful of the *Englischer* working among them.

For the most part, however, she found it nearly impossible to drag her gaze away from Jeremiah. The last barn raising at which he'd helped, he hadn't been able to contribute much to the physical labor because he was still recuperating from the gunshot wound that had brought him to Riverhaven in the first place. Today though, he seemed strong and vigorous enough to do his share of the harder work, even moving about without his cane for a few steps at a time.

Once, as if he'd felt her scrutiny, he glanced up and made a barely perceptible dip of his head in her direction.

Quickly, guiltily, Rachel put her proud feelings aside and turned to go back to the house, her face still warm with the awareness that Jeremiah had seen her watching him.

By the time the women served lunch, the entire barn had been framed. Not long after, the interior walls were in place. Before two o'clock the men working on the exterior framing had established their rhythm, hammering the boards and nailing them down, following the same routine as each piece was lifted into place.

They worked quickly but skillfully, the experience of the Amish men in patent display. The barn was going up incredibly fast. Gant ignored the fatigue that had begun to settle over him. In truth, he was enjoying being able to do more than hammer a few nails or stain a small piece of furniture.

It also felt good to be a part of a community, even if for only a day, to work alongside a group of men skilled at what they did, men who clearly enjoyed each other's company. He had been a loner most of his life. Even when he'd worked in the shipyards, he hadn't been much for mingling, and he had always sensed the need for a certain distance from his crew on the boat in order to maintain authority. For the most part, they had been a rough lot, and he was never quite certain but what a few might take advantage if they detected the slightest weakness in him.

This was a different kind of experience, and the fact that he found himself enjoying it came as a bit of a surprise. Indeed, the heaviness and ache in his bad leg seemed to pale in light of what they were accomplishing and the gratification to be had in doing it.

Nor could the resentful scowls of Samuel Beiler, frequent though they were, take away from his feeling of satisfaction in being included in the day's work.

He passed a hand over the perspiration that had gathered below the rim of his cap. All in all, it had been a good day, a fine day indeed. But as time went on, his leg and his back began to feel the need for the day, fine though it was, to come to an end.

It was dark when Gideon pulled the wagon into the barn. No more had Gant stepped down than Asa approached with a barely flickering lantern and a tense greeting.

"Captain...it's the boy, Silas. He's sick now. Acting a lot like the little girl, Tabitha, it seems to me."

Gant was so tired his mind felt like cotton. "Silas too?"

Gideon had started for the barn door but stopped to listen.

"A fever," Asa said. "Didn't Doctor Sebastian mention the possibility that the girl might have something more than rheumatism?"

Gant nodded. "So...is he separate from the others?"

"He's keeping his distance, but then he usually does. Only time he mingles is when he needs to give them orders. He usually stays off to himself."

"Aye, he's like that." Gant stopped to think. "Well, I can't call Doc out again tonight. He's likely just settling down from working on the new barn all day, and dead tired at that. Do we have plenty of that medicine Doc left for the girl's fever?"

"There's enough. Should I give him some?"

"No, you stay away from him. There's no sense in you coming down with this, whatever it is." Gant hated what he was thinking, but he couldn't ignore it. "Let's just hope it isn't influenza."

Asa waved off his caution. "I expect I've had enough fevers in this lifetime to be safe from most anything going around. How much of the medicine should I give him?"

"Let's try one of the powders first. We'll see if that helps. If need be, I'm sure Doc would come out tomorrow and check on him."

"I'll go for Doc first thing in the morning if we need him," Gideon offered.

"Good enough," said Gant. He turned to Asa and added, "Come to the house and get me if the boy should take worse. For now, let's try to get some sleep."

Even as he said it and turned toward the barn door, Gant knew it would be precious little sleep he'd get tonight. The very thought of a possible influenza outbreak among such a large group of runaways was enough to pose a wide-awake nightmare.

Asa had cautioned him more than once not to question the ways of the good Lord, but right now it was a hard thing not to wonder what was going on. Sometimes it seemed that the more he prayed about getting these people out of here and safely back on the road to freedom, the more bad luck arrived to hold them captive in his barn.

⇥ 25 ⇤

PASSING THROUGH THE FIRE

When you walk through the fire,
you shall not be burned.

ISAIAH 43:2 NKJV

By the next morning, Silas had a fever so high he was drifting in and out of consciousness.

Gant knew he dared not let the boy go on as he was much longer. He burned to the touch, even though Asa had plied him with cool cloths and cold drinking water all throughout the night. A few minutes before eight o'clock that morning, Gant roused Gideon from his room upstairs and sent him out to the farm to fetch Doc.

He didn't like leaving Asa alone to tend to the boy—he could see his friend was fairly worn out himself—but it might raise suspicion if the shop remained closed on a business day. So after he prepared a hurried breakfast for the fugitives, he left the barn and went to clean himself up a bit in advance of opening the shop.

He worried about Doc being seen on the premises too often. He hoped Gideon would remember his instructions, that Doc should pull his buggy up in front as always and come into the shop as he normally would. He could then exit through the back and make his way to the barn. Even so, there was no guarantee he wouldn't be seen. Still, with no vet in the area, it wasn't all that unusual for David Sebastian to doctor a horse now and then. Probably most folks would assume he was doing just that—if they wondered at all—should they happen to spy him coming or going at the rear of the property.

Not for the first time, Gant wondered how his friend managed to care for so many sick people on a regular basis and not end up sick himself. Heaven only knew how many different diseases Doc had been exposed to in his lifetime, and yet he couldn't recall ever seeing the man with more than a mild head cold. Maybe a body eventually became immune after so long a time of tending the sick.

Or maybe the good Lord simply had mercy on those who put themselves at risk to take care of others. Gant figured Doc had probably never refused to come when needed. If ever a man had challenged Gant's previously held conviction that humankind was fundamentally selfish, that man was David Sebastian.

His British friend had scotched much of Gant's earlier cynicism. He wasn't sure which of the two—Doc or Asa—owned the bragging rights to setting a stubborn Irishman straight on a fairly regular basis.

Long after the good Dr. Sebastian had left, Asa remained at the boy's side, attempting to cool the fire burning from him and soothe the tremors of his delirium. Now there was no smarting at the boy's insolent tongue, no occasional prick of irritation with that defiant lift of the chin. Nothing but unease for the youth's failing strength and the deadly heat that warred against his senses and battled for control of both body and mind.

Unease and a genuine pity mingled as he studied the young and surprisingly fragile features now fighting so valiantly against the enemy that had invaded his slight frame. How childlike and innocent he appeared in the grip of this unwelcome, deadly foe.

Scarcely did he apply a cooling cloth to the perspiration-soaked face than he needed to lift it away in exchange for another. Asa's other hand remained locked in the boy's tight, baking grasp as he moaned and mumbled incoherently. It was as if, at least for the time being, Asa had become the anchor that secured young Silas to this world.

As he tended to the youth, he prayed for him, seeking the healing only heaven could bestow. In an anointing of compassion and unconditional love, Asa bathed the boy—scarcely removed from childhood—in pleas for the Father's mercy and restoration, for strength to combat this debilitating weakness, for a divine infusion of vitality and wellness that would gain for him the victory over the destructive disease.

After Asa prayed, he bent to listen, lowering his ear to the boy's lips, trying to make some sense of the youth's fever-induced mutterings. He caught only fragments of phrases, rambling words and murmurings that fell away beyond recognition. Still he listened, for even as Silas clutched his hand, he seemed to be pleading, though for what Asa could not comprehend.

Burning. He was on fire, held captive inside a roaring furnace that threatened to draw him into an abyss from which there would be no escape. Only the hand he clung to kept him from falling into that blazing void. Only the soft, covering blanket of words protected him from crumbling into dust and ashes.

He couldn't fall...mustn't fail the people...had to lead them through... they were counting on him...they would never find the way without him, never make it through.

Who was holding him? So strong, that hand...and cool, so welcome in the fire...Mama...Mama Ari. No one else was that strong...no one else would be able to hold him from the flames. No one else would even try. Mama... He had thought she was gone...but no, not gone after all...she was here! Here with him, holding him, cooling him, keeping him from the flames, though he couldn't see her...

"Mama? Mama Ari..."

Asa caught an intelligible word now and then. Something about "people." Then "Mama..." The poor child was calling for his mama.

He strengthened his grip on the slender but weather-toughened hand for a moment, letting go only long enough to straighten and go for more water. But the feeble voice called him back.

"Mama...Mama Ari!"

Asa knelt again beside the boy sprawled atop the thin mattress on the wooden floor he and the Captain had laid out some months back. The Captain would not have people sleeping on the cold dirt floor below ground. "The least we can do is provide a real floor and blankets and what mattresses we can scavenge."

Now he riveted his gaze on the boy. Asa put a hand to his forehead, relieved to feel that the heat was subsiding somewhat. Though the water in the basin was warm, he again soaked the cloth thoroughly and pressed it to Silas's forehead.

"Can you hear me, son?" he asked, keeping his voice low as the others slept.

Silas opened his eyes slowly, his expression one of pain, as if even the small hint of light from the low-burning lantern was an agony to confront. When his gaze finally began to focus, it was one of confusion, sharpening to anxiety.

He ran his tongue over his lips. There was no mistaking the effort even this slight movement cost him.

"Where...what...happened?" His voice was merely a rasp, a ragged, scratching sound, like a knife being scraped over a piece of wood.

"You'd best not try to talk just yet, son," Asa cautioned him. "Save your strength. You've been sick. Bad sick."

The boy frowned. "Sick?"

Asa nodded. "Burning up with the fever. All the night through."

"Like Tabitha?"

"Maybe. Except Tabitha has the rheumatism trouble as well. Doc isn't sure now whether her fever came from the ague in her joints or the sickness like you've had. Could be both."

"She was really sick..." The boy's words drifted off as he again closed his eyes and fell asleep.

Asa stroked his forehead. "So were you, son," he murmured. "So were you."

He was relieved to see that this time the youth's slumber seemed more normal, less restive than the agitated, fever-driven sleep of before.

Asa watched him a few minutes more and then went to find a corner, not too far distant, in hopes of managing some rest for himself.

26

WHAT IF?

It seemed life held
No future and no past but this.

LOLA RIDGE

On Sunday morning, Rachel closed the barn door and stood looking around. Her milking and feeding chores done, she supposed she should head for the house to fix her own breakfast. Still she hesitated, taking in the crisp, frost-covered surroundings and watching her breath, clouded with steam from the cold.

She felt as if she'd been holding her breath for days now. Perhaps later today she would finally be able to release the tension.

On the other hand, the strain might turn to something worse. It all depended on how the lot was cast. As had been the way of the People for many years, the hand of God would direct one man to choose a hymn-book in which a paper had been placed—a paper on which a specific Scripture verse was written.

Abe Gingerich, Malachi Esch, or Samuel Beiler. Which man would choose the hymnal containing that paper? On this man would be conferred the power and authority to affect and even change the lives of many in their community—including Rachel.

More than once, the thought had entered her mind to pray about this divine appointment. But only for a fleeting instant before, overwhelmed by her own audacity—the sin of even entertaining such a thought—she had gone to her knees to plead for forgiveness. One must not, one dare

not attempt to interfere in the Lord God's work. There was no com-
prehending how great a sin it would be to pray for an event that would
benefit her personally!

Later today, she would know. She might be given a hint of hope, or
things could go on just as they were. Or just as likely, she might have to
face the shattering reality that any hope she and Jeremiah had was gone.

She assumed that should Malachi Esch be chosen, there might be
reason for optimism, not only for her and Jeremiah but for all the people.
Malachi was a kind and decent man, a man of wisdom known to be
fair and just.

As for Abe Gingerich, he had the reputation of being resistant to
change. Although Abe was known to be a steady, good-hearted person,
he had always stood on the side of tradition and was disinclined to
compromise.

Finally, the thought of Samuel Beiler as bishop caused a shudder
unrelated to the cold to roll over her. But why? Other than his ongoing
pursuit of her hand in marriage, Samuel had done nothing she could
point to that should induce uneasiness or apprehension in her. She had
no concrete reason for the feeling of dread he frequently evoked.

No, that wasn't quite true, she realized. More than once she'd had the
feeling he was threatening her. Not overtly. Not a heavy-handed sort of
menacing, but a vague sensation of warning, a sense that even the slightest
indication of defiance on her part would be met with severe consequences.

She realized now that her qualms about Samuel becoming the new
bishop weren't altogether related to her future with Jeremiah. True, such
an occurrence would almost certainly doom any chance of them ever
being allowed to marry. Samuel would never let Jeremiah convert to the
Amish church, would never accept him into the community.

But she also feared that as bishop, Samuel might instigate a rash of
changes in the People's way of life—unwelcome changes, perhaps even
some that would bring about dissension. Was it only her imagination,
which Eli had sometimes called too "fanciful," that made her think Samuel
would be a hard, unyielding leader? Was she being entirely unfair when
she envisioned him as a bishop who would rule rather than guide, who
would demand rather than direct?

Somehow she could never associate Samuel with fairness or kindness. Had she taken too much to heart an exchange she'd once heard between her parents about him?

She had no memory of the incident that had instigated their conversation, but Mamma had actually referred to Samuel as harsh and dictatorial, causing *Dat* to lightly scold her, although he hadn't sounded all that disapproving.

"Sam and his father before him have been friends of our family for years, Susan. He might be a little…judgmental at times, but that's just his way. He's a strong-minded man."

Rachel had sensed by her mother's low sound of disgust that she didn't share *Dat*'s opinion.

It occurred to her now that her father and Gideon were the only persons she could think of who ever referred to Samuel as Sam. She shook her head, thinking their supposed family friend was simply too rigid and authoritarian to be a Sam. Of course, her father had always been a man to see the best in others. As for Gideon, he most often employed the nickname in a derogatory manner.

Dat had indicated that Samuel might be somewhat judgmental. But now she wondered if she might not be the one guilty of that sin. Yet she couldn't help but side with her mother.

On Sunday morning, Gant tried his best to keep his thoughts on his own church service instead of allowing them to wander to the one taking place in the Amish community.

To save him though, he couldn't concentrate on Pastor Hartman's message. His mind was consumed with what-ifs, and one question loomed large above all others. What if Samuel Beiler were to become the new bishop? The very thought caused his stomach to knot.

He knew all too well, of course, what that would mean to Rachel and him: the loss of any hope of ever becoming husband and wife.

If Beiler were to have his way—and as bishop, he most definitely would—Gant would most likely not be allowed to show his face anywhere near the Amish community again. Ever. Indeed, if looks were any indication, Samuel Beiler, pacifist Amish man though he might be, would dearly love to tie his Irish nemesis to a stake and light a fire under him. Or just shoot him and have the deed done quickly. Whatever his weapon of choice, Gant thought sourly, Beiler would find a way to dispatch him without delay.

He glanced across the aisle just then and found Ellie Sawyer watching him with a questioning expression. Gant felt like a guilty schoolboy who'd been caught cheating in class. Of course, Ellie couldn't read his thoughts about Rachel and whatever might lie ahead for them. All the same, his recent awareness of the attractive young widow's possible romantic interest in him made for an unsettling awkwardness.

Gant quickly glanced away. Sighing, he chastised himself, not for the first time, for his lack of good sense. If Ellie Sawyer—young and pretty and available—really did have an interest in him, life might be a whole lot easier if he could simply respond instead of continuing to love a woman from afar, a woman he quite possibly could never love in any way other than at a distance.

He sighed again, this time more deeply. No point beating himself up over a situation he had no control over. Loving Rachel in the only way he could might not make much sense, but for now it would have to be enough.

After the church service ended, although he admittedly felt like the worst kind of scum for doing so, he cut out of the building as quickly as possible, scarcely acknowledging those standing close by and deliberately avoiding eye contact with Ellie Sawyer.

He rationalized that he simply didn't have it in him to be personable today, tense and short fused as he was. Somehow though, any excuse he came up with didn't take the edge off his self-contempt.

27

END OF A SEARCH

Is this my dream, or the truth?

W.B. YEATS

On Sunday night, Asa found the boy, Silas, considerably stronger. He was sitting up, eating a bowl of rice pudding. Not with gusto, perhaps, but at least he seemed not to tire with the effort.

"It's good to see you looking better," Asa said, watching him.

The boy nodded without looking up.

Asa put a hand to the youth's forehead. "I would say the fever is gone. Eat well. You need to get your strength back."

Again the boy gave a nod but said nothing as he scraped up the last few bites of pudding and then set his bowl aside. Asa studied him, relieved to see the improvement from only the night before.

Although he sensed no invitation in the boy's demeanor, he sat down on the floor beside him. Silas darted a brief look before pulling a blanket more snugly about his shoulders.

"Perhaps you'd best lie down," Asa said. "You don't want to overdo."

"I'm all right."

"You were very sick."

"I'm strong. I heal fast."

"You're fortunate then." Asa paused. "Last night—you were calling for your mama. Is she already in the North?"

Silas snapped around to look at him, his dark brows knit together in a frown. "What?"

"Last night. When your fever was so high. You called for Mama Ari."

The boy's expression suddenly shuttered, and he made no reply. Asa persisted, however, curious about this youth, wondering if he were a self-appointed leader of the runaways or if the responsibility somehow had been thrust upon him. "Is your mama already waiting for you in the North?" he repeated

Silas lowered his head slightly. "My mama is dead," he muttered, his tone sullen.

Taken aback, Asa drew in a long breath. "I'm sorry." He hesitated and then asked, "Has she been gone long?"

The boy shook his head. "She died on our last trip, a few months ago."

"I'm sorry for your loss," Asa said again. "Had she been sick?"

This time the boy looked directly at him, his eyes glazed with what appeared to be a combination of pain and fury. "No. A slave catcher shot her."

Sadness crept over Asa, weighing him down like a sodden blanket. "That's a hard thing."

He was surprised when the boy offered more. "They'd been after her a long time."

"They?"

Silas nodded. "She was one of the best conductors there's ever been. The catchers, they'd been trying for a long time to stop her, but they never could." He stopped. "They couldn't capture her, so they killed her."

"How did it happen?"

The boy looked off into the shadows. "They ambushed us. Meant to take us all. But Mama, she tricked them and took off in a different direction. Told me before she ran that I wasn't to follow, that if anything happened to her I was to take the people on. So that's what I did." He stopped but then added, "Guess they wanted her more than all the rest of us put together. There was three of them...and they shot her three times. We heard it all. And then I did what she said. We ran, and I led the way. I knew how...I'd been with her many a time, so we all got away. All but her."

Asa ached to reach out to the boy, to touch him and try to console him. But he sensed that young Silas would reject any attempt to comfort, so he remained still.

"Your mama was a hero."

The boy's expression cleared a little. "I know. They wanted her bad. Slave catchers had tried to get her other times too, but she was always too smart for them. This time she just...she let them kill her." He sounded as if he were about to strangle. "They hated her," he said, his tone edged with a strange note of pride. "All the slave catchers hated her. They hated her so much they didn't care about getting paid to trap her alive. They just wanted rid of her. They all wanted to be the ones who caught Ariana."

The boy's words struck Asa like a bolt of lightning. "Ariana?" he choked out. "That was your mama's name?"

"Uh-huh. Most folks called her Ari though."

Asa remained silent, thinking...*True, Ariana was an uncommon name, but not unheard of. Still, there was no point in stirring the boy's curiosity. Yet he had searched for her so long, looked in so many places, hoping, always hoping...how could he* not *ask?*

Finally he ventured another question. "Where...where are you from, boy, you and your mama?"

Silas shrugged. "Here and there. Nowhere special. We lived on the road a lot. Mama, she said once she came from Alabama but had me in Georgia." He eyed Asa suspiciously. "Why you asking so many questions anyways?"

Alabama...

His gaze swept over the boy's features, more white than black, for certain, but clearly mixed blood.

"Just wondering about you," he said. "How you got so far away from home, how you got involved as a conductor..."

"Mama was the conductor. I told you, I just took over after she...after she was gone. I learned all I needed to know from her."

"But how did she get caught up in it? You don't find too many women conductors."

Silas gave him a dubious look. "I reckon you know about Miz Tubman, don't you?"

"The one they call Moses," Asa said. "Yes, I've heard about her."

"There are others...other women besides Mama and Miz Tubman, I mean. Mama, she said she started to the North once all on her own.

Never made it though. Instead she met up with some people who had lost their way, so she took them as far as Ohio. She took sick not long after that. Came down with the pneumonia. A white man—a preacher—and his wife took her in and took care of her. She said she stayed with them, worked as their housekeeper for several months. A group of runaways who'd lost their conductor came through about that time, so she took them partway up North, then went back to Cincinnati and started helping other folks too. After that, a lot of people depended on her, I reckon."

He paused, lifted his chin, and added, "I heard tell from another conductor that Mama set hundreds of our people on their way to freedom and never lost a passenger, just like Miz Tubman."

Asa chose his next words with care. "And what about your daddy?"

Again a closed, glum expression locked the boy's features up tight. "Never knew him. According to Mama, she got sassy one time too many with the white man who used to own her. He up and beat on her and then sold her to one of them places where men go and do bad things to women. She finally got away from there, but she was carrying me by them. After she had me, she never left the life, just kept helping folks get to the North."

Asa's heart began to bleed a little and then hammer with reluctant hope. The boy's story lined up with the little he knew about his younger sister. His half-sister. They'd had the same mother but not the same father. Ariana's father had been the white master of the plantation where they'd both lived for several years. But eventually she had been sold from there—sold by her own father into a bawdy house because she was "mouthy...too uppity for her own good."

After that, Asa never heard of her again, though the Lord knew he had tried over and over throughout the years to find her. Everywhere he and Gant had gone, he asked after her but never found a trace.

Now, after all these years, was it possible he'd finally learned her fate? Was this boy seated beside him his sister's son?

"Have you no other family?" he ventured.

Silas shook his head. "No. There was only my mama." He stopped but then went on. "She told me once that she'd had an older brother. Sounded as though he'd been pretty good to her. But she hadn't seen him for years, not since she was taken away from the plantation where she grew up. She said it was just as well…she wouldn't have wanted him to know how hard things had been for her once she got sold."

A bitter, sick taste rose in Asa's throat, and he hauled himself to his feet in a sudden urgency to get away from the boy—far enough away to clear his head, to think about what he had just heard.

"I…I need to go the house for a spell and get some things," he said, rushing his words. "I'll be back…later."

The boy gave him a questioning look but said nothing.

Outside, he stood shaking, breathing in the cold air in huge gulps as if to cleanse the nausea churning up inside him. The blood thundered in his head as the full import of the story he'd just heard flooded over him like a tidal wave.

Could it be? If the Ariana Silas had known as his mother was actually Asa's sister, then she was dead. A guide to freedom for many, yes, but lost to him forever. But her son—if this Silas was truly Ariana's child—the boy was his nephew!

For the first time in years, he had family. Someone of his own blood, his own flesh. For so long, he had had no one. No one but the captain. A man he cared about as much as family, surely, but still not family.

Too overwhelmed to think, too shocked to do anything but feel, Asa braced himself against the cold, stinging wind, his head framed between his hands, his heart roaring like a storm at sea, and wept. He wept for the fragile, thin waif of a sister with the soulful eyes, torn away from him without warning. He wept for the battered woman he'd never had a chance to know, the woman who had given up her life to save the lives of a company of strangers. He wept for her son, who had known no real childhood, no home other than a road that led either to freedom or the grave.

He wept for the years that were now lost to him, the years that had passed without the help he might have given had he known his help was needed. He wept for the love he might have offered had he known that someone out there, his own flesh and blood, existed in a harsh and loveless life.

The pain was excruciating, and yet there was some small, tenuous comfort in knowing that the search that had driven him for years was finally over.

Gant sat at the kitchen table, the low, thin, flickering glow from a lamp the only light in the room. The tension that had been building in him all afternoon now threatened to burn a hole in his chest. One minute he felt as if he were going to be sick, and the next, he thought he might explode.

He knew he had no call to take on like this. What had he expected? That Doc would jump in his buggy right after the church service and roll into town with news about the selection of the new bishop? Hardly. But there was always the possibility he might have driven in to check on Silas and the still ailing Tabitha.

Well, he hadn't, so that was that.

More incredible still, had he actually thought he might hear the outcome from Rachel? That she'd suddenly appear at his door, flushed with excitement and good news?

He groaned, running both hands through his hair. This waiting was making a fool of him.

Ah, but then he had a thought to defend his fancifulness—what about Gideon? He often spent part of his Sundays with Doc and Susan. He didn't attend church with them, but surely he would know something of the day's events.

It was late though. Late enough that the boy most likely wasn't coming back to town until morning.

That hope dashed, Gant forced himself to get up and wash the dishes he'd stacked in the sink earlier. He took his time, stalling because he knew there was no point in going to bed. The thought that he was almost certainly destined for another sleepless night piled more coals on the fire of agitation already burning through him. He went to the bedroom to get his fiddle and then returned to the kitchen table. Mac's attention followed his movements, but he didn't offer to move from his cozy bed by the stove.

For several minutes, Gant attempted to play, but the music simply wasn't in him tonight. Every piece he started sounded raspy and thin, like a sick cat bemoaning its troubles.

Just then the real cat—the bobcat—made his presence known with a quarrelsome yowl.

Sounds like he doesn't care for my music-making tonight any more than I do…

"So where have you been?" Gant said aloud. "I haven't heard anything from you for some time now." He put the fiddle down and went to the window, but there was nothing to be seen in the darkness.

He was still standing, looking out, when Mac got up and scrambled to the door, but as soon as Asa stepped inside, the big dog went back to his bed. Gant watched his friend haul himself through the door, and in that instant his preoccupation with his own troubles fled.

"What's wrong?" he said. "You look like…are you sick? I told you to stay out of that barn. The boy is better, and the little girl is getting stronger. You don't need—"

Asa stood leaning against the door, and Gant stopped his tirade mid-stream when he saw that the other was trembling. "What is it? You *are* sick, aren't you!"

Asa shook his head and raised a hand as if to curb Gant's questions. "No, I'm all right. I just…no, I'm not sick, Captain."

"Well, you look sick!"

Gant crossed the room and yanked a chair away from the table. "Here… sit down."

Asa hesitated and then lowered himself onto the chair while Gant went to the sink and got him a cup of water. He waited until Asa drank the water and then sat down across from him.

"So…tell me."

His friend sat as still as a stone, not speaking for several seconds. When he finally raised his head to meet Gant's gaze, he lifted both hands in a small gesture that indicated he was overcome. Perhaps even dazed.

By now Gant was beginning to feel genuine concern. "Asa? What's going on?"

The other finally spoke, his voice as tremulous as that of a feeble old man. "You remember my telling you about Ariana...my sister?"

"I do, sure."

"Well, the boy...Silas...he was telling me about his mother..."

"You got him to talk about himself? That's real progress."

Asa shook his head. "Not so much about himself. A little. But mostly about his mother...Ariana."

Gant stared at him. "His mother was named Ariana?"

"She was. And she was originally from Alabama."

Gant looked up. "That's...surely that's a coincidence."

"I don't think so. Not after hearing the whole story."

He told Gant then. About the boy's mother being sold to a brothel, about her being a conductor of some reputation, about her saving the runaways from the slave catchers, and about her death.

Stunned, Gant sat listening to it all, trying at each pause in his friend's story to sort out the truth and finally realizing that what Asa had related was no coincidence, though for Asa's sake he almost wished it was.

Asa had hoped and prayed to one day find his sister alive, to have resolution as to her fate and be in a position to care for her. Instead, Ariana was gone. There would be no glad reunion, not on this side of heaven anyway.

After a long silence, Asa's question jerked him back to his surroundings. "So what do you think?"

Gant looked at him. "You're convinced the boy is Ariana's son? That would make him your nephew."

"What else can I think? He even looks like her."

"Could be that now that you've heard his story, he looks like her," Gant suggested. But even as he spoke, he remembered the sting of familiarity that had tugged at him the first time he saw the boy.

"It's true, I would never have noticed before he told me what he did. But can't you see it too?"

Thinking about the photograph he'd carried all these years to help Asa in his search for his younger sister and the only time he'd seen her, yes, Gant understood. The light skin, the dark and hooded eyes, the delicate yet strangely exotic features...yes, the boy resembled Ariana.

Even so, he continued to question Asa. "You're sure about this?"

Asa studied him. "How can I *not* be?"

Finally Gant nodded. "You mean to tell him, I expect."

Asa drew in a long breath. "Of course. But not tonight. Not yet. I need to think about *how* to tell him." He paused. "Do you think he'll believe me?"

Gant thought for a moment. "You carry his mother's picture. You know something of her beginnings and her life, at least as a child. Why wouldn't he believe you?"

Asa's features cleared. "That's so. Tomorrow then. Tomorrow I will tell him. For now, I'm going to think about my words, what I need to say."

"You should also concentrate on getting some sleep," Gant pointed out. "You've had little enough these past few nights."

With a nod, Asa got to his feet and started toward the hallway that led to the back of the house. He turned then, his face creased with a faint smile that wasn't altogether without a hint of sadness. "I should be happy about this, shouldn't I? But it's painful to think of Ariana gone. After hoping to find her for so many years, I can't think what it will be like to no longer search for her everywhere we go."

Without waiting for Gant to reply, he left the room.

Gant also had some thinking to do, and the realization was overladen with a blanket of guilt. The guilt had come with the reminder that many years ago he had actually found Ariana. In his search for her, he'd come upon the girl through a storekeeper who directed him to the local brothel. Once he found her, he'd attempted to convince her to wait for him while he negotiated with the brothel owner who had purchased her from her former master. But he'd returned from what had been a successful negotiation only to find her gone. He never saw her again.

He never told Asa. He hadn't told anyone except Rachel.

Asa's little sister, as he often called her, had appeared hard and bitter, having aged terribly from the lovely young girl in the photograph. Gant had assumed that she simply didn't want her brother to know what had become of her, and at the time he'd figured it would be easier on Asa if he *didn't* know.

Now, however, Gant wished he'd told him because now he had to decide whether he still should tell him. At the time, although he didn't like keeping anything so important from his friend, it had seemed kinder to say nothing.

He no longer knew if that decision had been right or wrong. He only knew that he dreaded the way Asa might look at him if he knew about the secret that had been kept from him all these years.

28

FROM HOPE TO GRIEF

Love is a fabric that never fades, no matter how often it is washed in the
waters of adversity and grief.

ANONYMOUS

Shortly before eight o'clock the next morning, Gant was in the shop, doing his best to avoid thinking.

Not that he intended to open for business that early. He simply couldn't stand the waiting any longer. At least if he were here in the shop, he'd be sure to catch Gideon when he first came in. In the meantime, he attempted to busy himself looking over new orders and scheduling deliveries for the remainder of the week.

As it happened, Gideon wasn't the first to show up. When somebody pounded at the front door, Gant looked up from his desk, surprised to see Doc standing outside.

This wasn't what he had expected, and his heart raced as he scraped back from the desk and hurried to unlock the door. Doc said nothing but merely gave a nod of greeting as he stepped inside. He was carrying a huge cooking pot, which he immediately hoisted onto the front counter.

"Soup," he said. "Susan and Rachel thought it might be of some help for your guests."

"Give them my thanks. It will be much appreciated."

Not for the first time, a hammer blow of guilt struck Gant. That, combined with the anxiety and frustration he had suffered throughout a long, sleepless night, rushed in on him, fragmenting his thoughts and feelings. How he wished his friends had never become aware of this business with the runaways, much less involved in it. Even Rachel and her mother knew what was going on, at least in part. In fact, they had known almost from the time he'd first arrived in the Amish community. Their friend Phoebe Esch had reluctantly filled them in on Gant's and Asa's involvement with the runaways, as well as Phoebe's own connection.

At the time, Gant had been so ill he hadn't realized what they'd been told until after the fact. If he'd any control over the situation, he would have made certain the entire dealings with the slaves and the Underground Railroad had been kept secret.

It wasn't that he didn't trust their confidence. To the contrary, Susan and Rachel were two of the most trustworthy persons he'd ever known. But their familiarity with the situation could place them in harm's way. Anyone suspected of aiding fugitive slaves, even from the sidelines, could be jailed. All it took was one neighbor with a grudge against another to make trouble.

Doc, of course, had grown ever more deeply involved, even giving some of the runaways medical care. Gideon had also been drawn in, having accompanied Asa on a trip north and making known his availability and willingness to go again whenever he was needed.

The entire family had been good friends to Gant. They were well-intentioned people, good people who were willing to help the runaway slaves however they could. Gant knew he could never dissuade them now to back away.

He knew because he had tried, more than once, to warn Doc off. But the last time he'd tried to caution his friend about the risks, Doc had replied with his typically British sniff. "Let this be. It's for me to decide what I will or won't do. I'll act upon my own conscience and God's directive, if you please. Only my Maker has a right to tell me what to do, certainly not some thick-headed Irishman."

Clearly, it would take more than a pointed caution from Gant to sway him. Besides, there had been a number of times when he couldn't think what they would have done without him. Especially when it came to his medical skills.

All these thoughts came flooding in on him in a matter of seconds while Doc tossed his hat and coat on a nearby table before following Gant to the back of the shop. Only then, when Gant turned to face him, did he realize that his friend had not made direct eye contact with him since he'd first walked into the shop.

In that instant, Gant knew that the news he'd been waiting for wasn't going to be what he had hoped to hear.

"Where's Gideon?" Gant asked, his eagerness for any news from Doc now rapidly draining away.

Still avoiding Gant's gaze, Doc rubbed his shoulders and then his hands, as if he were chafing from the cold. "He'll be along. I hope I haven't made him late. I asked him to bring in more wood before leaving."

"No, that's fine. As it happens, I don't really need him until later."

Finally, with unmistakable reluctance, his friend faced him.

Gant braced himself. "Well?"

Doc drew in a long breath. "It's Beiler. The lot fell on Samuel Beiler for bishop."

Gant felt as if his legs would buckle beneath him. A rush of dizziness hit him full force and then fled, leaving him weak to the point of nausea. He gripped the back of a chair with one hand to steady himself.

"I don't like it either," Doc said. His voice sounded harsh, even angry. But the look he settled on Gant held nothing but understanding and kindness. "I'm sorry. Truly sorry. I know this is an enormous disappointment to you, but—"

Gant put up a hand to stop him. "We both knew it could happen." He stopped, fighting to regain his composure. "I'll be all right. At least I will be once it sinks in."

Doc's expression gentled even more. "For whatever it's worth, I'm actually sick about it as well. For you...for the People..."

Gant nodded but only half-heard the rest of what Doc was saying. An image of Rachel filled his mind. Rachel looking at him with tenderness, smiling, that slight tilt of her head as if she didn't quite know what to make of him.

And then another image pushed its way in front of her. Samuel Beiler. Also smiling at Gant. A mocking smile. Head high, eyes proud, watching for any sign of defeat.

"Gant?"

He blinked, dragging his gaze back to Doc.

"Did you hear me? I said many of the People are grieved about this. In truth, they're worried what it will mean. Beiler has already been throwing his weight around, insisting on stricter and stricter regulations, settling punishment on anyone who challenges him."

Gant shrugged. So tight was he drawn that even this slight movement brought a pain to his chest. "But they believe this is God's will, right? Whoever the lot falls on...that's decided by God?"

"Even so, they're...anxious."

Gant locked eyes with him. "Rachel?"

Doc shook his head. "Susan said she's deeply upset. For that matter, so is Susan."

"But the People—they have no choice but to accept this. Isn't that right?"

Doc hesitated. "Well...for now, yes."

Gant shot him a skeptical look. "For now?"

"We have to wait. Wait and see how this works out."

"I may not know much about the Amish church, but I seriously doubt that anyone has ever booted out a bishop," Gant snapped back. "Only your ordinary, everyday sinner is subject to excommunication, right?"

Doc visibly winced. "Bitterness won't help, my friend. We're obligated to pray for each other, even those we perceive to be our enemies."

Gant studied him. "You may be obligated, Doc. I'm Irish, not Amish. And at the moment, I'm not feeling any special obligation to pray for *Bishop* Beiler."

"Gant, I understand how you feel, but—"

Again Gant lifted a hand to stop his friend's words. "I don't think so, Doc. You're too good a man to understand how I'm feeling right now."

The other gave a long sigh, his shoulders sagging. "No one is good, Gant. Certainly not me."

Gant suddenly felt a heavy weariness wash over him. "I know you mean well, Doc. And I thank you for coming to tell me this yourself. I appreciate that, I really do. But I'll need some time to get used to the idea. The finality of it."

Doc regarded him with an expression Gant couldn't quite read. A strangely sorrowful but carefully contained look, as if he wanted to say something he sensed he should not say.

Feeling too brittle, too close to splintering into pieces to deal with what he had just heard, Gant attempted a smile, which failed badly. "Just give me some time, Doc. We'll talk...later, all right?"

His friend delayed any reply but then gave a slow nod. "Yes. We'll do that." He paused and then added, "But I'm going to ask for your word on something. I want you to promise me you will pray about this." He waved off Gant's attempt to protest. "As my friend, and a friend of the People, I'm asking for your word that you'll pray for God's will in this situation. Pray for God to see and move and work His will. Just that, Gant. Will you do that?"

Gant studied him, keenly aware of the goodness he had found in this man almost since the day they'd met—the goodness and the wisdom and the unshakable faith so much a part of David Sebastian. And there was also the friendship the other had offered him, an unconditional kind of friendship. A rare gift, a gift previously unknown to Gant.

"All right, Doc. I'll try. Though for the life of me, I can't see what good it will do. If the Amish are right, the casting of the lot is God's doing. I'm pretty sure He's not going to change His mind for the likes of me."

Doc fixed a steady gaze on him. "I'm not asking you to try to change God's mind. Only to accept that He often works in mysterious ways. It's for us to trust Him, not question Him."

Gant was in no mood to argue theology. A simple shrug was his only reply. For now, it was all he could do to make a stab at getting through the rest of the day.

"Don't give up." Doc's quiet words caught Gant's attention. "Don't give up on Rachel. On any of this. Don't give up...not yet."

Gant's reply was equally as direct. "I don't think I can watch this play out over the long haul, Doc. I can't stay here indefinitely, knowing we can never be together. I've never been one to suffer in silence. You know Beiler will never let me convert, much less marry Rachel."

Gant could hear the scratch of pain in his own voice. Pain and perhaps self-pity? Maybe. Although he'd tried to keep any expectations buried, there was no denying he had hoped for better than this, hoped intensely that Samuel Beiler would not be chosen.

But Beiler *had* been chosen, and now there was nothing to do for it. Gant would shake off the hopelessness and go on. He could do no less. At the same time, he knew himself well enough to know he could never give up on Rachel as long as he was within reach of her.

"You know, I've thought for a long time that Rachel might not be the only reason you're here in Riverhaven."

Gant frowned, trying not to show his impatience. He found himself wishing Doc would leave, but just as quickly he felt a stab of guilt for the thought. The man had driven all the way out here on a bitterly cold morning after all, trying to ease what he'd known would be hard news for a friend. The least he could do was be civil.

"I don't take your meaning, Doc," he said.

"I'm not at all sure I know what it means either," the other replied. "It's just that when I pray for you—oh, yes, I pray for you, rogue that you are—when I pray for you I so often get this strangely ambiguous feeling that something isn't quite as…as clear-cut as it might seem. More and more, I'm coming to believe that you're here in Riverhaven for a reason that might be…well, if not entirely unrelated to Rachel, at least to some extent separate from her."

"Speak English, if you will, Doc. I don't follow you. You forget I'm just an ignorant Irish roughneck."

Doc uttered a sound of disgust. "You're as ignorant as a fox, though I won't argue the roughneck designation. In any event, I can't quite explain what I mean. But surely you haven't assumed that your ending up here as you did is altogether a matter of coincidence. Washed up from the river with an infected bullet wound that could have easily killed you, only to be taken in by an unlikely Amish family who just as easily could have left you to die in the midst of a rainstorm of nearly biblical proportions. And let's not forget that the Amish aren't usually given to entertaining strangers, even those who might turn out to be angels, which most defi-nitely was not the case with you. And how many times have you shown up at the scene of various nearly tragic occasions to lend your help, at the same time falling in love with an Amish widow who hasn't given another man a second look in years, and managing to win her love…a love that apparently has kept you fairly well anchored in place?"

Doc expelled a puff of breath. "Now I don't know about you, but that strikes me as a bit too much of a coincidence. Whether you're too pigheaded to admit it or not, I can't help but think you've had divine protection all along."

Gant stared at him, transfixed by what was almost certainly the most lengthy stream of words Doc had ever uttered all at once. Yet, despite his British friend's somewhat overblown method of speaking, he thought he actually understood what the other was getting at. "You're saying I'm not here by chance?"

Doc gave another long, exaggerated sigh. "Yes. I expect that's what I'm saying. And I'm also saying that no matter how much you fancy your situation with Rachel to be completely hopeless, it's possible that you're premature in thinking about leaving just yet. God might have another idea."

Gant continued to study him long and hard, but Doc didn't so much as flinch.

"Do you know something I don't?" Gant finally said.

"Absolutely not."

Weary to the point of exhaustion, Gant thought to placate his friend so he could collapse in a nearby chair and lick his wounds. "All right, I hear you. I'll pray."

Doc searched his face, his expression skeptical.

"My hand on it," Gant assured him.

Finally, Doc seemed to accept his words. With a small nod, he turned toward the front of the shop. "I need to go. I've several errands to see to. No doubt you've a busy morning ahead as well."

Gant followed him, waited while he donned his coat, and saw him to the door.

"I'll stay in touch," said his friend.

"Have a care," Gant replied, closing and locking the door behind him.

He stood, looking about at his surroundings for a moment before heading toward the back room. He was in no mind or mood to open for business, but Asa was with the fugitives and Gideon was going to be later than usual, so eventually he'd have to unlock the door and face the day.

But not yet.

David Sebastian drove away with a heavy spirit, knowing he had left his friend with a sick heart if not a broken one.

He hoped he hadn't said too much. In no way did he want to create even a glimmer of false hope that somehow, by some miracle, this present situation might change. From all appearances and based on everything he had learned about the Amish before and after his conversion, there would be no change.

Tradition was tradition, and rules were rules. The way they had always done things was the way they would continue to do things.

Or would they? The unforeseen change he had sensed moving through the community like an unsettling wind during the past few weeks—it wasn't the way they had always done things. He couldn't help but wonder where all this was going and what it would lead to.

His heart ached for Gant and for Rachel. His friend's stricken expression when he learned about Samuel Beiler had said it all. The man was distraught. And Rachel—the poor girl had nearly fainted when the selection was announced the day before. Why, she had turned absolutely ashen.

Those two truly loved each other, of that he had no doubt. This latest event must have had all the effect of a barred door closing on whatever hope they'd held. Perhaps he was simply too much of a romantic, but he thought it more likely that his fondness for both young people was at the heart of his distress for them. He could scarcely imagine the pain that must be tearing at them during this time.

Despite his own anguish for the two, however, he had to believe that God had His best will for both of them in mind. Somehow, He would bind up their wounds and give them a future, even if that future didn't include their sharing a life together. There was no limit to what the Creator could accomplish for His children.

If only he could help Rachel and Gant believe that.

Still numb and somewhat dazed by the events of yesterday, Rachel stood staring out her kitchen window. The day was bleak, entirely overcast with the gray dullness of an Ohio winter. Like her heart.

The announcement still seemed like a bad dream, like one of the many she'd had after Eli's death. She would wake up, for a moment almost relieved when it occurred to her that it *had* been a dream and everything was all right now. Then the realization that nothing was right, that the bad dream was real and would go on day after day, year after year, would pummel her in the stomach, leaving her weak and sick for the rest of the night and next day.

That's how she felt at this moment. Throughout the morning, she had drifted from room to room, slugging through her work, steeped in the same weakness and the feelings of helplessness that had overtaken her when she'd first learned that Samuel had been chosen as the new bishop.

Oh, she had tried not to hope, tried not to dream about being with Jeremiah. Every time the thought stole its way into her mind that a new bishop might actually make a difference, might reverse Bishop Graber's refusal to let Jeremiah convert, she would quickly attempt to suppress the bud of hope that began to open deep inside her. She never allowed herself to forget that things might not change, even under a new bishop.

Still, there had been that faint glimmer of possibility.

Now even that was gone. With Samuel as bishop, she was most likely relegated to widowhood for the rest of her years. And she could have accepted that, had Jeremiah Gant not come into her life. If she hadn't fallen in love with the one man she could never marry.

There was something else, something pressing on her apart from the finality of never being free to love and marry Jeremiah. Samuel himself. Did his new position of authority mean he would be even more relentless in his determination to convince her to marry him? Would he press her even more persistently? Was it possible that, as bishop, he could demand that she marry him?

A surge of revulsion rose in her. She couldn't. She could never be a wife to Samuel Beiler. She couldn't bear to even think about the possibility. Instead, she resolved to busy herself with her remaining chores for the day. It was midafternoon already, and she still had much to do. In addition to filling the lamps and bringing in more firewood, she badly needed to put the finishing touches on three birdhouses.

She had fallen behind on her orders. Since the vandalizing, she had all but lost her incentive to even go into the workroom. It was so painful to remember the damage and disarray she had found there that awful night when someone had broken into her house.

But she had orders waiting to be filled, and many were intended as Christmas gifts. She hated to disappoint those who were counting on her, so she really did need to overcome her reluctance to work. Besides, she knew the only way she would ever rid herself of the sick dismay this experience had foisted on her was to face it square on and return to her work. She must stay busy. The Amish had always recognized the reality that trust in God, work, and time enabled one to walk through grief without being crushed by it.

Rachel had lived through grief before and recognized it for what it was. She had survived it then, and God willing, she would survive it again.

But oh, how she dreaded the process.

⤳ 29 ⤝

FAMILY MATTERS

*What greater thing is there for human souls than to feel that they are joined
for life…to be with each other in silent unspeakable memories?*

GEORGE ELIOT

The note was delivered shortly after dark by a boy Gant had never seen
before. But he recognized Turner's handwriting all right, so he took
the message to the barn right away.

He found Asa putting a swatch of horsehair on the pony he'd whittled
for the little girl, Tabitha, while she was ill. As soon as he looked up and
saw Gant standing near the door, he handed the doll back to the child,
hauled himself to his feet, and walked over to the door.

"You need to go tonight," Gant said without preface. "Between eleven
and midnight. Is everything ready?"

The other nodded. "Everything and everybody. They've been waiting
a long time for this."

"I know. It's been hard on them." A thought struck Gant. "The girl,
Tabitha…she's able to travel now? And Silas?"

"Tabitha is still weak and a little wobbly in the legs, but she'll be all
right to travel. And Silas is itching to leave. I think he's going to be surprised when he figures out he's not as strong as he thinks he is yet, but
he's got gumption, that one. He'll do."

"Have you talked to him?"

Asa looked at him and shook his head. "There's been no good time
so far."

"You'd best get it done," Gant said bluntly. "He should know before you get on the road."

Asa sighed. "I suppose so."

"You worried about how he'll react?"

"A little maybe."

"He's young enough. I should think he'd be glad to know he has family."

"That's just the thing. He doesn't know me. I'm not family as far as he's concerned. I'm a stranger."

Gant studied him. "You're going to be on the road together. You won't be a stranger for long. In fact, this trip should be good for you both. Give you a chance to get to know each other. That's why you ought to talk to him before you leave. So he'll know who you are." Gant stopped and then added, "And so you can quit fretting about it."

Asa gave another nod. "No doubt you're right."

"Sometimes I am." Gant left him then so he could get the deed over with.

At first Asa kept Silas in the corner of his vision as he began to tell him the strange, mind-boggling story of how they were related. After another moment though, once he sensed that the truth had begun to settle in on the boy, he turned to face him directly.

"As incredible as this must seem to you," he said, "it's the truth, and you deserve to hear it. I don't know much about what might have happened to your mama since the time I last saw her at the plantation, but I can tell you whatever you want to know about the years before that, before you were born."

The boy's eyes seemed about to pop. The narrow look of cynicism that usually pinched his features had disappeared, at least for the time being. For now, young Silas was obviously a captive listener to whatever Asa had to tell him.

"You're sayin' my mama...she was your sister? You're the big brother she used to talk about?"

Asa nodded, watching him closely.

"So that makes me—what? What kind of relation to you then?"

"I'm your uncle. Your mama and I had two different fathers but the same mother."

The boy studied him. "You're darker than my mama. A lot darker."

"That's because your mama's daddy was a white man."

"I know that. Doesn't mean I like the knowing."

"Even so, it's true. He was the owner of the plantation where we lived when she was little." Asa paused. "Ariana never told you about him?"

Silas shook his head. "She never said nothing about him 'cept he wasn't a very good man and that's why she ran away from him."

"Well, now that's the truth. He wasn't a good man, especially where his slaves were concerned. He took some kind of sick pleasure in hurting us."

"So…you were a slave too?"

"I was. But no longer. I'm a free man now, thanks to Captain Gant. There are good white men, son. I've known a number of them, and the Captain is one of the best."

Silas's face hardened to a sneer. "Right. I s'pose you think he's your friend."

Patience, Lord. Give me patience with this boy…

"I *know* he's my friend. He took a bullet for me. That's why he walks the way he does."

The boy shot him a look of pure skepticism. "He got himself shot because of you?"

"He did. Nearly died as a result of it. So don't give me no sass. I won't tolerate unkind words about white men *or* black. We're all the same color in God's eyes."

The other glanced away, remaining silent for a time. "Mama, she believed in God too," he finally said.

"I know she did," Asa said quietly. "We used to talk about Him when she was just a little girl."

The boy turned to look at him. "She told me that. Told me her grown-up brother used to tell her stories about God and Jesus."

"She remembered that?"

Unexpectedly, Silas's expression turned softer, even thoughtful. "Yeah, she remembered. She…she thought real high of you, it seemed."

Asa's eyes burned. The boy was searching his face as if he were looking for something hidden. Finally he spoke. "So, just say you *are* my...uncle. What am I supposed to call you now? Uncle or Asa?"

"Best I can recollect, you haven't called me anything up to now, have you?"

Silas shook his head. "Didn't seem necessary."

Asa smiled a little. "Well, then...when it does seem necessary, call me whatever you want to."

The boy continued to watch him and then finally gave a nod. "I'll have to think on this, you know."

"Of course you will. In the meantime, there's something else you need to know, and our time is short, so I'll just fill you in. We're leaving in a couple of hours or so. Do you feel strong enough to travel?"

Silas's expression brightened. "We're leaving? About time!" Then he stopped. "You're going too?"

Asa looked at him. "You didn't know? Yes, I'm going. Is that acceptable to you?" he said dryly.

The boy's eyes narrowed. "I reckon it is. It's not like I need you to go though."

"I understand," Asa said, making an effort not to smile. "Still, you won't mind if I go along? I've had a good bit of experience with these trips north."

Silas studied him. "I s'pose you might be of some help then. But not because I'm still sick. I'm fine." He paused. "Well then, we'd better tell the people."

Asa hesitated, thinking. "Why don't you do that? They're used to taking their direction from you. I need to talk to the Captain about some things anyway."

Silas stood up, dusting his hands down the sides of his trousers. "I'll handle it."

As Asa walked away, he thought this new nephew of his could most likely handle just about anything that needed handling.

In any event, it promised to be an interesting trip.

➔ ✦

Later that night, Gant and Gideon stood watching as the last of the runaways were stowed in the wagons. Turner's oldest son, as promised, had arrived to help drive.

"You're sure I shouldn't go?" Gideon asked for the third time.

Gant shook his head. "No. Silas is used to doing this. He knows the way. He may be young, but he's smart, and he's experienced. And I expect Asa can handle himself and just about anything else just fine. No," he said again, "I need you here. And so does your family."

Gideon turned to look at him. "Why do you say that? About my family?"

Gant shrugged. "You know the trouble they've had. I just think you need to stay put for a while. Besides," he added, "with Christmas coming soon, I expect to be plenty busy. I'll need your help."

Asa walked up just then. "So, looks like we'll be on our way now."

Gant nodded. "You're sure you have everything you need?"

"We're all set. Even if we weren't, there's no more room in the wagons."

Asa smiled at Gideon. "I'll miss your company. Maybe next time."

"I wanted to go this time," Gideon said, "but the Captain thinks I should stay here for now."

"And he's probably right. Don't worry. There will be other trips." He shook hands with Gideon and then Gant.

"Have a care, *mo chara*," Gant told him.

Asa started off, tossed a wave over his shoulder, and then took off jogging toward the wagons.

"What's that mean?" Gideon asked. "What you said to him."

"*Mo chara*"? It's Irish for 'my friend.'"

Gideon looked from Gant to Asa, who was climbing up on the wagon bench in the lead wagon.

"I expect he's a good man to have as a friend," he said.

"The best," Gant replied, meaning it. "They don't come any better."

30

A Stirring of Rumors

A man reveals himself not by his words but by his deeds.

ANONYMOUS

It took only a little more than two weeks for Samuel Beiler to show what kind of bishop he would be.

There wasn't even a pretense that life for the Plain People would proceed as usual, that little would be changed under the leadership of the new bishop. Although Gideon Kanagy was no longer living Amish, he still had a number of friends who were, and those friends were talking. Talking and complaining and even worrying. Sometimes to Gideon.

Tonight, Reuben Esch and Solomon Miller both seemed particularly riled up as they sat in Gideon's rooms above the carpentry shop, plying him with the latest hearsay.

Gideon was surprised that either of his friends, Reuben especially, would visit him in his living quarters. Although both were in their *rumspringa*, neither had chosen to live outside the Plain community.

Solomon was actually preparing to make his vows to the church soon, and rumor had it that he and Sarah King would marry next year. Reuben, the son of Malachi Esch, had always been one of the male Amish youths who seemed disinclined to stray from his Amish upbringing. Even in his *rumspringa*, Reuben typically took little advantage of the freedom this Amish custom of a "running around time" offered. He was far more likely to stay close to home, helping with the farmwork.

Gideon was reminded that Reuben's father, Malachi, had never seemed to be as strict and unbending as some of the other Plain men were with their children. Malachi always appeared easygoing and good-natured with a soft spot for his family. So maybe Reuben had no worries that he might be rebuked for keeping company with a known rebel like Gideon Kanagy. Apparently Solomon didn't either.

In any event, he was glad they were here. He sometimes missed being around his Plain friends. Although he still saw the other fellows now and again, being together with his two oldest pals was different. He had grown up with Reuben and Solomon. Sometimes it seemed as if they'd known each other forever. The three of them had always shared matters they wouldn't have confided to others. There were some things best left unsaid except to the most trusted of friends.

Tonight, his two companions seemed to have plenty to confide, and Gideon's surprise and anger grew by the minute at their stories about their new bishop. Maybe he shouldn't be surprised by the tales he was hearing about Beiler. He had never liked the man, had never quite trusted him, partly because of the accounts he'd heard growing up about Beiler's harsh treatment of his own sons. Even so, he was surprised by some of his friends' tales.

Over the years, Gideon and some of the other fellows had actually come to feel sorry for the Beilers, especially the two older boys. Aaron, the oldest, was now in his own *rumspringa*, and according to Solomon and Reuben, he was inclined to spend more time with the *Englisch* in the area than with his own Amish neighbors. Noah, the middle son, was a couple years younger than Aaron and a quiet, seemingly shy boy. Once he was finished with his schooling, he went right to work on the farm, and that was still where he spent most of his time. As for Joe, the youngest, he was thought to be a little slow in the head.

Tales had circulated for a long time that Aaron and possibly Noah were routinely mistreated and maybe even beaten by their father.

It wasn't unusual for an Amish man to be strict with his children. But strict was one thing, and cruel was another. Gideon didn't know if many of the adults were aware of the stories about Beiler, but the young people talked. They talked about the bruises they'd seen on Aaron, particularly in warm weather when more of his skin was exposed. And when they were younger, there had been many a morning when Aaron and Noah had come to school with swollen red eyes that hinted they might have been crying the night before.

No one knew for certain, of course, but tales were told, and some were believed. But even if anyone had known for sure, most likely nothing would have been done about it. A man's dealings with his family were his own business. That was just the way things were among the People.

Now that Gideon was older, he appreciated his own father more than ever. His *dat* had been stern at times and expected hard work and right behavior from his children, but Gideon couldn't remember a time when he'd ever been frightened or cowed by Amos Kanagy. His father had always seemed comfortable in showing his love for his family.

When he realized that his mind had wandered away from the conversation, he tugged his thoughts back to what the others were saying.

"He actually told them they couldn't get married this month, like they'd planned?" Reuben questioned.

"Who's that?" Gideon broke in.

"Miriam Zook and Mervin Fisher," Reuben supplied. "Seems Beiler heard they were seeing each other too often and disciplined them. He made them postpone their wedding."

"Made them?" Gideon asked.

Solomon gave a shrug. "The bishop has the say-so about weddings."

"Sounds as though the new bishop has a say-so about everything," Gideon put in.

"You don't know the half of it," Solomon said. "He's even putting restrictions on how often a husband and his wife can..." he stopped, his face flaming. "You know."

"What?" Gideon burst out. "Since when does a bishop have the right to interfere in the People's marital matters? That's never happened before!"

Reuben, usually a respectful and reserved type, grated out, "Bishop Beiler seems to think he has the right to interfere in whatever he wants." He shook his head, brushing away a shock of dark hair that fell over his forehead, and added, "The people are getting mighty upset with him."

"Rightly so, it would seem," said Gideon.

"He ordered Thomas Schrock to close down his blacksmith shop,"

Solomon said. "Told him he needed to spend all his time farming. And Thomas started smithing in the first place because he couldn't make a living with just his small acreage, what with his big family and all. *Dat* said Thomas is worried sick about finances now. The People will help him, of course, but Thomas won't like being beholden to the community."

Anger surged in Gideon. He got to his feet and began to pace. "This just isn't right! Somebody needs to do something."

"Like what?" said Reuben. "Beiler is the bishop."

"He's sure not acting like any bishop I ever heard tell of, " Gideon shot back. "He shouldn't be allowed to get away with this."

"Nobody can stop him," Solomon pointed out. "He has all the control."

"Bishop Graber would never have behaved like this," Gideon said. "No bishop ought to have this kind of power."

"It's getting kind of scary," Reuben said quietly. "People are beginning to wonder what's going to come next."

"Well, he's already set down a new rule about Christmas," Solomon said, his expression sullen.

Gideon stopped pacing and turned to look at him.

"No gifts are to be exchanged. Nothing. No homemade presents, not even food—nothing at all. Not among family members or friends. Not even for the children."

"But Bishop Graber always let us exchange gifts, so long as they were homemade and not elaborate," Gideon put in.

"The *new* bishop has reversed that," Solomon said, his tone sour.

Gideon shook his head. "This is so wrong."

Reuben had been quiet for some time but now spoke up. "You think maybe it would do any good for Aaron to talk to him? Maybe if Samuel realized that he's stirring up resentment among the People, he'd ease up a little."

Solomon shot him a wide-eyed look. "Are you serious? Aaron would never dare to disagree with his father! He's afraid of him."

"Aaron's a grown man," Gideon reminded the others. "He has no call to be afraid of his own *dat*."

"Maybe not, but it's no secret he and Noah do whatever they can to keep him off their backs."

They stayed silent for the next minute or two, each obviously thinking his own thoughts. Reuben finally broke the silence again. "What about your sister, Gideon? Could she maybe speak to him...to the bishop?"

Gideon, now standing at the window, turned. "Rachel? Why would she talk to Beiler?"

Reuben and Solomon exchanged glances. "Well, rumor has it that they might have...an understanding," Reuben said.

Gideon tensed. "That's not true," he said, his tone rough.

"You sure?" Solomon seemed to form the words carefully, but his gaze was intent. "There's been talk for a long time that the bishop means to marry her."

"I'm about as sure as I can be of anything that Rachel has no intention of marrying Samuel Beiler," Gideon said, not even trying to hide his irritation. "And that's all I have to say about my sister."

The other two nodded and glanced away.

Gideon felt close to going into a sulk. It made his blood boil to think of people talking in such a way about Rachel. The idea of her name even being mentioned in the same breath as Samuel Beiler's was insulting.

They spent the rest of the evening talking about inconsequential things, and Gideon soon lost interest. The sense of good fellowship and contentment he'd enjoyed earlier had been mostly spoiled by the revelations of Beiler's behavior and particularly by the thought of him being linked with Rachel.

He was almost relieved when his friends left so he could be by himself to think through the unpleasant and worrisome accounts that still continued to nag him after he went to bed. During a long and restless night, he increasingly felt a need to talk to somebody about the things he'd heard tonight, someone who could be trusted not to go ratting to the bishop. But who?

Besides, what good would it do? It wasn't as if anyone could change the way things were, after all. Whatever a bishop decreed was final.

This *would* have to start up just when he was actually considering going back home and living Amish again. He'd been thinking about it for quite a while, in part because of his feelings for Emma, but also because the *Englisch* life was losing its appeal for him. The main thing keeping him away from the Plain community now was his job. He purely enjoyed working in the carpentry shop for Captain Gant. Farming was all right, and he didn't mind the hard work, at least part-time. But he'd much rather work in the shop—work with the wood itself, make deliveries, and be a carpenter instead of a farmer. He'd learned a lot from the captain and wanted to continue to learn while working on the job and gaining more experience. He had earlier wondered if Bishop Graber would approve his working in the shop. And now that he would need Samuel Beiler's approval, he knew it was even less likely that he'd be allowed to continue as Gant's apprentice.

Reuben was right. This was getting kind of scary.

Still, as futile as the effort might be, he wished he could hash all this out with someone he trusted. Someone wise who understood the People's ways but who didn't necessarily believe everything that the bishop ordered was sacred and untouchable.

It occurred to him that that someone just might be Doc. With that thought and an extended time of mulling it over, he finally found enough peace to drift off to sleep.

31

A Secret Meeting

When men meet with a mission, let truth be in their midst.

ANONYMOUS

Christmas came quietly in the Riverhaven Amish community and passed without leaving much of an imprint.

To an observer watching from the outside, the holy days of the winter season looked almost like any other days, common and ordinary with nothing to mark them as special.

For many of the Plain People, it was a bittersweet time, although still a special time of reverence, for remembering and rejoicing in the Savior's birth. This year, however, rather than being a day of great brightness and high cheer, it was a time when some, especially the children, wondered why it had to be spent without the usual scent of evergreen in the house or the annual small gifts of love and friendship so carefully handcrafted and exchanged between family members and friends.

This was a quiet and carefully scripted Christmas, one to tread through softly rather than dance through joyfully.

As the old year faded into the new, David Sebastian kept his concerns regarding Samuel Beiler to himself. He longed to discuss the matter with Susan, but she was burdened with her own worries about the new bishop's flagrant bullying of the People. Besides, he had come to realize by now that Amish men simply didn't discuss matters of church leadership with their wives, and although it went against the relationship he had with Susan, in this particular case he felt obligated to maintain his silence.

He was reluctant to add to her troubled state of mind by letting her know just how serious the situation had become. It wasn't fair to use her as a sounding board for his own disquiet. He couldn't even bring his closest friend into his confidence because Jeremiah Gant was *Englisch*. No matter how much the community had come to respect him, he was still an outsider.

David couldn't help but wonder if the meeting he'd been invited to tonight had anything to do with Beiler. To his surprise and puzzlement, he'd been asked to come to Malachi Esch's house after supper for some kind of a gathering even though he was a fairly new convert and not in any way involved in leadership. He had no idea who else would be in attendance. Malachi mentioned only "a few who want to discuss some concerns of the People."

He was just putting on his coat when Susan came down the steps.

"Will you be late, do you think?" she said.

"I hope not. I can scarcely keep my eyes open now. I'm still reeling from that delicious dinner you cooked at noon. Between that and the leftovers we had for supper, I expect I'll fall asleep on my way home."

She lifted her face for his kiss, and he obliged. "Woman, I'm going to be as big as a house if I keep eating the way I have been."

"You haven't gained a pound in ten years, David Sebastian," she said, tugging the front of his coat more snugly about him. "I should be so fortunate as you."

"You," he said, pulling her back into his arms for another kiss, "are perfect just as you are."

"Plump as a mother hen," she said with a sigh.

"Pretty as a peacock and twice as sassy." He clucked her under the chin, and she gave him a look. "By the way, you can make some more of that cinnamon egg pudding we had for Christmas anytime you're in the mood."

She smiled. "I noticed you seemed to like it."

"Now there's an understatement." He gave his middle a thump. "So, you're sure you don't mind being alone for a bit?"

"I won't be alone. Fannie and Thunder will keep me company."

"I'm sure they will."

Reluctantly, he let her go and turned toward the door, but she stayed his hand before he could open it. "David?"

He waited.

"You'll be careful?"

"Careful of what? I'm only going as far as Malachi's."

"I know, but…well, just be careful."

He touched the palm of his hand to her face. "I always am, dear," he said quietly, touched by her concern yet regretting that she obviously felt uneasy.

In truth, the entire community seemed to share that need these days.

Even if David Sebastian had deliberately tried to figure out the purpose of that evening's meeting at Malachi Esch's house, he would have been hard-pressed to imagine most of it. As soon as he saw the bishop who had officiated at his and Susan's wedding—Bishop Schrock, from a neighboring district—David knew something unusual was afoot. And by the time Malachi finished a brief few words in recognition of the bishop, David was more puzzled than ever about the reason he—a recent convert—had been invited. Especially since only he, Abe Gingerich, and John Lapp, Abe's brother-in-law, were gathered around the kitchen table with Malachi and the bishop. Some of the older men, longtime members of the Riverhaven Amish community, were conspicuously absent.

"As I said," Malachi offered in his familiar way of often repeating himself, "Abe Gingerich and I, as your ministers, took some of our concerns—and those of a few other men from our district—to Bishop Schrock to seek his wisdom and advice."

He gave more details about some of the complaints that had been brought to him and Abe by a number of the Plain People. Some were problems David had already heard about; others were new to him.

All had to do with Samuel Beiler.

David tensed when Malachi's gaze roamed down the table and settled on him. "I asked Doc here even though he's pretty new to the church because he's been a doctor and a *gut* friend to our people for many years now. We've learned to trust his judgment, and none of us would question his faith or his wisdom in spiritual matters. And John..." He inclined his head toward Abe's brother-in-law, seated across the table from him. "John has a particular concern that he just recently brought to our attention." He paused. "It's a matter that might concern you, as well, Doc."

Little by little, David grew even more tense as John Lapp began to speak. In a quiet, hesitant tone, the local farmer related a story that sent a chill of dread coiling through him.

"You all know my boy, Jacob?"

The others at the table nodded, waiting. "Well," John Lapp went on, "he and Bishop Beiler's middle son, Noah, they spend a lot of time together. They're good friends, those two."

David noted the way John had begun to wring his hands atop the table as he spoke. Self-consciousness or controlled anger? He wasn't sure.

"The Beiler boy, he's some younger than my Jacob, but he's tagged along after him ever since the two were just little tykes. Noah is a quiet sort, on the bashful side, and has never seemed real happy. Never laughs or acts *schtupid* like some boys when they're that age. He's never been much of a talker."

Where was this going? David knew what John meant about the Beiler lad. He had treated him once or twice for the usual boyhood broken bones and sprains. He had never been able to coax anything more from him than a ghost of a smile and a shake of the head. But what did Beiler's son have to do with tonight's odd meeting?

"A few weeks back," John continued, "Noah told Jacob a mighty troubling story. I'm not sure what gave rise to him bringing it up. I think it might have had to do with some of the fellows talking among themselves about that *Englischer* boy who was in court back then for beating on a relative. You know the one? He beat up a younger cousin to get back at his uncle. Seems the uncle turned him in for stealing."

Again the men gave a nod of acknowledgment.

"Anyway, something apparently was said while they were all together that upset the Beiler boy, and later that night, when he and Jacob were by themselves, he let it be known that his *dat* beat him and the oldest son, Aaron, pretty regular."

The men had fallen totally silent. David caught himself holding his breath. Finally, Abe Gingerich spoke up. "I asked John about this, and he said he questioned his boy, Jacob, pretty thoroughly. Jacob maintains that Noah Beiler insisted he and his brother were often beaten. Not paddled, but beaten. Hard."

John Lapp went on, his hands balled into fists on top of the table. "At first I figured Noah had exaggerated. Boys will do that sometimes. You know...to get attention. But my boy stood up for him. He said Noah wasn't one to say things that weren't true. Even so, I wasn't all that concerned. After all, which one of us hasn't had to discipline a son for some kind of misbehavior?"

Malachi Esch interrupted at that point. "There's a difference between discipline and a beating, John," he said quietly.

"*Ja*," John agreed. "And I pointed that out to Jacob. I told him he mustn't exaggerate and that Noah might have used too strong a word."

He stopped, glanced around the table, and dropped his gaze slightly as he continued. "There was more. Noah claimed his *dat* also beat his mother when she was still living. Said he beat her till she cried."

The others exchanged looks, but David caught his breath. Unless the Beiler boy had exaggerated—or worse, outright lied—his darkest suspicions about Samuel Beiler had just been confirmed.

Over the years, he had noticed a number of behavioral traits in Beiler's wife that he found suspect: the way she seemed to shrink within herself when her husband was in the room, her obvious uneasiness at his presence during the delivery of two of their sons, the nervous glances she sent his way when he wasn't looking, and a number of unexplained bruises and broken bones.

In his medical practice among the Amish, he had come across more than one wife who had been beaten. The Amish were inclined to handle or even conceal any disturbing conduct within their own communities rather than involving the *Englisch* authorities, but physical abuse wasn't that easy to conceal from a doctor. Twice he had actually confronted husbands he suspected of such despicable mistreatment. One had flatly denied David's accusations and, furious, refused to allow him to treat any member of his family again. The other man seemed to have been shamed by the confrontation and, as far as David knew, had discontinued the appalling behavior.

He had never been certain about Samuel Beiler, only suspicious. The signs had been there but not any conclusive evidence. But now, as much as he hated to face the fact that his suspicions had most likely been justified, he found himself believing the witness of John Lapp's son.

David was roused from his thoughts as Malachi asked, "Doc, the bishop and I need to ask you something, and whatever you say won't leave this room. Did you ever know about any of this in regard to Samuel's wife and his sons? Could what the boy told Jacob be true?"

Bishop Schrock also faced David with a question. "You can understand, I'm sure, Doctor Sebastian, why your friends brought this information to me and why we need to find out if there's truth in it."

In that moment, David was genuinely at a loss for words. If he had ever been able to prove his suspicions, most likely he would have gone to Bishop Graber. But he had never had proof. Did he and the others really dare to take the word of a child? The Beiler boy, Noah, couldn't be more than thirteen or fourteen at most. How on earth could they even begin to handle a thing like this?

"There's more, Doc," Malachi put in.

David looked up to find his neighbor's face creased with a troubled expression.

"I think maybe there's another reason you should know about what the Beiler boy told John's son, whether it was true or not."

David waited.

"It's…about Rachel." Malachi looked uncomfortable, as if he were embarrassed about what he had to say yet convicted that he needed to say it.

"Rachel? What about Rachel?"

"Well…Samuel has been way too open about the fact that he's wanted to marry Rachel for a long time now. He should have kept that kind of thing to himself, but he hasn't. And he seems awful sure he can convince her to agree."

Malachi shook his head. "It's not right that he should talk about such things to others, but he does. Now, Doc, we know it's none of our business. But what with Rachel being Susan's daughter and your stepdaughter, and given what his own boy has claimed about the beatings…well, that's another reason we thought you should be here tonight. As I said, we all know it's none of our affair, Samuel's talk about marrying Rachel, but I imagine you can see why we thought you should know."

David's throat was so tight, his mouth so dry, he wasn't sure he could speak, but somehow he forced a reply. "I've known…for some time that Samuel wants to marry Rachel. She's refused him. More than once."

The look Malachi settled on him held both sympathy and understanding. "Can you tell us anything about the other, Doc? About the beatings? Do you believe young Noah?"

David hated this. Who was he to accuse a man—his own bishop—of such a heinous, detestable act? And yet hadn't he known? When Martha Beiler was still alive, hadn't his uneasiness about Samuel even then been more than mere suspicion? Hadn't he seen her draw back in what seemed to be an involuntary shudder from her husband's hand on her arm or her shoulder? And the bruises, the fractures. He had asked her about them of course, but she always blamed them on a fall or offered another excuse.

More often than not, Samuel had been in the room with them, and the way he glared at his wife had made David wonder if things might not go even harder for her if he questioned too much. More than once, he'd considered confronting Beiler, but some instinct always warned him off—perhaps because he was afraid he would only make things worse for Martha.

And what about now, if he should admit his qualms? What then? What could possibly be accomplished by adding his own suspicion to the tales of a child? Samuel Beiler was a bishop, after all. The spiritual leader and the authority figure for an entire Plain community.

In that instant he thought of Rachel. She had made no secret of the fact that she didn't love Samuel, that she had no inclination whatsoever to marry him. She was in love with Gant, after all. Gant was the man she wanted to marry. But they couldn't marry. That was more certain now than ever. As bishop, Samuel Beiler would never allow Gant's conversion, never ease the way for Rachel and Gant to wed.

What if Beiler somehow found a way to *make* her marry him? David couldn't conceive of that happening, couldn't imagine any way the man could ever change Rachel's mind—and certainly not her heart. But even the most implausible idea that it could happen made him ill.

Well, but forget Rachel for the moment. It was almost a foregone conclusion that Beiler would marry someone. Amish men seldom remained single for any length of time, but Beiler was still unmarried after a number of years. It wasn't all that unrealistic to assume he would find someone eventually. Some unsuspecting, vulnerable woman who might be subjected to the same treatment Martha Beiler had endured.

Chilled, David knew then that he had kept his silence about Samuel Beiler long enough. Perhaps too long. Perhaps if he had told someone long ago what he suspected about the man, he might have spared Beiler's wife and his sons a great deal of pain.

He met Malachi's questioning gaze. "Yes," he said, his voice strained and unsteady, "I...I suppose I do believe Noah Beiler. Yes," David said again. "I'm afraid the boy most likely is telling the truth."

32

A GIFT FOR RACHEL

Set me as a seal upon thine heart.
SONG OF SOLOMON 8:6-7

Gant waited a week into the New Year before going to Rachel. He had made a gift for her before the holidays, but since the practice of exchanging Christmas gifts had been outlawed by Samuel Beiler, he'd deliberately delayed giving her the gift until now.

Of course, he shouldn't be giving her a gift at all. In the Amish community, a man wasn't to give a woman gifts, nor was she to accept them, especially anything personal, unless they were engaged or married. But he wasn't Amish, and since it was no longer Christmas, he was just stubborn enough not to care about Samuel Beiler's new rules one way or the other. Besides, the Amish rules didn't apply to him, and if he wanted to give Rachel a gift, then he would.

That didn't mean she would accept it, but Gant thought she would.

It wasn't much, nothing extravagant, and not really anything personal except for the fact that he believed she'd like it. Knowing her love for birds, especially waterbirds, he'd carved a swan from a piece of black teak he'd put aside years ago after a trade with a Burmese sailor. He had thought the day might come when he'd want to do something special with it, and it finally had. He'd shaped it and stained it and polished it until it gleamed like satin, and then he wrapped it in a silk sleeve and tied it with satin.

He hadn't carved anything for a long time, and when he'd first started to work on the piece a few weeks back, he wondered if he could fit it to his imagination and have it look the way he wanted. It had cost him a few late nights, but it came out rather well if he did say so himself.

At first he'd wondered how much of his desire to give her a gift had to do with the sideboard Samuel Beiler had commissioned him to make as a birthday gift for her. Was it possible the idea had been born once he'd started working on Beiler's gift? And he *was* working on the sideboard in spite of the anger it evoked in him. All too often he had to remind himself the piece was for Rachel and therefore worth his best effort, or he would have destroyed it before it was ever finished.

Well, tonight he was taking her *his* gift. Admittedly, he was looking forward to giving it to her, but more to the point, he wanted to see her, needed to see her. In truth, he felt as if he couldn't put in another day without seeing her. It was even more important, given the way he'd been thinking lately.

He forced his mind to cut away from that direction. Some other time he could punish himself with the pain those thoughts leveled on him. Not now, not tonight. He had no intention of carrying that heaviness into Rachel's house.

Of course, Rachel might not even let him inside her house now that their future seemed to be sealed.

More like their doom was sealed.

Well, somehow he had to convince her to let him in. He wasn't sure exactly what was driving him other than the need to be with her, to soak up her presence. He had to see her tonight or he would surely snap. That was all he knew, and it was enough.

He scowled at his own dark mood and determined to shake it off before he reached Rachel's house.

He'd left the buggy back at the shop. A single horse tethered at the back of her house wouldn't be all that noticeable to anyone happening by. But before going half the distance, the cold had begun to seep through his body like river ice. He wrapped his coat more snugly about him and ducked his head against the rising wind.

Riding home would be a misery.

When Rachel cautiously opened the door and saw him standing there, her first inclination was to refuse to let him in. She shivered, but not from the cold blast that struck her from outside. Something was on the wind tonight, something wild and unnatural about the night itself, and when she met Jeremiah's eyes she saw it reflected there too.

At first she thought he was angry. But a second look and she recognized the fierce determination that virtually trapped her in his gaze. She had seen that look before.

"Jeremiah…"

"I need to see you, Rachel. May I?" He gestured toward the inside.

Without waiting for her reply, he stepped in, easing himself carefully past her.

Still she hesitated, long enough for him to reach around her and push the door shut. Ignoring any formalities, he shrugged out of his coat, doffed his cap, and gave both a careless toss over the wall peg.

Suddenly irritated with him—he knew he wasn't supposed to be here—Rachel stood watching him. He faced her with a quirk of a smile. "I'm near frozen. Do you have any coffee?"

"Won't you come in, Jeremiah? Please, just make yourself at home." Rachel despised sarcasm and was surprised to hear it lacing her own words. But he deserved it.

He didn't stop until he reached the middle of the kitchen and turned to face her. She was so close on his heels she nearly ran into him.

"Coffee? Please?"

"I still have some left from supper. Or would you like me to make fresh?" she said grudgingly.

Her eyes went to the brown-paper wrapped package he held, and in spite of her best intentions, her curiosity stirred. Her gaze followed his movements as he placed the package on the table with obvious care.

"Just so it's hot," he said. "Leftover is fine."

Rachel wanted to be angry with him. She had every right to be angry. She should tell him to leave. She should *insist* that he leave. But what she saw in his eyes and what she felt in her heart pressed her to keep silent.

She drew in a long, shaky breath and motioned toward a chair at the table. "Sit down," she said, her voice unsteady. "I'll get your coffee."

He seemed to slump with relief and then sank down onto the chair and sat waiting. He said nothing, but Rachel felt him watching her as she heated the coffee and poured him a cup.

She managed to keep her hand from trembling as she set the cup on the table in front of him. "You know you shouldn't be here. If anyone finds out…" She let her words fall away unfinished.

He looked up at her. "I won't stay long. Sit down with me?"

Rachel hesitated but then, deliberately ignoring the chair closest to him, sat down across the table. "What do you want, Jeremiah?"

He pushed the package across the table toward her. "This is for you. I heard that you weren't supposed to receive Christmas gifts this year, so I waited."

Rachel looked at him and then the package.

"It's not a Christmas gift," he said with a knowing smile. "Christmas is over."

She continued to eye the package but made no move to touch it.

"Open it," he said quietly. "Please." His gaze went over her face, and Rachel felt as if he were touching her.

Finally, she loosened the brown paper wrapping and then sat staring at a beautiful, multicolored sheath of material that seemed to shimmer in the lamplight. She glanced across to see him watching her, his eyes reflecting the light. Now her hands did tremble as she carefully pulled away the soft fabric to reveal an intricately carved black swan that seemed incredibly lifelike in its gleaming perfection.

Rachel couldn't stop a sharp intake of breath or resist touching it. She put one finger to its head, tracing the line of its long neck down its back. The wood felt cool and smooth, smoother than anything she had ever touched before.

"Oh, Jeremiah…" She breathed the words more than spoke them, and when she met his eyes she knew in that instant that he had made this, made it with his own hands...for her.

"You shouldn't have done this." She felt tears burn her eyes and didn't know if the beauty of the swan or the idea that he had actually made something so exquisite for her was responsible for her emotion. "It's the loveliest thing I've ever seen."

The intensity and tenderness of his gaze nearly undid her. "And you," he said, his tone hoarse, "are the loveliest thing I've ever seen."

"You made this?" she said, already knowing the answer but desperately needing to quiet her heart and ease the tension hanging between them. "For me?"

"I did. I had thought to give it to you for Christmas, but then I heard that the rules had changed, so I thought I'd best wait."

"I don't know what to say...I've never seen anything so beautiful, so... perfect. But...I shouldn't—"

"Don't," he broke in. "Don't say you shouldn't take it. It's important to me that you keep it."

"Jeremiah..."

Rachel's every instinct was screaming that she should give it back to him—now. They shouldn't even be together like this, alone in her kitchen with the night and the soft light from the lamp wrapping around them like a blanket of warmth...and desire.

And yet how could she not accept it? The time and the work and the emotion that must have gone into this—how could she refuse to keep it? She sensed that rejecting it would hurt him, would wound him terribly.

And so she made her decision. "Of course I'll keep it."

He closed his eyes, just for an instant.

Trying for a lighter tone, she added, "You couldn't pry it away from me. I've never had anything so lovely. I just...I don't know how to thank you."

He shook his head. "Your willingness to keep it...that's my thanks."

Unexpectedly then, he got to his feet. "I know my being here makes you uncomfortable. I'll go now. And I'll try...I'll try to stay away this time. But tonight," he shook his head, "tonight I just couldn't."

Relieved and yet disappointed at the thought of his going, Rachel also stood. "I wish…" She stopped, knowing she didn't dare finish what she wanted to say. *I wish you didn't have to go. I don't want you to go. I wish we never had to be apart.*

For a moment they stood looking at each other. Something in the way he was studying her caused a chill to seize Rachel. She felt as if she'd been shaken. And suddenly she felt afraid.

"Are you leaving?" she choked out.

He frowned. "Yes, I'll go. I didn't mean to stay this long, I just wanted to give you—"

"No," she said sharply. "I mean, are you leaving? Are you going away?"

A startled look darted across his face, but his expression quickly stilled and in that instant he seemed to withdraw from her. "Do you want me to leave?"

She couldn't breathe. A deep, throbbing pain rolled over her and something inside her seemed to cry out. But she didn't answer him.

"Would it make things easier for you if I left, Rachel? Is that what you want?"

He said it with such a sadness, such a soft, lonely tremor in his voice that Rachel thought she would weep.

"No, Jeremiah. That's not what I want. It's totally selfish of me, I know, but I don't ever want you to go away." She felt as if she were strangling on the words she had no right to say, but she couldn't stop. "Even if we can't be…together, I don't want to completely lose you. I don't think I could bear it if you left."

He stood, unmoving as a stone. Was it relief that stole across his features? "Then I'll stay," he said quietly.

Without warning then, he closed the slight distance between them, caught her up in his arms, and kissed her with a gentleness so sweet it stunned her. It was as if in that moment a sacred vow had been sealed.

Almost as quickly as he'd touched her, he backed away, leaving Rachel to stare at him, speechless.

"I won't apologize for that," he said. "I've just…missed you so much. This whole week, I've been a little crazy to see you."

Rachel knew she should be angry with him. She should tell him to leave her house and not come back. He had no right to touch her, much less kiss her. But the words stayed buried. What she saw in his eyes and what she felt in her heart whispered for her to keep silent.

"I'll go now," he said. He hesitated before adding, "But you know where I'll be, Rachel. If you ever need me, you know I'll come."

Without saying another word then, Rachel let him turn and walk away.

She didn't move again until she heard the solid thud of the front door closing behind him.

✦33✦

A MATTER OF TRUST

Do not trust all men, but trust men of worth.
DEMOCRITUS

On a whim, Gant told Gideon to close up the shop for lunch, grabbed his coat, and started walking.

The afternoon air was brisk but not uncomfortable. He wasn't particularly hungry, so he walked all the way to the park, where he now stood watching the river.

He needed a break from the shop, but lately he'd been avoiding taking lunch at the inn, mostly because of Ellie Sawyer. He'd begun to see what Gideon had insinuated, and because of that he now found himself awkward around the young widow. She *did* seem to find ways to spend time with him, and he feared there was something in her eyes when she looked at him that he couldn't share. So for several days now he'd been eating leftovers in the kitchen at home or a quick sandwich in the shop.

He liked Ellie, but if she wanted more from him than a simple friendship, it wasn't in him to give. After her husband's death, he had tried to make sure she and the baby got along all right and wanted for nothing. Now, however, he was backing off from being with her as often as before. She had her job and a nice apartment above the restaurant, and she seemed well settled. He had no intention of leading her to believe he wanted anything more than the friendship they already had.

It occurred to him that perhaps the problem had already been taken care of. He'd seen Ellie and the new doctor, Wyatt Tanner, walking together down the boardwalk last week. He had felt both pleased and relieved.

In any case, there simply wasn't another woman for him but Rachel, and he couldn't imagine there ever would be.

Looking around, he spied a massive old tree stump and eased himself down on it, following the water with his gaze as far as he could see. Mac padded around a bit but soon plopped down at his side and joined Gant in studying the river.

This part of the Ohio was quiet today. A small flatboat loaded with kegs and boxes passed by a weathered old barge. In the distance, a side-paddle moved slowly and was eventually overtaken by what looked to be a store-boat, though it was too far upriver to make out any identifying sign.

A familiar feeling much like homesickness washed over Gant. Not unusual, that. The river became home after a time. He still missed it. Most likely he always would.

It could be a lonely life, but he had found it to be a good one, even a peaceful way to live. Most of the time.

In a way, a man became a part of the river, melded with it, flowed through life with it. Even when the wind was up in a storm, there was a oneness. You didn't fight the river, you worked with it. You were together in a kind of balance only a pilot could sense.

Asa had his own unique way of likening the river to the attributes of God. He often compared a river to God's mercy flowing into the children He created and flowing out from them to others—a continuing, unstoppable stream.

Sometimes he also referred to God as the Great Navigator. A man could navigate a river, Asa claimed, just as he navigated through life. But God was the one who "walked the wheel," and the river's power was beyond any mortal's ability to defeat.

Gant saw the wisdom and the truth in his friend's observation, but all the same he had once taken a kind of defiant pleasure in the contest. A storm on the river tested a man, and it was usually a foregone conclusion that the storm and the river could easily triumph, but in another time he had occasionally viewed such events as a competition and enjoyed the challenge.

Long ago, however, he'd conceded the folly of his young and foolish behavior.

These days the competition had no face, no identity. Once again he'd thought himself up to the challenge of defeating an adversary, this time the shadowed enemy of the Riverhaven Amish. The People's tormentor continued to harass the community with increasingly harsh, even dangerous incidents.

At times he almost felt as if he were somehow a catalyst in the enemy's attacks, as if he'd only made matters worse by intruding upon their world.

Unexpectedly, Mac shot to his feet and gave a chuff.

"Gideon told me I might find you here."

Gant jerked around to see Doc Sebastian approaching with a smile. "Is this your thinking place?"

Gant shrugged. "I like it here. So what brings you to town?"

"Errands…and you, actually."

David Sebastian came around to stand in front of Gant. Immediately, Gant's big hound leaned into him, demanding attention.

After a minute, Gant called the dog back to his side with a short "Down," and the dog settled beside his owner.

"So what do you need? I'll go back and open the shop—"

"No, there's nothing I need from the shop. It's still open, by the way. Gideon looked to be writing an order for Paul Shelton."

"Huh. I told him he could close up for lunch when he wanted." He looked at David. "So what can I do for you?"

David hesitated a few seconds more, knowing there would be questions he couldn't answer. Finally, he decided to just jump in. "You recall telling me about the sideboard Samuel Beiler asked you to make for him as a birthday gift for Rachel?"

Gant nodded, his expression darkening. "What about it?"

David knew he needed to be cautious in the way he handled this. "Have you finished it?"

"No. Why?" Clearly, Gant didn't even want to talk about the matter.

"Then don't. Don't finish it. Don't let Beiler have it."

Gant's head came up with a quizzical look. "I agreed to do it. It's too late to back out on it now. What's this about?"

David sighed. "I knew you'd have questions, and I can't answer them. I shouldn't even bring this up, but I have a valid reason."

Gant got to his feet, his puzzled expression turning to a frown. Mac got up as well, watching him, but when Gant made no move to leave, the dog lay down again. "I can't cancel Beiler's order now. I told him I'd make the sideboard, and even though I wish I hadn't, I'm not one for going back on my word."

"Just this once, I'm asking you to."

"Doc—"

"I need you to trust me. Don't give Beiler the sideboard."

Gant studied him, clearly expecting an explanation.

When David offered none, he shook his head in apparent frustration. "I trust you, Doc, but you have to admit this is an odd request. You're asking me to break my word without a reason. How am I supposed to handle that?"

David's mind raced, groping for a way to satisfy Gant's bewilderment without divulging what was told to him in confidence. "I wish I could explain, but some matters have come up that I can't discuss. At least... not at the moment. You need to take my word for it that I have Rachel's best interests at heart, and just do as I ask. Please."

He saw Gant's attention sharpen at the mention of Rachel's name.

"What does this have to do with Rachel?"

David sighed. "I think I went over this with you once before, but let me explain again. An Amish man has no right to give a woman an extravagant or personal gift unless they're married. It simply isn't done. Even an engaged couple must use restraint when it comes to the gifts they give each other. Beiler and Rachel are neither engaged nor married, so he has no right whatsoever to give her that sideboard."

That piercing blue gaze of Gant's threatened to impale him, so fierce was the man's stare. "I know that. So why do I get the feeling you're trying to tell me something without actually saying anything?"

David shook his head. "That's all I can say." He paused, then added, "I should think you'd be relieved. I know you've regretted accepting Beiler's order for the sideboard all along."

"I have, that's true. But since I did accept it, it seems that I ought to go through with it."

"Well, now you don't have to."

"And just what do I tell Beiler?"

David waved off the question. "Tell him you're too busy. You are busy, aren't you?"

"Too busy lately, but that's no excuse for canceling an order this far along. Rachel's birthday is less than three weeks away."

David settled a meaningful look on his friend, trying to communicate what he mustn't allow himself to say. "I know when Rachel's birthday is," he said evenly. "But in this case, let the fact that you have too much work serve as an excuse. For now, at least, until I'm free to tell you more."

He hesitated and then added, "It's for Rachel's good, my friend. It truly is. If Beiler should attempt to give her that sideboard—or any other significant gift, for that matter—she'd refuse it. And rightly so. All your effort would be in vain. But it might stir up trouble Rachel doesn't need. And there's also the possibility that she might be royally upset with you for building the thing. You wouldn't want that."

Gant locked gazes with him, obviously searching for what remained unsaid. Finally, he nodded. "All right," he said. "I'm not comfortable with this, but I wasn't comfortable with any part of it. I expect it was sheer stubbornness, and no doubt a bit of spite, that made me agree to accept the order in the first place. It seemed to me at the time he was sure I wouldn't take him up on it, so I decided to call his bluff." He paused. "Can I assume that you'll eventually fill me in on what's behind all this secrecy?"

"I hope so," David said. "But even if I can't, just know you're doing the right thing."

"Why do I find that to be small comfort at the moment?" Without giving David the opportunity to reply, Gant went on, his tone dripping with sarcasm. "Now then, since I have no idea when I might be seeing Beiler, and because I'm so *terribly* busy, would you do me the favor of delivering a note to him?"

David considered it. "Yes, that's probably the best way to handle it."

"You mean he's not as likely to trounce you as me?"

David let his gaze rake his big, powerfully setup Irish friend. "The Amish aren't inclined toward 'trouncing,' but even if they were, I can't quite see Samuel Beiler getting the best of you."

Gant uttered a low sound of disgust. "Let's go back to the shop then, and I'll write my note of excuse."

David expelled a long breath, relieved that the exchange he'd been dreading was over.

⇥ 34 ⇤

MEETINGS THAT MATTER

He leadeth me, O blessed thought!
O words with heavenly comfort fraught!
Whate'er I do, where'er I be,
Still 'tis God's hand that leadeth me.

JOSEPH H. GILMORE

Captain Gant had already left the shop, leaving Gideon to lock up early, as he almost always did on Saturday afternoons.

Gideon was about to pull the shade on the door when he glanced across the street and saw the Beiler brothers coming out of the feed store. His curiosity piqued, Gideon opened the door and waited while they crossed the road.

It was unusual to see all three of Samuel Beiler's sons together at the same time. He hadn't seen Aaron, the oldest and the one closest to Gideon's age, for several weeks. Like himself, Aaron was in his *rumspringa*. Also like Gideon, he seemed to spend most of his time around the *Englisch*, although he still lived at his family farm.

Gideon lifted a hand as they approached. The two younger boys grinned and returned his greeting, but Aaron merely gave him a glum look and a short nod.

Only when they drew closer and stepped onto the boardwalk did Gideon notice the dark bruise just below Joe's eye and the vivid red scar that looked like a recent cut trailing down the opposite side of his face. The youngest of the three, Joe must be about ten or eleven years by now. It had long been assumed that the boy was a little slow in his head.

For the Amish, this was no disgrace, but rather a trait that made him "special," to be treated kindly and with gentle care. Indeed, all children were special to the People.

In that instant, the same memory that had crossed his mind a few nights ago, when he and his friends had been discussing Samuel Beiler, again edged its way into Gideon's thoughts. For some years now, the two oldest Beiler boys had been seen bearing signs of mistreatment, giving weight to the rumors that their *dat* beat them. Now Gideon couldn't help but wonder if Samuel Beiler had taken to roughing up his youngest son as well.

Anger collided with a wrench of sympathy as Gideon observed the boy's mottled face. Yet Joe's expression was cheerful. He actually appeared happy to see Gideon, in contrast to his older brother's sullen behavior.

At the moment, Aaron was glaring at him as if Gideon had stolen his horse out from under him. His expression was so filled with dislike it was almost like a physical blow.

And then as quickly as it came, it was gone, replaced by a bland, unreadable gaze.

Gideon almost felt that he'd imagined the loathing he'd seen in the other's eyes only a moment before. Confused, he had to make an effort not to trip over his words. "So where are you fellows off to? Big Saturday night in town?"

Both Joe and Noah cracked halfhearted grins while their older brother gave a shake of his head. "Just finishing up some errands for *Dat*," Aaron said. "We have to be on our way now. Still work to do. Church is at our house tomorrow."

He stopped, settling a look on Gideon that would have appeared to be wholly innocent had it not been for the faint smirk that followed his next words. "You should come."

Gideon replied with a steady gaze and a slight smile. "Not this time."

Aaron's look of disdain remained fixed, but he merely gave a nod, saying, "Well, it was good to see you. We need to be going now."

Gideon watched the three of them make their way down the road to where their buggy was parked in front of the harness shop. After another moment he turned and went back inside.

For more than one reason, the encounter had unsettled him. The marks on young Joe's face and the contempt he'd sensed in Aaron had left him troubled and uneasy. As best he knew, he'd done nothing to merit Aaron Beiler's resentment or dislike. They had never been best buddies, but they had spent time together with some of the other Amish young people.

He was convinced, though, that he hadn't misread the other's feelings.

His thoughts remained cluttered and uneasy as he finished locking up. Finally, he decided to spend what was left of the weekend out at the farm. He'd delayed long enough the talk he'd been wanting to have with Doc.

Besides, there was always a chance he'd catch a glimpse of Emma while he was out her way, maybe even have the opportunity to manage a few words with her.

Emma. She was on his mind constantly these days. He missed her something fierce, but any contact with her was almost impossible.

That wouldn't be the case if he'd do as his mother was always asking him to do—go back to his life among the Amish, make his vows, and start over. But he couldn't return just because of Emma. Even Mamm wouldn't want him to do that. He could only go back and live Amish if he were convinced it was the right thing to do, the thing God meant for him to do with the rest of his life.

On the heels of that thought came the uneasy awareness that lately something seemed to be urging him in that direction, pressing him to return to his roots. At times, an inexplicable longing rose up in him, and he would unexpectedly find himself actually missing his old life. In spite of his desire to hold on to his job with Captain Gant, and despite the enjoyment he'd once found in the comforts and conveniences of life among the *Englisch*, there were times now when much of what he had once prized so highly—including his "freedom"—felt strangely empty and meaningless. During those times he almost felt as if he were treacherously close to shucking it all and heading back to the People.

What was happening to him anyway?

Halfway out to the farm, a memory struck him with such force he actually gave himself a shake, as if to throw it off. When he and Rachel were younger and had done something that wasn't quite right, something that left them feeling guilt-heavy and needing to confess—admittedly, those times were far fewer for Rachel than for him—they'd say Mamm must be praying for them.

They would try to laugh it off, but once, when they were grown, Rachel told him in all seriousness that she didn't take those words lightly. "Honestly, Gideon, I'm not so sure but what we weren't right. It wouldn't surprise me to find out that Mamm's prayers were behind our attacks of conscience."

He smiled a little at the memory. Sometimes now he also wondered if the idea that Mamm could pray a "conscience attack" on him was all that unlikely. He had always believed that if anyone's prayers had that kind of influence with God, it would be the prayers of his mother.

After Gideon let it be known that he'd like to talk to Doc alone, his mother shooed them out of the kitchen with coffee and cookies while she enlisted Rachel and Fannie's help to clean up the dishes.

They'd had a nice time at supper, what with Rachel giving in to Mamm's coaxing to stay for the evening meal and Fannie's exuberance, no doubt due to having her entire family together at the table—these days a rare event. Rachel, too, had seemed more lively than usual, teasing and laughing with Gideon as they once had when they were both still at home.

Now, seated across from Doc in front of the fire, Gideon found himself feeling blessed—not for the first time—by the family he'd been born into. Even given the troubling conversation he was about to launch, he knew a warm sense of contentment as he studied the older man he'd always greatly admired and respected.

Strange how lives sometimes converged in the most unexpected ways. Who would have thought Doc Sebastian, trusted friend and family physician, would one day end up as his stepfather and an Amish man himself?

He was genuinely happy for his mother. These days she seemed always cheerful and content. That Doc adored her was never in doubt. Of course, Gideon had seen the way he'd looked at Mamm long before they became man and wife, as though she were far more like a blessing on his life than a good and faithful friend. They suited each other well.

"So what's on your mind, son? You said you wanted to talk."

Gideon nodded and decided to jump right in. "I wouldn't want you to think I've mentioned this to anyone else, Doc. I wouldn't do that. But there are some things that have me plenty bothered, and I need to talk about them to someone I trust."

Doc remained quiet but inclined his head as if to encourage Gideon to have his say.

"Just so you know, Doc, all this is connected in one way or the other to Samuel Beiler. You'll see what I mean."

Now Doc leaned forward a little, his previously mild expression turning more solemn. "All right. Go on."

Gideon made no attempt to soften the remarks he'd heard from Solomon Miller and Reuben Esch the night they'd visited him, nor was he able to completely conceal the feelings of disgust and anger their comments had stirred up in him. And when he related the rumor supposedly circulating about Samuel Beiler and Rachel having an "understanding," he saw those same feelings mirrored in Doc's expression.

"So he's actually insinuating they're to be married?" Doc's tone was sharp.

"That's what the fellows told me."

Doc stood, and with his hands knotted into fists behind his back, he began to pace back and forth in front of the fireplace. He stopped only when Gideon spoke again.

"That's not all, Doc. Something else happened today that's got me upset too."

He went on to explain then about his encounter with the three Beiler boys. "True, there's no way to know just how Joe got those bruises and marks on his face. But what with the stories I've heard over the years about Samuel's treatment of his sons, I don't mind telling you I got a strange feeling when I saw Joe."

Doc turned to face the fire but only for a moment. When he again turned back to Gideon, his expression was taut with emotion. "You're right—there's no knowing how the Beiler boy got those marks. He could have been injured in a fall or another accident. I know you won't repeat any of this, Gideon, including your suspicions. It wouldn't be fair to

Samuel, nor to his sons either. We'll keep our concerns between ourselves. But I'm glad you told me."

Gideon also got to his feet. "What do you think about all this, Doc?"

"If you don't mind, son, I'd rather mull it over for a time before saying something I might regret later. Anything I'd say wouldn't be based on fact, after all."

Disappointed, Gideon gave a long sigh. He'd counted on getting Doc's opinion. "Maybe I shouldn't have mentioned any of this—"

"No," Doc interrupted. "I'm glad you did. Let's just say you're not alone in your concerns. That's all I dare say for now, but you did nothing wrong in coming to me. Nothing at all." He paused before going on. "We'll be talking about this again. Perhaps soon I'll be able to explain more than I can now. All right?"

His even tone gave no indication of any hidden meaning. Even so, the way Doc was looking at him gave Gideon a strong hint of something being left unsaid, possibly something important.

Clearly, he would have to be patient. He wasn't surprised when Doc changed the subject. But his next words did surprise him.

"Perhaps I'm out of line asking you this, son, but I've wondered...do you ever think about coming home? Back to the People?" It was as if Doc somehow knew the direction his thoughts had taken on the way out from town.

Gideon fumbled for a reply. "I...suppose I do. Sometimes."

Doc remained silent, as if waiting for more.

"Why would you ask me that?"

Doc shrugged. "I'm curious, that's all. And your mother...well, you know. She never stops hoping. But I imagine you know that."

Gideon gave a nod. "I'm sure."

He hesitated before saying anything more, and in the meantime Doc brought up another remark Gideon wouldn't have expected. "I want to be certain you understand that there's always a place for you here. Just because your mother remarried doesn't mean the farm isn't yours for the future. This place is your inheritance by rights, and I wouldn't want you to think I'm unaware of that. We'd welcome you back with open arms. I hope you know that."

Gideon stared at him. "Doc...I don't want the farm. Farming just isn't for me. I want to earn my living doing exactly what I'm doing now—working as a carpenter. Maybe even having my own business someday."

Doc was obviously caught off guard. "Well...I hadn't realized. You're quite certain?"

Again Gideon nodded, even more vigorously. "I've known for a long time. In fact, my job is one of the reasons I might shy away from coming back. I don't want to give it up."

Doc frowned. "Why do you think you'd have to give it up? You could still work in town and live Amish. I know Gant values your work. And I'll admit we could use your help around here, at least on a part-time basis, but I see no reason you couldn't manage both. Whether you want to farm or not, this place is going to be yours someday."

"Samuel Beiler would never let me keep my job with Gant!" Gideon burst out. "And as bishop, he has the power to make me quit."

Doc studied him. "Is that the only reason you haven't come back?" he asked quietly. "Your job?"

"No, not at all. But it's important to me. And so is Emma!" he blurted out, not thinking. "But I know I can't come back just because of her. That wouldn't be right."

He stopped, feeling heat flame his face at the realization that he'd said more about his personal feelings than he should have. An Amish man had no right bringing up a relationship—or even the hope of a relationship—to anyone else, even a family member.

Even so, he added, "Besides, I don't know if she'd have me even if I did come back. Her *dat* probably wouldn't even let me in the front door. Levi doesn't like me, not a little bit."

"Emma?" Doc gave a faint smile, as if Gideon's words weren't exactly news to him. But his expression quickly sobered. "Well, I can't tell you what to do, of course. But I will say this. If the time comes when you're sure you'd like to come back and live Amish, I don't think you should let the threat of losing your job stop you, nor would I worry all that much about Levi Knepp. Things have a way of working out."

He drew in a long breath before going on. "The most important thing for you, son—for any of us—is to heed God's will, though His will may not always seem like a possibility. Sometimes it won't even seem to make sense. But as I said, things have a way of working out in the long run if we let the Lord put us where He wants us. You just follow where He leads and let Him take care of any obstacles."

The strangest feeling settled over Gideon as he listened to Doc's advice. He knew in that instant he had to think through very carefully what he'd just heard because he sensed he'd been given something that might be really important. Something that might actually make a difference in his life.

→ ←

"Are you going to tell me what you and Gideon talked about?"

Susan waited until Gideon had gone upstairs before asking the question Doc had been expecting. He had to smile a little. His wife was seldom predictable—except when it came to Gideon.

He moved a little closer to her on the sofa. "Nothing much really, at least nothing that should concern you. He was just looking for a bit of advice."

"And he came to you? I'm glad, David. He's always respected you, you know."

She really did look pleased by the idea. "And I've always liked your son, Susan. He's a good lad with a good head on his shoulders."

As he would have expected, she obviously was still curious. "Advice about what?"

He smiled even more. "Really, dear," he chided.

"Well, I can't help but wonder. You have to admit it's unusual. Gideon seldom seems to want advice from anyone."

"As I said, it's nothing for you to fuss about. We had a good talk together, that's all. Man to man."

Her mouth tightened, but David could tell she wasn't actually upset. She seldom became genuinely aggravated with him, but when she did, there was no mistaking the signs.

→ ←

Inside his boyhood room, Gideon stood, looking around. For some reason, anytime he spent the night, he found comfort in its very plainness. There was nothing decorative or "fancy" about it, of course, although the bed quilt Mamm had made just for him warmed and brightened the surroundings.

She unfailingly kept things the same here. A couple of wooden toys he'd played with as a child, a few small mementos he'd made in school, and a slingshot were neatly lined up on his chest of drawers, just as they always were. No doubt there was plenty of oil in the lamp beside his bed, and knowing Mamm, the linen was most likely changed on a regular basis even though he didn't spend all that much time here.

The thought brought a smile…and a bittersweet tug at his heart.

Things had been so simple then. The boy who once slept here night after night, like most young Amish boys, had thought life would probably always be uneventful and uncomplicated. When he wasn't too tired to stay awake, he had daydreamed a little about the future, but he never imagined the challenges or trouble that waited there.

Admittedly, he had also thought about going away, seeing more of the world than this farm and the small, sleepy town of Riverhaven. He had even thought about following the mighty, mysterious Ohio River to unknown places and the adventure he would never find in the Plain community.

He sighed. Now he would give a lot to believe life could ever be that simple and problem free again. At the moment, he simply felt tired and troubled. He was tempted to flop into bed without changing clothes and find the peace that only sleep could bring. Old habits took over though, and he found himself unable to tumble into Mamm's clean bedding in his everyday work clothes. He kept a change of nightclothes here, so he took the time to change and then went to bed.

And stayed awake. Tired as he was, he couldn't sleep. He didn't feel the least bit drowsy. He heard every creak in the old farmhouse, every outside noise that filtered in through the windows, and he finally thought he could hear his own heartbeat.

Before long, the fatigue he'd been feeling earlier completely disappeared, giving way to an uncommon tension that made his body feel as tight and drawn as a brand-new chicken-wire fence. His head actually ached from the strain.

Yet amid the physical discomfort, all he could think about was what Doc had said regarding God's will. Just how was he supposed to know what God wanted for him, what His will for his life might be? He didn't like to think he might make a mistake about something this important, something that could change—or not change—the direction of his entire life. That was a pretty scary idea.

After another hour or so of tossing and turning, questioning himself and wondering, Gideon couldn't stand it any longer. Ignoring the chill that he knew awaited him once he threw off the quilts, and paying no heed to the cold that gripped his feet, he got out of bed. Then, for the first time in a very long time, Gideon Kanagy knelt beside his bed and began to pray.

CONFRONTATION

None but one can harm you,
None but yourself who are your greatest foe.
HENRY WADSWORTH LONGFELLOW

David Sebastian knew the moment Samuel Beiler began to read Gant's note that the man was fighting hard to control his temper. His face flushed crimson, and the hand holding the note trembled.

"He has no right to do this," Beiler said in his heavily accented English. "No right. He made a commitment to me."

David managed to keep his tone mild when he replied. "Unfortunately, he found himself unable to keep that commitment. He wasn't sure when he'd see you, so I told him I'd deliver his apology. He's sorry not to give you more notice."

When Samuel made no reply but simply stood studying the note with a white-knuckled stillness, David decided to move on to the more difficult part of what he'd planned to say. "More to the point, Samuel, as a member of Rachel's family, I found your idea of a birthday gift for her entirely inappropriate."

There was no mistaking the flare of rage in the other's eyes. "It's not for you to say what's appropriate for me and Rachel." His tone was as harsh as if it were laced with ground glass.

David now struggled to hold his own temper in check. "There is no 'you and Rachel,' Samuel. You're not a couple, and it's wrong for you to pretend that you are."

They were standing just outside the barn. The evening was cold and damp and dreary. There would be rain or sleet later. The chill that coiled through David when he met Beiler's eyes, however, had nothing to do with the weather. The man was looking at him as if he'd like to gut him with the nearest pitchfork.

He turned to go, but Beiler's next words stopped him.

"So it's your doing then. You talked Gant into reneging on our agreement. You had no right."

Painfully mindful of the truth in Beiler's words, David slowly turned to face him, choosing his words with care. "And you have no right to allow others to believe you have some sort of understanding with Rachel. That's not the case, and you know it. It doesn't become you as a man, and certainly not as our bishop, to foster such an untruth."

"Rachel is simply being young and stubborn. Given enough time, she'll see what's best for her. I'm quite certain everything will work out well for us."

David nearly choked on the acid taste of his own outrage. He was finding it more and more difficult to control himself, but he was determined not to let Beiler provoke him any further. Even so, he could hear the anger rising in his voice. "Rachel's not that young, Samuel. And she's never been stubborn. What is it going to take for you to accept the fact that she has no intention of allowing you to court her? Do you actually believe she'll change her mind if you continue to pressure her? Surely you're not that naive."

As if Beiler suddenly realized his behavior belied the proper demeanor of a bishop, he seemed to grope for self-control. The angry flush paled slightly as he crushed the note in his hand and threw it to the ground, taking on the air of arrogance David had come to associate with him.

"Watch your words, Doctor Sebastian," he said with what David knew to be a deceptive calm. "The Amish do not insult their bishop."

"As an Amish man myself," David said pointedly, "I have no wish to insult you, Samuel, nor any intention of doing so. I'm trying to reason with you. You're doing yourself no benefit by misleading others about having a relationship with Rachel. No good can come of such a pretense. You need to look for a wife and a mother for your sons elsewhere. There are a number of widows and unmarried women among us. Why not concentrate your attentions where they're wanted?"

As David watched, Beiler knotted his fists, drawing himself up to a rigid stance. "It would be best if you leave now, Doctor. We have nothing else to say to each other."

With a slight shake of his head in frustration, David turned and started up the field. He could almost feel Beiler's icy stare following him like a knife in his back.

He sank into the buggy, feeling depleted and totally disgruntled. What in the world was to become of the Riverhaven People with a man like Samuel Beiler as their bishop and spiritual leader?

For one of the few times in his life, David Sebastian came close to questioning the work of his Creator, the choice He had made in allowing such a man to assume the authority over an entire community. But instead, he willed himself to pray.

He was still praying when he reached home.

⇥36⇤

STALKER IN THE SHADOWS

Stars, hide your fires;
Let not light see my black and deep desires.

SHAKESPEARE

It was a lousy night to keep watch, what with a cold rain starting up and the wind on the rise. But he was trying to get an idea of Gant's nightly routine, and this was the only way. Trouble was, the man seemed to change everything on any given night, from his trips in and out of the house to the time he turned his lamps off for the last time.

He'd been out here four nights straight now, and Gant hadn't done the same thing twice. Was he that unpredictable or just absentminded?

That big, mean-looking dog worried him too. There had already been one night when he'd nearly panicked, thinking the dog had spotted him or at least got a whiff of his scent. Gant had let him out, and he'd bounded up the hill, growling. But when Gant called him, he'd hesitated only a moment before turning and racing back to the house. Ever since, he hadn't dared to move in as close as before. That animal looked as if he could bring down any man or beast he chose to.

There was another problem too. In addition to the dog, he was pretty sure something else was lurking around Gant's place, maybe some kind of a wild animal. Night before last when he was out here, he'd stayed high on the hill, like tonight, keeping well away from the house. Even though there hadn't been a breath of wind moving, more than once he thought he heard leaves rustling and crunching a ways down the hill. He'd also seen a shadow slinking around, low and fairly close to the house. A shadow that two or three times made a strange, growling sound.

The faint sound of music had been coming from the house most of the time he'd watched. He assumed it was Gant. He hadn't seen anyone else around, and there was no sign of a buggy or a horse parked in front or back. From this distance, the music sounded as if it were coming from a fiddle. Gant hadn't stopped playing for more than a minute or two, so apparently he wasn't aware that there was something skulking around right outside his house.

He hadn't stayed to watch any longer. Whatever that was creeping around the shrubs and woodpile, he wasn't going to take any chances.

So far, he hadn't accomplished what he'd set out to do: find out when Gant was likely to be at home or away. It was beginning to look as though tonight wouldn't be any different. It was getting late, and he needed to get back to the farm. Besides, Gant wasn't likely to be going out anywhere on a night like this.

He'd give it another few minutes and then go back to the vacant lot behind the livery, where he'd left his horse tied to a tree among the high grass and overgrown weeds.

Just then, he heard the dull snap of wet twigs not far from him, just a few feet across the hill, where the ground dipped. He froze, his heart pounding. Squinting into the distance, he saw a shadow emerge from the trees, and that was enough to spur him to unlock his legs. He took off at a run, holding his hat down tight against the wind.

Did he hear something growl not far behind him, or did he imagine it?

Whether he imagined it or not, he kept running as if a demon were at his back, gaining ground and set on hauling him down. He ran so fast and so hard his heart pumped and his chest burned as though they would explode at any second.

Twice he slipped in mud and almost fell, but he made it to his horse. Gasping for breath, he yanked the rope from the tree and took off toward the road at a full gallop. Only then did he dare to toss a look over his shoulder. He saw nothing.

Nothing but the windblown rain and a darkness dappled by the faint lamplight that flickered behind the curtained windows of a few nearby houses.

Maybe he had imagined it after all. Maybe he'd just got spooked and *thought* the thing, whatever it was, was chasing him.

Maybe. But even so, he was finished with this risky business of prowling around, hiding in the dark and the cold. Next time he came out here, it wouldn't be to stand watch. It would be to finish the job and be done with it—and done with Gant.

➔ 37 ➔

AN UNHOLY PROPOSAL

Dust is the end of all pursuit.
GEORGE CHAPMAN

Monday afternoon, Rachel opened the door to find Samuel Beiler standing there, a grim look of determination darkening his features.

Her first instinct was to shut the door without inviting him in. She had seen that look before, always when he had set his mind on something and wasn't about to be denied. But Samuel was bishop now. She could hardly slam the door in the bishop's face.

Instead, she waited, giving merely a small nod of acknowledgment. "Samuel."

"I need to speak with you, Rachel. May I come in?"

She delayed but then reluctantly opened the door wider, saying nothing.

He wiped his boots and then stepped inside. Normally she would have taken his coat, offered him coffee, and indicated that he should take a chair. Not today. Something in that fixed, severe countenance told her this was not to be a friendly visit. For that matter, his last visit hadn't been a cordial one either.

They stood in the middle of the kitchen, facing each other. Rachel was beginning to wonder if he was going to simply stand there, staring at her. She could hardly have been more uncomfortable.

When he finally spoke, his low, almost gentle tone surprised her. "I think you know why I'm here, Rachel."

"No, Samuel. I've no idea."

He sighed as if he were disappointed and somewhat impatient with her reply. He seemed to draw himself up to his full height, which was considerable, and stood holding his hat, watching her. "I've come as a friend, Rachel, but as your bishop as well."

Her instincts instantly went on alert, her mind racing in search of something she might have done to trigger his visit.

"You might want to sit down," he said in the same quiet tone of voice.

Rachel ignored the suggestion, continuing to face him while bracing herself for whatever she was about to hear.

When she remained standing, he hesitated before going on. Rachel forced herself not to look away as he studied her, annoyance now visible in his eyes.

"I've heard talk, Rachel," he said heavily. "Talk that disturbs me."

Rachel waited, saying nothing.

"Some say that you and the *auslander*, Gant, have disobeyed Bishop Graber's warning that you must not see each other."

"We don't," Rachel said, her voice thin with tension.

"What?"

"We don't...'see' each other."

"That's not what I'm told."

"Whatever you've been told, Samuel, Jere—" Rachel quickly corrected herself. "Captain Gant and I don't see each other. Not alone. Unless it's by accident."

Guilt swept over her as the memory of Jeremiah's recent night visit pushed against her conscience, the visit when he'd brought the black swan he'd carved for her.

His mouth tightened. "Don't compound your wrongdoing with a lie, Rachel. His horse has been seen here, at your house, at night." His look darkened still more as he added, "And apparently you have been together at other times as well."

Caught off guard, Rachel fought to hide her surprise. *How did he know? Had he been watching her house?*

To deny his accusation again would be an outright lie. There had been other times, such as the night he'd walked her home, the night of the break-in. At the moment she was too stunned to remember others.

She felt trapped.

"Well?"

His accusing gaze was locked on her, and in spite of her resolve not to back down, Rachel felt angered and at the same time disgusted with herself for allowing him to humiliate her.

"Why are you doing this, Samuel?"

"I'm your bishop now, Rachel. It's my duty to address any wrongdoing on the part of my people and take the necessary steps to correct it." He paused before continuing. "What do you have to say for yourself?"

Rachel glanced away, physically ill with the emotions rioting within her. She didn't trust herself to speak, so she made no reply.

"Rachel, I have to say that ever since that Gant person arrived here, you have behaved foolishly, even recklessly." His voice took on volume. "Taking him into your house—an unknown *Englischer*—caring for a total stranger, nursing him back to health, as you might a husband! You've been in his shop in town, you've been with him in your home, just the two of you alone. You haven't conducted yourself as a godly Amish widow at all. *Nee*, you've acted shamefully and sinfully with this man!"

"That's not true, Samuel!" Rachel snapped. "If you knew me at all, you'd know you have no right to accuse me of anything of the sort! You're judging me by chance, by appearances."

Anger warred with weakness so fiercely she felt as if her legs would buckle under her at any moment. Yet she refused to let him bully her. He might be her bishop, and although she had to admit that at times her behavior might have appeared questionable, in her heart she couldn't believe she had committed sin with Jeremiah.

No? She had let him kiss her. She had loved a man she was forbidden to love...and she still did.

If only Bishop Graber would have given Jeremiah a chance to convert, he wouldn't have been forbidden. *If only...*

"Please leave, Samuel," she choked out, turning away from him. "I can't listen to any more of this."

"You will listen!" he demanded. "Rachel, don't you realize you're in danger of being placed under the *Meidung*?"

Rachel wheeled around, her heart thundering. "You can't...you wouldn't..."

But he could. He was the bishop now. But would he actually order that she be shunned? "Samuel, are you threatening me?"

He impaled her with a look that left no doubt in Rachel's mind. He *was* threatening her.

"I've done nothing deserving of the *Meidung*! You know I haven't!"

Fear seized her like an icy wave. She could imagine nothing worse. Being cast out from her family, her friends, the entire Plain community... She would rather lose her very life!

"I can't believe this," she said, the last fragile shell of her composure treacherously close to shattering. "I can't believe you think so poorly of me that you would jump to such false conclusions."

He made a gesture of frustration with his hands. "You're leaving me no choice. What kind of bishop would I be to let you set such a poor example for the other women in our community? To let you endanger your own soul?"

"Endanger..." Rachel's voice broke. Fear knotted inside her. She felt as if she were suffocating. Something flared in his accusing eyes that told her he'd seen her fear and was gratified by it.

To think that he had once declared affection for her, had even asked her to marry him. There had been a time when she'd actually thought of him as a friend.

As if Samuel had read her thoughts, he suddenly shifted his tone of voice from that of her accuser to the reasoning and kind tenor of a friendly advisor. "Rachel, it doesn't have to be this way. It shouldn't be this way, not between you and me. Don't you realize that this is difficult for me too? I care about you. I don't want to do anything to hurt you. I especially don't want to see you jeopardize your relationship with the Lord God because of sin in your life."

Confusion now entangled Rachel's emotions. Her mind went spinning, struggling to grasp the meaning of this abrupt turn in his behavior. In spite of the turmoil roiling inside of her, she found herself sensing a ray of hope in this unexpected change.

"I don't understand…"

He smiled, and for a moment he looked like the old Samuel who had once taken meals with her family. The friend who had taught Gideon how to gentle a horse. The good neighbor who had helped bring in the harvest the year her *dat* had been down with a broken leg.

But the words he was saying now pierced the fog of her thoughts, and her mind strained to clear.

"I want to help you with this, Rachel. I hope you believe that. But you need to make a complete turnaround in the way you've been living, and you need to trust me, as your friend and your bishop, to help you do that."

As Rachel fought her way back to clarity, she watched him with a growing feeling of uneasiness. She sensed that something lay behind the seeming kindness in his eyes, something that belied the rational and reasonable words coming so smoothly and easily from his lips.

"Haven't I always been a good friend to you? Didn't I try to comfort you after Eli's death and advise you as to finances and the management of your farm? I know at times you've resented my advice. You've always had an independent spirit, Rachel, we both know that. But surely you realize I've only meant what's best for you."

"Samuel—"

He waved off her interruption. "*Nee*, I want you to listen to me now, Rachel. This is for your own good."

Rachel stiffened, immediately irritated by this familiar insinuation that he was far wiser than she and capable of making the right decisions that she couldn't.

Either he didn't notice the flush of anger she felt flame her face or he chose to ignore it. "Let's forget for a moment any hard things I've said. Just…hear me out. If you're willing, Rachel, we can put all this bad business about the *auslander* behind us. We can still salvage your reputation and undo any damage done by your impulsive behavior."

He paused, his fingers kneading his hat over and over again. "I've said this to you before, Rachel, but I'm going to speak of it again. I need a helpmate. A wife…and a mother for young Joe. Aaron is older now and will soon be on his own. And Noah gets along without much guidance, although he's too stubborn by far. But Joe is still young enough to need plenty of guidance and discipline. He needs a mother. And I'll admit that I need a companion. A man isn't meant to be alone, nor is a woman."

He stopped and took a long breath before continuing. "Rachel, you know I've always cared for you."

Not this again. It had been so long, she'd actually thought he had given up. "Don't, please, Samuel—"

Again he warded off her attempt to speak. "Let me have my say, Rachel. This is important…for both of us."

He took a step toward her, but Rachel instinctively stepped back. Her earlier uneasiness was quickly altering to suspicion.

"I believe we can be good for each other. I'm already extremely fond of you, and I believe you could come to care for me in time. I'd be good to you and good *for* you. You would be the wife of a bishop and looked upon as a virtuous, godly woman. There would be no hint of…of wrong living or disobedience to the *Ordnung.* You would be highly regarded and respected. Marriage to me would allow you to put to rest any past mistakes in judgment or behavior. It would enable you to start anew, and it would benefit me also, as I would no longer need to shoulder all the household responsibilities in addition to my work on the farm."

Searching her face, he added, "As your husband, I would count it a blessing to teach you how to make good decisions and train you in right living. And…you would no longer have any fear of being shunned."

Rachel nearly gagged at the hot wave of nausea that rose up in her. So this was his real motive for frightening her with the threat of shunning! The truth slammed into her like a physical blow. "You dare try to deceive me, Samuel? You mean to force me to marry you in order to avoid the *Bann?*"

From somewhere deep inside her, she found the strength to meet his challenging eyes without flinching. "Get out! Get out of my house! Now!"

His face flamed. Every semblance of reason and kindness that had gentled his appearance only a moment before now bled into a fiery mask of outrage and anger. In that instant, Rachel recalled dark rumors and hints of questionable behavior on Samuel's part, especially during the time since he had become bishop. But over the years things also had been whispered about his temper, his heavy-handed methods of dealing with those who supposedly violated the *Ordnung*. It was rumored that even his deceased wife and his sons had suffered from his bad temper at times. And her friend Barbara had let it be known that some believed he was abusing his authority as bishop in a variety of ways.

"Be careful what you say to me, Rachel!" He hurled the words at her like stones. "You'd best think carefully about what I'm offering you before you insult me!"

"What you're offering me? I would die before I'd accept what you're offering me! You shame me, Samuel Beiler. And you shame the office of bishop!"

In two strides, he was in her face, his eyes ablaze with unmistakable contempt and fury. He raised a hand to her. Rachel somehow found the strength to lift her face to his and meet his furious gaze straight on. Silently, she dared him to strike her. Slowly, he dropped his hand away.

"You will regret this, Rachel," he ground out, his menacing bearing and tone of voice a visible threat. "You refuse me, and you give up your last chance to continue living a decent life among us."

There was no pretense about him now, nothing but a dark, thunderous rage.

"Get out," she again demanded.

Rachel managed to wait until she bolted the door behind him before falling to her knees and collapsing into a shuddering torrent of anguished weeping.

Hours later, Rachel sat in the darkened kitchen, still shaken and sickened by the unthinkable episode that had occurred earlier.

At first she had been unable to claw her way through the bewildering shock that had left her weak and dazed in Samuel's wake. Finally though, her mind had begun to clear, and she forced herself to comprehend the reality of what Samuel had proposed—and threatened.

As if his presence still hovered over the room, she gradually came to realize that his accusations of poor judgment and unwise behavior might hold some truth. Perhaps she *had* acted at times on impulse instead of wisely, but hadn't she acted mostly out of love and not from willful sin or the intention to deceive? And despite whatever truth his allegations might have contained, surely his rage against her and his attempt to force her into an unholy marriage had been just as wicked.

As the awareness of her mistakes came to bear on her and the shadow of guilt weighed heavily on her, she prayed from the deepest well of her being for forgiveness. She prayed for mercy and a clean heart, as well as God's intervention, that He would somehow stay Samuel's hand and stop him from carrying out the threat of the *Meidung*.

She didn't doubt that he intended to have her shunned and held the power to do so. But the peace that gradually began to dawn on her as she prayed seemed to whisper that in truth she had done nothing to deserve being placed under the *Bann*. Guilty of impulsive, even foolish actions at times, yes. But not guilty of the sins Samuel had hinted at.

Rachel also knew that hers would not be the only heart to break if Samuel carried out his intention. She sobbed and groaned aloud to think of the pain and sorrow it would bring her family.

If she had done something so terrible that the shunning would be justified, that was one thing. But she couldn't believe Samuel actually believed such wickedness of her. The more she thought about it, the more convinced she became that this was his way of trying to force her hand, to coerce her into a marriage that in itself would be a sin—on both their parts.

"*O Lord God, what am I to do? What* can *I do?*"

She had to tell someone. Someone she trusted, someone who could help. Someone must know what had happened here today.

Mamma? Her mother was the one she always went to when she was troubled or needed help.

She instantly discounted the very thought. She couldn't bring such a blow down on her. If there were any way at all to keep Mamma from knowing about this ugliness, she must somehow shield her. She couldn't bear the thought of what Samuel's threats would do to her gentle, sensitive mother.

Then she thought of Doc. Hadn't she always trusted his quiet wisdom, his kindness? But Doc was a new convert. Well liked and respected by the People, yes, but he would have no influence where a bishop was concerned. Besides, if Doc knew, she couldn't expect him to keep such a secret from her mother. It would be altogether unfair to ask it of him.

Malachi Esch. Unexpectedly, her good friend Phoebe's husband came to mind. Malachi had been a friend to her and her family since she was a little girl, and he was kindness itself. Everyone knew him as a good man, a fair and wise leader.

He was also a compassionate man in every way. He and Phoebe had sometimes even helped hide the runaway slaves, at the risk of their own safety, just like Jeremiah and Asa did.

Even more importantly for her situation, he was a leader in the church, one of their preachers, so he would have some influence and authority.

Rachel knew she had to tell *someone*. Why not Malachi? Although the thought of confiding the personal nature of Samuel's accusations to anyone made her feel shame, she sensed that Malachi would listen to her with an open mind. And somehow she knew he would believe her and not condemn or humiliate her.

There was still plenty of daylight left, and Malachi lived close by. She felt an urgency to not delay, to go now. She feared Samuel would waste no time sending a messenger to impose the *Bann* on her. If she had any hope at all for help, she needed to act as soon as possible.

Her decision made, albeit reluctantly, she rose from the kitchen chair and went to get her coat. She delayed only a moment before leaving the house, just long enough to whisper one more prayer, again asking for God's mercy and understanding, this time on the part of Malachi, one of His godly servants.

38

MESSAGES

Ye faithful!—ye noble!
A day is at hand
Of trial and trouble,
And woe in the land!

JAMES CLARENCE MANGAN

On Tuesday afternoon, Gant received a note from Asa, letting him know that the "shipment had been delivered to the supplier," where it would be "loaded and transported on to the north warehouse."

As for Asa and John Turner, they would "lay over in Canton long enough to make repairs on the equipment and let the horses have a rest before heading home."

Gant quickly translated all he needed to know. They had reached the station just outside of Canton, where Paul Frazier and his brother would take over as conductors and drive the refugee slaves the rest of the way north with fresh horses. Asa and young Turner would also have a rest and then head home.

He breathed a sigh of relief and continued to read. Silas, as expected, had gone on with the "shipment." Asa had given him money for a fresh mount of his own, asking him to return to Riverhaven and stay with them a spell once the trip was completed. Was that all right with Gant? He doubted he'd be able to convince the boy to spend much time "off the road," but he hoped Silas would at least stay long enough to get some rest and visit awhile before going on. Did Gant think they could make a place for him?

Clearly, Asa wanted to spend as much time as possible with his newly discovered nephew. Happy for his friend, Gant hurriedly scrawled a reply and passed it to the waiting messenger. Silas was welcome for as long as he wanted to stay.

As he continued his work on the kitchen set he was making for Hap Carter and his widowed daughter, Gant remembered to give thanks for another safe "delivery." They had been fortunate so far in setting hundreds of runaway slaves safely on the road to freedom, either by land or on the river. Over the years, they hadn't lost a one of them, and other than the gunshot one of Cottrill's men had inflicted on him, neither he nor Asa had suffered any major injury.

Truly, they had been exceedingly fortunate. No, he corrected himself, they had been exceedingly blessed. Blessed and divinely protected.

Malachi Esch knew he could wait no longer to contact Bishop Schrock and at least one other bishop—most likely Jacob Lehman—both from neighboring districts. Bad enough what he had learned from Rachel Brenneman the past evening. But today, his boy, Reuben, had seen with his own eyes a sight that not only outraged Malachi but sorely grieved his heart.

Early this morning, he had sent Reuben into town to pick up feed and a few store supplies. When the boy returned, he told a tale Malachi might not have believed had not his own son been doing the telling. Reuben was a *gut* boy and had always been truthful to the bone. Malachi knew if his son said it, it was so, and that was that.

He still shuddered as he recalled Reuben's words. "I saw Noah and Joe Beiler on the road coming back from town, *Dat*. I don't know what happened to Joe, but he looked a fright. As if he'd been beaten, and badly so. His face was all bruised and puffed, and one eye looked as if it was swollen shut. And he was walking like it hurt him some to move."

Reuben had hesitated before going on, but finally, as if he couldn't stop himself, he'd burst out, "Is it true, *Dat*, what's been told about Bishop Beiler beating on his boys? And his poor dead wife as well?"

Malachi hadn't known how to answer his son's question. There had been a time when he would have simply cautioned the boy not to repeat rumors—rumors he had heard himself but refused to spread. Even now, there was no proof Samuel was responsible for his youngest son's painful appearance. Still, after what he'd heard told at the meeting a few days before, plus Rachel Brenneman's account of Samuel Beiler's threat against her, and now this incident his own son had related to him, it seemed the truth had to be faced.

He had answered Reuben carefully but with candor. "It is said, son, that where there's smoke, there's bound to be some fire. I fear there may indeed be some fire behind these stories."

"But he's a bishop now, *Dat*!"

"So he is, Reuben, but he's still a man, and though we don't like to think it, he's just as prone to weakness and sin as we all are."

After Reuben went out to the barn, Malachi forced himself to confront the reality that something had to be done about Samuel Beiler. But it was beyond his authority or right to make decisions in such a serious matter. So with a heavy heart, he wrote identical notes to the two bishops in districts nearest Riverhaven, asking them to come as soon as possible for a meeting of utmost importance.

Then he called Reuben in from the barn and instructed him to deliver each message to the two bishops. "Go on horseback—that will be faster than taking the buggy. And waste no time, son," he told him. "There are important matters that must be dealt with right away."

Late into the evening and night, he longed yet again for his beloved wife, Phoebe. Not that he could have discussed private church matters with her—that simply wasn't done. But with her at his side, he always felt stronger, wiser—more a man. Not a typical or a particularly righteous way for an Amish man to feel, but he thought God would understand. They had been so close, he and Phoebe. Most of the time they seemed more one than two. Small wonder he missed her so much he sometimes thought his heart would break for the pain of it.

39

CONVICTION

My soul, wait thou only upon God;
For my expectation is from him.

PSALM 62:5

Gant worked late in the shop, mostly cleaning up paperwork and organizing new orders. Gideon had offered to stay and help, but something about the boy's restless mannerisms and air of distraction lately told him to give his young apprentice some time for himself. Besides, when it came to paperwork, Gideon's mind seemed to wander off to anything else but what he was doing.

Something was eating at the lad, he was almost certain. His work hadn't suffered so far, but clearly he had something pretty heavy on his mind.

Ah, well. He was young. Probably girl problems. Maybe that pretty Emma Knepp, although he would hope the boy had enough sense not to get tangled up in a forbidden relationship with an Amish lass. A sure road to heartbreak, that. Not to mention trouble.

And hadn't he learned enough about *that* himself?

Gideon Kanagy knew what God was prodding him to do. He had sensed it for days and fought against it for just as long. He had little doubt that carrying out the Lord God's will in this instance would cost him his job.

Yet in moments of brutal clarity, he had to admit that the loss of his job with Captain Gant might be not be the worst of it. It might cost him something even more precious. The loss of Emma. Because even if he were to give up his employment with the captain, there was still no guarantee that Samuel Beiler, in his power as the new bishop, would grant him permission to return to the People. It was well within Beiler's authority to question Gideon's repentance for so long he wouldn't be able to make his vows and join the church for years.

By then, Emma would have forgotten about him and married some-one else. For that matter, Beiler might never allow him back into the community of the People. He might end up always standing outside and looking in. Who could predict what a man like Samuel Beiler might do?

He shivered a little as he walked the riverbank, although his coat was heavy and usually more than enough to ward off the early evening wind. A chill seemed to run all through him, and he had a hunch it wasn't from the January weather.

Gideon wasn't one to dwell too much on what he couldn't change, but lately he'd taken to brooding about his future. Ever since he'd finally given up on his own judgment and begun to seriously pray for God's guidance, he'd felt what Rachel called a "conviction" to return to his Amish faith and way of life.

He wasn't exactly sure how he could know whether God was convicting him or he was just bringing it on himself. It was a kind of pressure, as if someone or something were bearing down on him, continually pushing at him with the same thoughts time and time again. It was a little like when he'd seen Mamm or Rachel kneading bread, pressing carefully but firmly into the dough over and over.

At first, hoping he might be wrong, he'd tried to ignore the pressure. When it didn't go away, he tried to push back, mentally defending his own reasons why he couldn't afford to give up the life he'd made for himself among the *Englisch*. He had to make a living, didn't he? And he had no desire to do it by farming. He wasn't cut out to be a full-time farmer, and he knew it. Besides, it wouldn't be right to leave the captain on his own. The man had treated him well right from the start, paying him a fair wage and training him as a carpenter. He'd been patient with his mistakes and not short on praise when he approved of his work. He'd feel uncomfortable walking out on the captain after all this time.

But trying to justify his reasons for staying put didn't help either. He had eventually accepted that the changes inside him must be God's doing. There didn't seem to be any other explanation.

If that was the case, he'd better deal with it. He'd done a lot of foolish things in his life so far, but he wasn't about to defy God, at least not knowingly.

The problem was, he didn't quite know where to start. Should he tell his family first? Or would it be better to talk to Emma before anyone else, to try to get a sense of how she really felt about him? That didn't seem right either. If God really was guiding him to go back and live Amish, he needed to do it out of obedience, not because he wanted to court Emma.

Maybe the right thing to do was to talk with Captain Gant before anyone else. After all, he would be the one most affected by his leaving.

No. He should probably face Samuel Beiler first thing, before mentioning his decision to anyone else. After that he'd speak with the captain.

He dug his hands down deeper into his pockets and ground his teeth at the thought. He'd rather take on a wounded bear. But sooner or later he'd have to steel himself and approach the man.

The man. He still found it almost impossible to think of Beiler as the bishop. Somehow he just didn't fit the title.

✧40✧

IN SEARCH OF GUIDANCE

For one thing only, Lord, dear Lord, I plead:
Lead me aright.

ADELAIDE A. PROCTER

Four days later, as January was nearing an end, an unannounced meeting assembled at Samuel Beiler's farmhouse. Only Malachi, the two hastily summoned bishops, and Abe Gingerich, the other preacher besides Malachi, attended.

Samuel Beiler was told only that they would meet with him and each of his sons one at a time, and that there would be no conversation among them between meetings.

One after another, the men entered, walking heavily, as if burdened by the awareness that after this night the community might never again be the same. Every face was serious, even grave. No words were spoken before the meeting commenced except for a brief and solemn greeting. No smiles were exchanged, for this evening held nothing to smile about. The deepening twilight, this gloaming time of day, somehow seemed appropriate for the events to be discussed and the decisions to be made.

They questioned Beiler's sons first, warning them not to discuss their meeting with their father. They brought them into the room one at a

251

time and talked to each alone. The two younger boys were reluctant but ultimately cooperative, although the youngest, Joe, was obviously shy and nervous about saying anything against his father.

As a preacher and without the authority of a bishop, Malachi would be asking no questions. All the same, he would be listening closely.

He knew Jacob Lehman to be a kindly and thoughtful bishop. Clearly, the man was doing his best to put young Joe at ease during his questioning. "Understand, Joe, you are in no trouble. None at all. But some are concerned about how you received those bruises and marks on your face. We mean merely to help you, but you must be completely truthful with us. Now, tell us what happened."

The boy's glance darted around the room as if he were looking for a way out. At first he shrugged, but Bishop Lehman prompted him. "It's all right, Joe. Tell us who did this."

Joe's gaze swung back to him, but still he hesitated.

"Was it your *dat*?"

Finally the boy nodded. "*Ja.*"

The bishop drew a long breath. "Why, son? Why did he strike you?"

The boy shook his head. "He didn't say why. He was mad at me, I guess."

"He struck you with his hands?" Bishop Schrock asked.

Joe looked at him as if he didn't quite understand. "*Ja*, his fists."

Malachi saw the bishop wince.

"But he didn't explain why you were being punished?"

Again the boy shook his head, his expression confused and seemingly embarrassed. "Sometimes he says I try his patience. He tries to make me a better boy." He lowered his head, not looking at any of the men across from him.

"I'm sure you're already a very good boy, Joe," Bishop Schrock said gently.

Malachi's heart wrenched at the child's look of shame. He had explained to both bishops that young Joe was known to be a little slow in the head. He could tell they remembered, for they were being extremely kind and patient with the boy.

As soon as they excused Joe from the room, they brought his brother Noah in. Malachi was pleased to note that both bishops showed the same restraint and kindness toward the older boy as they had toward Joe. Even so, there was no mistaking their intent to learn the truth about the kind of man and father Samuel Beiler was.

They had to press Noah more firmly about his father, but not for long. The boy's natural good nature found it hard to dissemble. Although his demeanor was awkward at first, he soon answered any question submitted to him with what appeared to be complete candor.

Yes, he admitted, his gaze only slightly diverted, he too had suffered numerous "punishments" at his father's hands. And like his younger brother, the reason for those beatings—Malachi couldn't bring himself to call them "punishments," for both boys' words spoke of beatings, not mere incidents—was never really explained. He mentioned only his father's anger and his intention to make him, like Joe, a "better boy."

The two bishops seemed to go out of their way to be gentle, but the longer Noah's questioning continued, the more disturbed Malachi grew. It was no secret that some among the People believed in the "severe" disciplining of their children. He suspected that in all cultures there were those who trusted more in beatings to achieve their desired results than in less extreme methods of discipline.

But Samuel Beiler had often crossed the line in dealing out even the harshest of punishment. Malachi could not believe that the Lord God approved of a father beating his son with his bare hands to the point of disfigurement.

The oldest of Samuel's three sons turned out to be an unpleasant surprise. Aaron Beiler was still in his *rumspringa*, so he might have predictably been more candid about his father than his younger brothers had been. He was known to be an independent sort, surly and gruff, intelligent, and often displaying a streak of belligerence. Malachi would have expected him to be the most outspoken about his father, even blunt.

He was anything but. At first, he seemed openly defiant, tossing off slick and empty remarks in reply to every question he was asked. When pressed to be more serious and sincere, instead he became curt and disagreeable.

Malachi was completely caught off guard when, rather than supporting his brothers' remarks about their *dat*'s severe punishments and beatings, Aaron sneered. "*Lecherich*! They're both such *boppli*! Carrying on like babies when their punishment is no more than what they deserve!"

He flatly denied any mistreatment from Samuel and stuck to his story that his brothers were spouting half-truths. "Our *dat* is a hard man, but he's also a fair man."

After a long pause, Bishop Lehman leaned forward and said, "Are you saying then, Aaron, that you have never received harsh treatment or beatings by your father?"

At first the youth delayed, but then he shrugged. "Nothing more than I had coming to me."

There seemed nothing more to say after that, so the boys were allowed to leave. The two youngest were instructed to go to the home of Samuel Beiler's sister and spend the night with their aunt.

When they called Samuel Beiler in, they gave him an account of the accusations leveled against him, concentrating more on the reports that he had abused his authority as bishop, issued directives not in keeping with the *Ordnung*, and inappropriately "threatened" a widow in the community with the *Bann*. Unwilling to invite even more severe beatings on Beiler's sons, they deliberately didn't dwell on the charges about the previous beatings he had inflicted upon his wife and children, although they would, of course, have to take all this into consideration.

Malachi thought Samuel might have been able to talk his way out of most of this had it not been for the final charge—his attempt to coerce Rachel Brenneman into marrying him by threatening to have her shunned.

Beiler appeared to seethe with what Malachi sensed to be a scarcely contained fury, but he said little throughout the meeting other than to deny each accusation. His delivery of each reply was given with a steely-eyed, tight-mouthed control and a strange tone of contempt.

Only at the end of the meeting did Beiler's self-control clearly desert him. He rose from his chair and hurled a red-faced volley of objections at his questioners. "You dare to insult me, a bishop, a leader like yourselves, with such lies? Gossip! Rumors! That's what you bring into my house—to me and my sons—and demand that I defend myself against such ridiculous lies? This is the work of the devil! You are all guilty of carrying out his mischief! Well, I don't have to listen to this any longer and I won't!"

He stormed out of the room, ignoring Bishop Schrock's attempt to stop him.

Shocked by Beiler's behavior, Malachi and the others left immediately to continue their meeting at Malachi's house.

For a time, the two bishops, Abe, and Malachi sat in silence. Finally Bishop Schrock broke the silence. "Well then, it seems that our brother will make no attempt to explain or defend himself, so we must take what we know to the Lord God and ask for His guidance. We know what his sons have confided, and we know what Malachi has shared with us about Samuel's attempt to force the widow Brenneman into marrying him by threatening to place her under the *Meidung*."

He paused. "I'm sure we can trust Malachi's word about Rachel's virtue, that she is an honorable and God-fearing widow and in no way deserving of being shunned. I would suggest that she avoid the company of this *auslander*, Gant, but I sense that her only sin, should we choose to label it such, would be poor judgment on occasion. However, even if she were guilty of more than that, your bishop had no right to attempt some sort of forced alliance."

He turned to Bishop Lehman. "Jacob? I'm sure we want to hear your thoughts as well."

Bishop Lehman knitted his hands together on the table, saying in a thoughtful tone of voice, "I'll admit that I'm somewhat confused about Aaron Beiler's refusal to support the remarks of his brothers and his attitude in general. Nevertheless, I tend to trust what we heard from the two younger boys. And I'm grieved to learn about Samuel Beiler's treatment of one of your widows. That's nothing less than shameful!"

"We will, of course, need to speak with Samuel again," put in Bishop Schrock. "He must be given every opportunity to defend himself—or repent."

"But even if he repents," said Jacob Lehman, "he will need a time for restoration. Perhaps a very long time. A decision has to be made about the People's need for a bishop."

Ordinarily, as Bishop Schrock had earlier explained, they would delay making such a decision for a longer period of time. But because they feared that Beiler's sons might suffer repercussions from the situation, and because of Beiler's threat to have Rachel Brenneman shunned, they were in agreement that a decision in this most serious of matters should not be delayed.

So after the bishops had had their say, there seemed nothing else to do except to spend a lengthy time in prayer, seeking God's wisdom and guidance as they tried to come to a fair and right conclusion about Samuel Beiler.

"Tomorrow, then," said Bishop Schrock, "we will speak with Samuel again, and then, after an additional time of prayer, come to a decision."

Malachi almost spoke up at one point to voice his concern about Rachel. More than once he had felt a twist of genuine fear for her safety. Bishop or not, if Beiler were the kind of man who would beat his own sons, attempt to force an unwilling woman to become his wife, and raise a hand as if to strike her when she refused...what else might he be capable of?

In the end, he kept his silence, reminding himself that it wasn't his place to add his opinions to those of the two bishops. No, he would take his private fear to his Lord and trust Him to protect Rachel as well as Samuel's sons. He wasn't at all sure his own personal concern was important enough to enter into the bishops' decision, a decision that would affect the entire Riverhaven Amish community.

But he believed with all his heart it would be of great importance to their heavenly Father.

→ 41 ←

A HIGHLY UNEXPECTED TURN OF EVENTS

A person's own folly leads to their ruin,
yet their heart rages against the LORD.

PROVERBS 19:3 NIV

Had Malachi tried to predict how Samuel Beiler would react to his visit from the two bishops the next day, his most far-fetched ideas would not have come even close.

Not that Malachi witnessed the meeting in person. Only the bishops visited Samuel, arriving at his house unannounced. But later that same day, they gave Malachi a detailed accounting of what took place.

Malachi's son, Reuben, had a saying when he got surprised in a not so good way: "It made my mind hurt." That's how Malachi felt after hearing from the bishops what had transpired at their meeting with Samuel Beiler. It made his mind hurt. It also made his heart hurt.

He had known Samuel for years, had lived close to him, watched his children grow up, worshipped with him, and prayed for him, especially when his wife died. That such a man, a man upon whom the lot had fallen to serve as bishop, would openly defy the very messengers God had sent to hear his defense, pray for him, and counsel him…that Samuel would turn on them and on his God was beyond all imagining.

And yet it had happened. According to Jacob Lehman and Amos Schrock, Samuel had appeared to snap. He openly scorned their charges of misconduct, misuse of his authority as bishop, and bad behavior in general—behavior out of keeping for not only a spiritual leader but for any Amish man. He had as much as called the two bishops liars and perverters of the truth—them and all those who had made the accusations against him, even though two of his own sons were among those he condemned.

"Like a madman he was," Jacob Lehman had said, with Bishop Schrock nodding in agreement. "For a while there, I thought he had lost his mind altogether."

That Samuel was a proud and at times a seemingly headstrong man was no secret to Malachi or, he imagined, to anyone else who knew the man reasonably well. Too many times he had displayed those traits in matters involving the church and individual members of the community.

But this? Along with all the other troubling aspects in his character that had recently come to light, now to hear that he had behaved like a crazy man, cursing people he had lived among for years and even coming close to blaspheming the Lord God in his tirade while displaying absolutely no sign of repentance—it was too much for Malachi to take in. His head was not only hurting, it was swimming by the time the bishops left to report the events of the day to Abe Gingerich.

By late afternoon, Samuel's position and authority as bishop had been revoked, and he had been placed under the *Bann*.

Now, as Malachi sat at the kitchen table, considering all that had happened over the past few days and grieving the ugliness of the entire situation, he tried to sort through the clutter of his mind. He thanked God that he hadn't witnessed Samuel's outburst, for seeing it with his own eyes no doubt would have scalded his soul with a memory he would never forget.

As it was, his shock and confusion were now giving way to concern for those Samuel believed to have turned against him. Over the past few days, Malachi had been relieved that no further word had come to Rachel about being shunned, yet he'd remained uneasy, wondering when and if the man would actually carry out his threat to her.

Now, of course, he couldn't have her shunned. Still, in light of all that had recently transpired, he was beginning to question Samuel's mental state and couldn't help but wonder if the man might not attempt to exact some kind of revenge on those he felt had wronged him. In addition to Rachel, there were the Beiler boys to think about. There was no refuting the fact that Samuel had beaten them before. What might he do now?

Malachi was already sick at heart. Now he began to feel physically ill as well.

He must go yet this evening to the home of Dr. Sebastian and his wife, Susan. By tomorrow the word about Samuel's shunning would be all over the community. He had to talk with them now and caution them about Rachel—just in case. He understood why Rachel hadn't wanted to go to her mother with this trouble before, but now, Susan and Dr. Sebastian had to know.

He didn't like the way he was thinking about Samuel. He fervently hoped he was letting his imagination run away from reality, but he would take no chances. It was best for Rachel and her family to know about the troublesome situation yet tonight so they could take precautions.

Malachi had long been a man of prayer. Many of the People simply relied on the Lord's Prayer in all their approaches to the Almighty, but Malachi was more inclined to openly share whatever was on his heart with the Lord God. A few years ago, his family and others in the community had accepted God's offer of salvation instead of clinging to the belief that His salvation was not free, but had to be earned. From that time on, they had learned to pour out their hearts in earnest prayer, knowing their Lord would hear them and answer.

These days, it was hard for him to get to his knees. His legs didn't work so well as they had when he was younger. Even so, he struggled to kneel by the kitchen table, where he prayed in the language of his people, the language God also understood, just as He understood the tongues of all His children.

"Lord God, in Your mercy and by Your power, protect these, Your people, from harm in the aftermath of these ugly and sinful events that have taken place among us. Guard from further harm, O Lord, those who sought only to speak the truth and shield their loved ones. And if it be Your will, have mercy on this one who has strayed from the path that leads to You."

Clumsily, he got to his feet and went for his coat, reluctant to leave and yet knowing his visit to the Sebastians could not be avoided.

It had been an awkward time, a painful time, but David Sebastian could not have been more grateful for Malachi Esch's promptness in coming to them. His account of the past few days' events and especially those of today had been candid and obviously prompted by his concern for Rachel.

David assumed his good friend wouldn't have divulged as much as he did had it not been for that concern. As it was, his quick action would enable them to take measures to protect Susan's daughter.

In fact, as soon as Malachi left, David went to fetch Rachel. At the moment, he was still trying to ignore the disappointment he felt that Rachel hadn't come to them earlier and made them aware of the burden she'd been carrying, particularly Samuel Beiler's threats. That she had spent the last few days bearing her terrible secret alone wrenched his heart.

Yet he thought he understood why she'd acted as she had. She'd doubtless been trying to shield her mother. And knowing Rachel and her sensitive spirit, she had most likely been feeling shamed by Beiler's accusations.

From where he was standing in the hallway, he glanced upstairs. Susan was still with Rachel in her old bedroom, no doubt attempting to comfort and reassure her. Of course, Susan was badly shaken herself. But he knew his wife. She would hold steady as long as her daughter needed her strength.

For that matter, David was also finding himself somewhat stunned and struggling to take in this entire situation. It boggled the mind to think of all that had transpired in such a short time.

In truth, he had never actually felt any liking for Samuel Beiler—having distrusted the man for years because of the suspicion of cruelty toward his wife. But even so, he couldn't stop a pang of sorrow for the predicament Samuel now found himself in. He couldn't imagine the horror of being cast out from everyone and everything he'd ever known.

His first concern for now, however, had to be for Rachel. She could not stay alone, at least not until this worrisome situation with Samuel Beiler had been resolved somehow.

Many decisions would have to be made, and all of them significant. For example, what would be done about choosing a new bishop? David was, for the most part, completely unfamiliar with how the church worked in matters such as these, but he knew enough to assume that another lot would have to be cast for a new bishop to be chosen. And this time, that decision would most likely be made between Malachi Esch and Abe Gingerich, their two remaining preachers and church leaders.

As Susan had once explained to him, the position of bishop wasn't typically coveted by Amish men. The overwhelming responsibility for the spiritual direction of an entire community, the often onerous decisions that needed to be made, and the time and effort involved weren't for the spiritually or physically weak.

Feeling a need to be with Susan and Rachel, he sighed and started up the steps. So many people would be affected by the shunning of Samuel Beiler. Some lives had been damaged, some would be changed. Although it was probably a forbidden thought, he couldn't help but wonder, and not for the first time, about God's plan in allowing the lot to fall on such a man in the first place.

In that instant, however, it occurred to him that if Samuel had never become bishop, his true nature might never have been revealed until it was too late and he had done even more damage. Sometimes a man's depravity was concealed until surprised by the light.

In any event, he decided, God always knew what He was doing, so man shouldn't need to. And with that thought, he shook off the troubling questions about the unknown future in order to face what needed to be done in the challenging present.

GANT'S DILEMMA

God keep you every time and everywhere.

MADELINE BRIDGES

I want to see Rachel, Doc."

David Sebastian took in Gant's condition at a glance. Clearly the man was strung as tight as the fiddle he sawed on, standing there, waiting to come inside, his eyes desperate, his mouth hard, his hands clenched. He looked as if he were about to lunge through the door right past him.

"Gant...this might not be the best time—"

"I have to see her! Is she all right?"

"She's quite all right, but it's still not a good idea for you to be here."

"Because I'm the reason Beiler threatened her, right? At least part of the reason."

Doc took a long breath. "Gideon talked with you, I suppose."

"As soon as he came to work this morning."

Of course he had. The boy had stopped by the house last night, not long after they'd come back with Rachel. He heard the whole story, and they'd had quite the time keeping him from tearing out of the house and going after Samuel Beiler. Only Rachel's pleading had stopped him.

He'd finally relented but insisted on staying the night. He was still seething when he left for town this morning.

"Doc, I'm going to stand right here until you let me in."

And he would. David sighed and opened the door wide enough for him to enter. "You and I will talk first," he said firmly.

"Where is she?" Gant was already looking for her, his eyes scanning the hallway and then the living room.

"She's upstairs with Susan and Fannie. She really is all right. Now calm down because you're not going to see her until you do."

The man must have raced that big red horse of his all the way out here from town. His face was flushed, his breath ragged, his cap askew.

"Come and sit down. I'll get Rachel in a moment."

Gant followed him into the living room but remained standing. He doffed his cap, still looking as if he might spring into motion at any moment.

David sighed. The thing about the Irish was their impetuous nature. In truth, he felt sorry for his friend. Clearly he'd come as fast as he could, most likely knowing he'd meet with some measure of resistance. All the man wanted was to comfort the woman he loved, after all.

But that was the problem. He was forbidden to comfort her or to love her.

What a dilemma for a man like Gant. What a dilemma for any man. Didn't he know as much from his own experience?

"You're sure she's all right?" Gant said.

"Well, she's still a bit unsettled, given everything that's happened. At first, she was feeling somewhat responsible for Beiler's being placed under the *Bann*, which was ridiculous of course. Anyway, after she learned the rest of the facts—his cruelty to his wife and sons, his abuse of his authority as bishop, and his blatant bad behavior in some of his dealings with the People—I believe by now she's accepted that he had to be shunned and that it was none of her doing at all."

"Aye, I've got all that. Gideon was pretty thorough with the gritty details," Gant said with a look of disgust. "Can I see her now?"

"Just a moment," David cautioned. "There's something else I think you should know."

Gant frowned, obviously impatient.

"I don't know exactly what she told Susan, but it seems she's still shouldering some guilt about you."

"About me?" Gant's expression of impatience changed to that of confused hurt. "What *about* me?"

David hesitated, at a bit of a loss as to how to explain. "Apparently, Beiler's accusations that she'd...that she'd behaved wrongfully with you... well, it gave her pause." He hesitated, struggling to find the right words. "I don't mean to imply anything. As I said, I don't really know what she told Susan, and Susan was quick to assure me that the concerns Rachel is fretting about aren't all that...questionable. Even so, Beiler's harangue is still troubling her."

Gant's face had gone crimson. "Doc, I promise you we never...there was never anything improper between us." He broke off, his mouth tightening. "Maybe Gideon didn't tell me everything. Doc, surely you know I would never compromise Rachel. I know what kind of woman she is. I couldn't respect her more—"

David waved off his friend's fierce protest. "And I know what kind of man you are. I know you wouldn't do anything to harm Rachel in any way. But you have to understand that the Amish don't believe in even sharing an embrace or a kiss—not that I'm saying you did—unless a couple is at least engaged. And even then, things are supposed to be kept very chaste."

Gant looked at him. "Are you going to tell me you never kissed Susan before you were engaged?" His expression was openly skeptical.

David now felt a flush creep up his own face. "I'm not going to tell you anything other than how Rachel seems to be feeling...according to Susan." He cleared his throat. "So when you do talk with her, keep your distance or she's likely to react."

"I understand. *Now* can I see her?"

Rachel walked into the living room slowly, even uncertainly, as if she almost dreaded their meeting. Gant drank in the sight of her, troubled by the signs of fatigue, the shadows smudging her eyes, and the way she averted her gaze.

"Rachel," he said, keeping his voice as soft as he could manage. "I just...I wanted to make sure you're all right."

Still avoiding his gaze, she nodded. "*Ja*, I'm fine."

"Is there anything you need, anything I can do?"

She shook her head slightly. "I'm all right, really."

He discovered that now that he was here, he didn't know what to say. "I hope it's all right...that I came."

She turned a hand in a vague gesture of reply. "I...suppose so. But we can't really be alone together anymore. It's not right."

"I was worried about you—"

"Don't be," she said, her tone unexpectedly sharp.

"Rachel..."

Something in his tone of voice apparently made her finally turn and look at him. He saw her expression soften, but her eyes held a wounded glaze that cut to the core of him.

"Jeremiah," she said softly, "I don't think we should talk right now. I'm sorry, but I just...can't. I need time. There are some things I need to think about."

Gant saw the slight trembling of her hands, the drawn lines about her mouth, and the weakness shuddering through her. It occurred to him that she probably hadn't slept at all the night before.

"Rachel, you and I...we haven't done anything wrong. No matter what Beiler may have said to you, what we've shared has never been wrong. We couldn't help loving each other."

He saw her flinch and for just an instant squeeze her eyes shut.

He realized then that he was only making an already difficult situation harder for her. He ached to hold her but knew he couldn't. He wanted to stay with her, at least long enough to comfort her, but that wasn't possible either.

Reluctantly, he made the decision that seemed to be best for her. "I'll go now, Rachel," he said, lowering his voice and keeping his tone as gentle as possible. "I'll come back...later. Please, just get some rest. Will you do that?"

She glanced away but nodded.

"Rachel? One thing..."

She looked at him.

"You'll stay here, won't you, with Susan and Doc...for now? You won't stay alone?"

She studied him and then actually managed a faint smile that brought a sudden surge of warmth to his heart. "Yes, Jeremiah. I'm staying here for a while. I'll be all right. I'll be safe here."

"*Please, God,*" he prayed as he left the house, "*please, let her be safe... here and anywhere she happens to be.*"

⇢ 43 ⇠

TIME TO GO HOME

Home is where our family lives and love abides.

ANONYMOUS

A week later, both Doc and Gideon informed Gant that according to all accounts, Samuel Beiler was gone, not only from the Plain community but from the Riverhaven area itself.

The three of them stood talking in the shop in the middle of the morning. "Does anyone know where he went?" Gant asked.

"Nobody seems to," replied Gideon.

"Not even his sister?"

"Nope. He just took up and left, according to Malachi." Gideon pulled a sour face. "And good riddance, I say."

"Don't forget the point of shunning, son," Doc put in. "It's not to punish. It's done for the good of the person shunned and to protect the church."

"I still don't understand that," Gant said.

"Hopefully, it will help the one being shunned to see the error of his ways and change those ways," Doc explained. "Being cast away from the flock, so to speak, is a very difficult and painful situation for an Amish person. It's hard for those outside the faith to understand, but it really is done in hopes of bringing about repentance and restoration, as well as to keep the body of believers pure."

Gant shook his head. "For a man like Beiler, this must be about the worst thing that could happen to him."

Gideon still looked skeptical. "I wonder. Old Sam always struck me as too bigheaded to be bothered about anything."

"Well, let's hope you're wrong," Doc said. "We would want to think that no one is beyond repentance and forgiveness."

"But I heard Beiler refused to accept the *Bann*, that he just left. No one seems to know where he went or if he's coming back."

"There's no acceptance or nonacceptance to the *Bann*," Doc replied. "It is what it is, and for someone to say they don't accept it doesn't make any difference. A person is shunned and that's all there is to it unless he repents and comes back to his faith and the church."

"So what about Beiler's sons?" Gant asked.

"They wouldn't go with him," Gideon put in. "Reuben Esch told me they're out at Samuel's sister's place. At least for now, they're staying with her."

After Doc left and Gideon took off with the day's deliveries, Gant sat at the table in the back room for a long time, thinking. He couldn't help but remember that this shunning practice was exactly what Beiler had threatened Rachel with unless she agreed to marry him.

He cringed at the very thought. He knew Rachel well enough to know that for her to be cast away from her entire family, her friends, and her church would have absolutely devastated her. In his warped, conniving way, Beiler had come up with the very thing he figured just might coerce her into marrying him.

That the man had sunk that low still enraged him. The very fact that Beiler had threatened Rachel made Gant want to trounce him.

Some Amish man *he* would make.

In that instant it occurred to Gant that he'd better start working on that potential for violence just in case the next bishop, whoever he happened to be, might have a more open mind about allowing him to convert.

Did he still hold out any real hope for that possibility? And if he did, did he actually believe he could ever become the man he would need to be—a man who could live with the pacifist and nonviolent beliefs of the Amish? Could he ever become the man Rachel would want him to be, the man she deserved?

Only God knew the answer to that. But Gant was certain that if he was given the opportunity, he would try.

When he'd been talking with Doc and Gideon, he had also realized that even though Beiler was now gone from the area, he still felt a sense of unease that something wasn't quite right. He found it hard to believe that a man like Beiler would go off just like that and leave behind his sons, his land, and all his possessions. After all, according to Doc, he didn't have to leave the area. He was banned from the church and fellowship with the People, but he didn't actually have to go away.

So why did he? Pride, maybe? An unwillingness to submit to being shunned? That seemed to be the only thing that made sense. The strong sense of pride and arrogance that had always appeared to be inherent to Beiler's character might be the only way to account for his swift exit from the Amish community.

Even so, Gant still felt uneasy.

Or was he just being overly anxious about Rachel? He couldn't forget how fragile she'd looked the last time he'd seen her. He'd worried about her ever since that day. Every protective instinct he had cried out to guard her, to take care of her. Instead, he couldn't even spend an hour alone with her.

At least she was still staying with Doc and Susan. He had no doubt that they would keep her close and look after her.

Even so, he still wished he could be the one taking care of her.

He had to smile a little at his own thought. If Rachel were to know the way he was thinking, she'd no doubt inform him that she didn't need anyone taking care of her, that she could manage quite well on her own.

Rachel decided that morning that it was time for her to go home. She had relied on Mamma and Dr. David's strength and attentive care long enough. She had to get back to her own house, her own way of life, and her own resources before too much dependence on her family set in.

Mamma was the soul of patience with her, and Dr. David couldn't be more kind. Fannie loved having her here, but Rachel was afraid her younger sister was beginning to want her here all the time. In fact, only yesterday, she had asked Rachel if she couldn't just move home to stay.

It was no good to let Fannie get her hopes up about that, and it wasn't right that Rachel should go on monopolizing her mother's time and attention either. She sensed that even Dr. David was spending more time at home, staying closer than usual. Goodness, they'd been put out enough already, what with fretting over her, keeping an eye on her house, and helping to tend her animals as well as their own. She needed to convince them that she was ready now to go home, that indeed she wanted to go.

And in spite of sometimes still feeling a little unnerved and confused by everything that had happened, she did want to get back to her usual way of living. Apparently Samuel was long gone now, so she no longer had to dread the thought of him showing up at her door again or carrying out the threat he'd made about having her shunned. Even though a shadow of sadness seemed to trail her every movement, and though she couldn't completely shake the guilt that edged its way into her mind when she remembered his insinuations about her and Jeremiah, she had to admit she was beginning to feel a subtle sense of freedom that Samuel could no longer plague her with his insistent visits and proposals.

Later that morning, she took advantage of the time when Fannie was walking Thunder to tell Mamma what she planned to do. She would talk with Fannie later, but she wanted to tell her mother first while they could be alone.

At first, Mamma was visibly upset. "Oh, Rachel, are you sure you're ready to be alone so soon? It hasn't been so long, after all, and you know we enjoy having you here. Why, Fannie will be so upset to hear you're leaving!"

"Mamma, Fannie's getting too used to my being here all the time. It's not good for her. We know I have to go home sometime. Besides, I'll make sure she knows I want her to come and stay with me as often as she likes, just as she always has."

She took both her mother's hands in hers. "I can't tell you how much it's meant to have you and Dr. David to lean on these past few days. You've been so good to me! But it's time I get back to my own home now, it really is. And after all, there's nothing but a big field between us, Mamma. It's not like we don't see each other every day."

Susan nodded and squeezed her hands. "I know, I know." When she looked at Rachel, tears were in her eyes. "But I'll miss you, daughter. It's been wonderful-*gut* having you here under the same roof again."

Her grasp on Rachel's hands tightened. "Oh, when I think what Samuel threatened you with—I can't even bear the thought of it! He had to know how much the very idea of the *Bann* would frighten you, how it would hurt you! He knew that, and he still—"

"Don't, Mamma." Rachel lifted her hands away to clasp her mother's face between them. "It's all right now. Samuel won't hurt us anymore. And I'm all right now. I'm just going home, nowhere else. I'll always be close by."

Her mother wiped at her eyes with both hands. "Still, you'll be careful, *ja*? You'll lock your doors and...just take care, won't you? There's still somebody out there up to no good, Rachel."

"Don't you worry, Mamma. I'll be careful. Of course I will."

Rachel dropped her hands away, but her mother quickly covered them with her own again. "And, Rachel...there's something I want to say to you. Something I want you to know."

Rachel looked at her, waiting.

"When you told me about how you felt when Samuel accused you of being...wrong in your behavior with Captain Gant, you admitted..." Her mother's face flamed for an instant, but she went on. "You admitted you had let him...kiss you."

"Oh, Mamma, I'm so sorry. I didn't want to hurt you...I was just so upset that night—"

"No, no, I don't mean to accuse you. Just...tell me this. Do you think I'm a bad woman, Rachel?"

Rachel reared back in astonishment. "Mamma! How can you ask such a thing? You're a wonderful woman! Everyone knows that. You're the best mother ever, a good wife, a friend to everyone in the community... why, you couldn't be a finer, more godly woman!"

"Then let me tell you something. I thought perhaps it would help you to feel better if you knew. And I would tell no one but you. We

Amish women, we don't usually share such things, but you seem so full of self-doubt right now. And you're feeling bad about yourself. But you shouldn't, daughter. You see, truth be told, David kissed me too…before we were married. More than once. Even before he converted to the faith, he kissed me. And I let him." She stopped. "We had loved each other for so long. So I understand…about you and Captain Gant. And if you don't think I'm a bad woman for wanting to be…close to the man I love, then neither should you think of yourself as one, Rachel."

Rachel sat staring at her crimson-faced mother, who seemed in that moment unable to meet her eyes, and then gently pulled her into a hug. "Oh, Mamma, thank you! Thank you for telling me that!"

Mamma met her gaze again, and then, as Rachel watched, she seemed to struggle to find her sternest motherly expression. "That doesn't mean, of course, that you should allow it to happen again."

For the first time in days, Rachel smiled—really, genuinely smiled. "No, of course not, Mamma."

STALKING RACHEL

Oh! Thou, who comest, like a midnight thief,
Uncounted, seeking whom thou may'st destroy;
Rupturing anew the half-closed wounds of grief,
And sealing up each new-born spring of joy.

JOHN KEEGAN

S he took her time about coming back to her own place.

He'd been waiting, hiding in the trees and watching every night for a week now, growing more and more furious when she didn't show up. He wasn't dumb enough to try to get to her while she was still at her mother's place. Not with her family around. Even Gideon was there sometimes, and that Gant fellow had stopped by as well. No, there were just too many people watching her who could ruin his plans again.

He just wanted *her*, Rachel. Gant, too, but he might have to be satisfied with just Rachel at first. Gant and that big hound of his were a risk. He hadn't figured out yet how to take him.

At first he'd thought getting rid of Gant would solve everything. But once he realized the man wasn't going to leave, he tried to scare Rachel into staying away from him. That hadn't worked either. Now that she'd gone and ruined everything, he just wanted revenge.

He would have been content to just scare her, but not actually hurt her. He'd thought she would eventually lose faith in Gant and even suspect him of the trouble happening all around. But oh, no. The more bad things happened, the more she seemed to cuddle up to him.

He hadn't meant things to go this far. At first, it had been mostly pranks. Fun. Just stirring up a little trouble to liven things up a bit. The fires, the teasing of the little sister, nobody had really got hurt. But after the accident with the Esch woman, his so-called *Englisch* friends had quickly deserted him. Only by threatening to implicate both of them in the Esch woman's death and the other troubles did he manage to convince them to keep their silence.

He was on his own then, and everything just got worse.

He tried to stop once, but he kept being drawn back in. Something in him craved the excitement. Now this. What a mess. And it was all Rachel's fault. Hers and Gant's. If she'd only acted like a decent Amish widow instead of getting mixed up with that outsider like a common tramp, nothing would have come to this point.

His two cowardly brothers blabbing to the bishops about the beatings. His *dat* losing his temper like a wild man and taking it out on *him*, now that the other two had run off to hide at their Aunt Rebekah's. And now *Dat*'s shunning.

He rubbed his shoulder and his cheekbone, where a big, painful bruise had raised up after the last beating. As if everything was *his* fault, when in truth it was all *Rachel's* fault. Hers and Gant's. If she'd only acted like a decent Amish widow instead of getting mixed up with that *auslander*, nothing would have come to this point. *Dat* would still be the bishop, he wouldn't be taking his temper out on *him*, and his brothers would still be at home.

What a mess.

Well, Rachel had herself to thank, now that he'd completely given up any thought of being careful with her so as not to do her any real harm. There was no longer any reason to avoid hurting her. Now he intended to give her what was coming to her. And somehow, later, he'd get Gant as well.

They had spoiled everything—every plan he'd had, every attempt he'd made to put things right, to make things work out the way they were supposed to. So things would get better for him. So things would be better for his whole family. Instead, everything was a disaster.

The two of them were now going to pay. First her, then Gant. Starting tonight.

→ 45 ←

ENCOUNTER WITH
THE ENEMY

*A starless landscape came
'Twixt that scene and my aching sight.*

THOMAS D'ARCY MCGEE

A t times like this, Gant got more impatient than ever with his bum leg.
And in weather like this, it was more of a handicap than at any other
time. Consequently, he'd been downright black tempered most of the day.

It started early this morning before the sun ever came up. He'd been
restless all night. Jake—even a bobcat deserved a name, didn't he?—had
screeched on and off since bedtime the night before. Probably that's why
Mac had been restless too, sleeping light and uttering a low growl every so
often. Gant got up once to look outside, hoping Mac might quiet down
if he knew his owner was up and alert. Nothing he could do about the
bobcat, of course. He would probably soon be slinking off to wherever
it stayed during the daylight hours.

Gant supposed he couldn't really blame the animals for his own
sleeplessness. He simply couldn't shake the increasing uneasiness he'd
been feeling since he'd learned from Gideon the day before that Rachel
had returned to her own place. He had just about decided that the only
way he was going to put his apprehension to rest was to keep watch over
her himself.

Was he being totally irrational? What did he think he was going to do in case of trouble? His leg had gotten so stiff in the recent cold, rainy weather he could scarcely walk. He had had to take up the cane most of the time now just to get around at any reasonable pace. Not likely he'd be able to chase somebody down. In case of an intruder or something of the sort, the best he'd be able to do would be to beat him off with his cane.

In a spurt of raw frustration, he brought his fist down on the table with a growl of disgust. From his place by the door, Mac roused and shot him a cranky look.

"Right," he muttered. "*Now* you want to sleep. Too bad. You had your chance last night."

By the time Gideon came back from deliveries midafternoon, Gant was walking the floor more than working. He felt like a caged lion with a sore foot. But over the past few hours a growing urgency had nagged at him until he sensed he had no choice but to give in to it.

He motioned Gideon over as soon as the boy came through the back door.

"You have any plans for tonight?" he asked.

Gideon shook his head. "No. Why?"

"I could use your help."

"Sure, Captain. What do you need?"

"Two good legs, but you can't do anything about that. So how about going with me to keep watch out at Rachel's for a while tonight?"

The boy frowned. "Keep watch?"

Gant tried to explain how he'd been feeling since learning that Rachel was back home. He didn't like being that open with the boy or anyone else about his emotions, especially when it involved asking for help. But pride allegedly went before a fall, and in his case that could probably be taken as a literal truth.

Gideon's reply surprised him. "To tell you the truth, Captain, I've been kind of uneasy about things myself."

Gant looked at him. "You have?"

The other nodded. "Well, we've still got a troublemaker out there somewhere, maybe more than one, and if you think about it, my family seems to have been the target for a lot of his orneriness. If I had my way,

Rachel wouldn't be staying alone out there right now, so close to the woods and all."

Learning that Rachel's brother shared his apprehension cinched Gant's decision to do something about his increasing uneasiness.

By dusk they were on the road in Gant's buggy, buttoned down as snug as possible.

"This is quite a buggy, Captain. I expect you did most of the extras on it yourself. That so?"

Gant nodded. "I did a lot of it, except the frame, of course. I'd have to say I wouldn't want a future as a buggy builder."

"Those leather flaps may come in real handy tonight while we're sitting out in the cold. And that seat in the back works real good for Mac."

The dog chuffed his agreement.

"I appreciate your coming along with me, by the way," Gant told him.

"Well, Rachel is my sister, after all. Why wouldn't I come with you?" They rode in silence for a time before Gideon asked, "Do you have any idea who might be behind all the trouble, Captain?"

Gant shook his head. "I wish I did. What about you?"

Gideon didn't answer right away. Then, "Ever consider that it might be Samuel Beiler?"

Gant looked over at him. "You suspect him?"

"I don't know. Just wondering, that's all. If it was him, and he's really gone to stay, then maybe there won't be any more problems."

"That'd be good," said Gant.

"But you don't think so?"

"I don't know what to think. I just know that whoever is behind all the trouble belongs in jail. And I'd like to see him there."

Gideon nodded. "So would I. The sooner the better."

It turned out to be a thoroughly miserable night, with rain splattering the roof of the buggy and a thin but cold wind rushing through the trees. Even though Gant was considerably older than the boy next to him, he wagered Gideon was just as uncomfortable as he was. Even Mac had taken to whimpering now and then as if to remind them that he was a bit put out with their present situation too.

They spent the next three nights in the same spot in the same kind of weather, huddled under the warmest blankets they could find. And saw nothing—including Rachel. They never caught so much as a glimpse of her, nothing but the faint golden glow of lamplight filtering from her windows.

For once Gant was relieved not to see her. It meant she was staying safely indoors.

Their second night there, he heard a sound that caught him up short. A screech, echoing through the darkness, not all that far away. A bobcat. But it couldn't be *his* bobcat. Not all the way out here. And yet he had heard it once before, or at least he'd thought he heard it. The night he sat in this same spot, keeping watch after Rachel's break-in. That night, too, he couldn't believe his ears, and yet he'd been almost certain.

"You hear that?" Gideon whispered.

Gant nodded.

"That's a bobcat, isn't it?"

"Sounds like one."

"You don't think that's the one that's been hanging around town, do you?"

"Doesn't seem likely," Gant said. "They like to prowl, but I doubt he'd wander out this far."

Or would he?

On their third night—actually, it was past two in the morning—they decided to go back into town a little earlier than before. Gant's leg was one large throbbing pain, thanks to the weather and sitting hunched up in the same position for so long a time. Then too, Gideon seemed to be coming down with a cold and was feeling pretty rough himself.

Gant had begun to feel hopeful that their troublemaker *had* been Samuel Beiler, having seen nothing out of the ordinary the past two nights. Maybe things would now settle down in Beiler's absence.

He was just pushing the blanket away to reach for the reins when Gideon put a hand to his arm. "Captain—"

Gant turned to look at him, but Gideon had leaned forward and was staring at Rachel's house, at this time of night a lightless, indistinct shell.

"Look," Gideon whispered. "See that?"

Gant saw it, all right. A faint light, flickering in the darkness, illumining a figure with a lantern. Someone was headed for the back of the house.

At the same time, somewhere on the hill a bobcat cried again.

Something awakened Rachel. She sat upright, not as if she'd been dragged out of a drowsy, confused deep sleep, but instead suddenly wide awake, listening.

To what?

She heard nothing, yet her heart raced, and her blood pounded as though something had set her spinning into a panic.

She waited another minute or so, but when she still heard nothing, instead of lying back down, she got up, shrugged into her robe, and crossed to the window. It was totally dark with rain pattering on the roof and splashing against the window.

Seeing nothing, she started to turn away but then stopped.

Was that a light moving toward the house?

She waited...and saw it again. It flickered, wavered, and then disappeared.

But no, there it was again. Moving toward the back of the house.

Frozen in place, she clutched at her throat and made a small moaning sound.

What to do? Should she cry out, try to frighten them away? Or hide? That was it. She would hide. But where?

She glanced around. There was nowhere to hide in the bedroom.

Where, then?

No. With all the strength she could muster, she forced herself to shake off the fear. This was her house. Her home. She wouldn't be frightened into crawling under a bed or creeping into a clothes closet. She would find some other way out of this.

She looked around the room, her eyes going to the lamp on the bedside table. Maybe if whoever was out there saw light in the house they'd know she was awake, watching, and they'd go away.

Her hands shook wildly, but she finally got the lamp lighted and set it closer to the window, where it could be seen from outside.

She thought of the kitchen drawer where she kept the knives. But no, she'd never be able to use a knife on someone—the very thought made her cringe. Besides, a knife could just as easily be turned on her.

But there was the mallet for pounding meat. And the rolling pin.

She pulled her robe tighter and started for the kitchen. To find a weapon…and wait.

An icy chill coiled all the way down Gant's spine as he watched the light weaving its way from the trees to the house.

"We need to move," he said, his words a harsh whisper as he tossed the blanket away. Cautiously, he unhooked the lantern from the side of the buggy and lighted it, shading it as best he could with one hand and then giving it to Gideon while he reached for his cane.

Gideon jumped from the buggy, stopping to wait for Gant. Mac stood in the back, stiff legged, on alert with a menacing, low growl.

Gant waved both of them on. "*Go!* I'll be right behind you! Mac—*forward!*"

With that, Mac cleared the buggy with one leap, taking off ahead of Gideon, both of them crashing through the grove and onto the road.

Gant wouldn't have thought he could take the mud-slicked road as fast as he did, and he did stumble a couple of times, almost falling. But he righted himself and kept going, following the trail of light from Gideon and the lantern.

He looked up and saw a faint light seeping through an upstairs window—a light that hadn't been there a moment before. He remembered the night he'd searched the house, after the break-in. *The light was coming from Rachel's bedroom.*

So she was awake. Was she aware that someone was just outside the house?

Rachel tiptoed into the kitchen, the plank floor cold on her bare feet. She went to the cabinet and opened the drawer where she stored most of her larger utensils, rifling through it in the darkness with trembling hands. She found the mallet, her hand lingering on it for a moment. Then, with a ragged breath she lifted it from the drawer, ran her hand over it, and put it back.

Everything in her, everything she'd been taught, believed, and grown up with screamed deep inside her that she could not, must not resort to violence, even if she were physically capable of defending herself.

"He is my refuge and my fortress: my God; in him will I trust…"

After a moment she stepped quietly into the shadows and waited.

Gant pushed himself to move faster, finally catching up with Gideon, where he was waiting for him at the side of the house. Mac, restrained by Gideon's hand on his head, stood watching Gant expectantly, clearly waiting for a command.

With one hand behind him, palm outward to caution the dog from charging ahead, Gant, followed by Gideon and Mac, now moved slowly and as quietly as possible toward the back of the house.

They were halfway there when they heard a blood-chilling screech from the hill close behind the house. Gideon lunged on ahead, dangling the lantern close in front of him while Gant followed, with Mac overtaking him as he pushed ahead.

They reached the back porch and stopped dead.

A snarling Mac, on his hind legs and stretched to his full length, had pinned a man to the porch wall. The kitchen door stood open, revealing nothing but darkness.

Gant glanced to his right at the hill behind the house, where a hissing, growling bobcat—*Jake*—stood poised halfway down as if about to leap, at the same time eyeing Mac and his captive.

Gideon scanned the entire scene, including the hill where the bobcat waited. Gant held his breath, locking gazes with the wintry-eyed bobcat before stepping onto the porch.

Gideon lifted the lantern higher, trapping Mac's prey in the flickering light. "*Aaron?*"

A white-faced Aaron Beiler stood trembling, his eyes glazed with what looked to be rage and something akin to terror. One hand still held a lantern. On the floor of the porch, where he had dropped it or thrown it, lay a dangerous-looking iron pipe.

Gant ordered Mac to release and then to stay. The big dog dropped to all fours but moved little more than an inch away from the boy he'd held captive until a few seconds ago. The dog stood panting, teeth still bared, a threatening stare solidly fixed on Samuel Beiler's eldest son.

At that moment, Rachel appeared in the open doorway. She wore a stunned but defiant expression. With her left hand, she clutched her robe tightly around her. "What—Gideon? Jeremiah? What are you doing here?"

Her gaze went to Aaron Beiler and to Mac and then cut to the bobcat. She was pale and visibly shaken. Yet, all things considered, Gant thought she appeared remarkably steady.

In that instant, Aaron Beiler made a move as if to run, but Mac stopped him dead by blocking him with his heavily muscled body and a fierce warning snarl. The boy shrank back.

"Gideon," Gant said quietly, "take the buggy and go fetch Carl Nielson. We need the law out here. Mac and I will stay with your sister and make sure Aaron doesn't go anywhere." He paused. "Maybe when you get back with Carl, Aaron would like to explain what he's doing here." He glanced at the iron pipe and motioned to it. "With a weapon."

That said, he put a hand on Rachel's shoulder, waiting for Mac to herd Aaron Beiler inside before moving to follow them.

They stopped when the bobcat uttered one final cry—a growl of dismissal, Gant thought. He watched as the creature turned his back on them all and took the hill in broad leaps, stopping when he reached the crest only long enough to cast an impatient look down on them.

Then he was gone, leaving Gant to strengthen his grip on Rachel's shoulder as he led her indoors.

46

RACHEL'S ANSWER

My beloved is mine, and I am his.

SONG OF SOLOMON 2:16

Three weeks later, Susan and David Sebastian invited Gant and Gideon to a "very special late supper," which they planned to host on Sunday. It was their way, Doc explained when he stopped in town to invite Gant, of sharing their thankfulness and appreciation to him for helping to keep Rachel safe.

Gant wasn't concerned about their showing appreciation for anything he'd done—they had already expressed that to him many times over. The only thing he was interested in was whether Rachel would be there.

As it turned out, she was.

Susan, in her usual style, had prepared a feast.

The woman was a wonder in the kitchen. Gant declared himself to be "royally stuffed" as he finished off his last bite of apple pie. "I'll probably topple over and cave in your mother's floor when I get up from the table," he told Fannie, who was seated next to him and, as always, found him highly amusing.

Indeed, the gathering did turn out to be very special, and for more than one reason. A few days earlier, Gideon had announced his intention to return to the community and make his vows. He would again be living Amish. Susan was fairly beaming throughout the evening.

Gideon had told Gant of his plans two days earlier, at which time he expressed his concern about keeping his job. Gant had quickly assured him that for his part, he would definitely hope to keep him on. It all depended, of course, on what the new bishop decided about the situation, but the fact that Samuel Beiler was no longer their bishop boosted Gideon's hopes considerably.

Gant had noticed another area in which Gideon seemed to be hopeful. Without referring to Emma Knepp by name, Gant had offhandedly inquired as to whether Gideon had any other news, given the fact that he would be living Amish again. The boy had merely grinned and granted that indeed he might, in the near future, have more news.

Good for him.

There was some conversation, as might have been expected, about Aaron Beiler. The young troublemaker was now in jail and awaiting trial, not only for the havoc he had wreaked upon the community for more than a year but also for what the boy claimed to be the accidental death of Phoebe Esch.

"It will be up to his lawyer to prove Phoebe's death was truly an accident, of course," Doc pointed out while they were still at the table. "But I tend to believe the boy on that score. I think it likely that what began mostly as mischief, probably as an attempt to frighten Phoebe—and thereby unnerve the rest of us—took a tragic turn. My opinion is still that Phoebe died of a sudden heart attack."

"But he'll still have to pay, won't he?" Gideon asked.

"Certainly he will," Doc agreed. "And for all the rest of his bad doings as well. Aaron insists he was only trying to get rid of..."

He paused and stole a glance at Gant, who nodded, saying, "I know what the boy was up to, Doc. He's already confessed part of it to Carl Nielson. He thought he could run me off, and then Rachel would turn to his father. In fact, according to Carl, just about everything the boy did was provoked by his desire to make things better for Samuel—and thereby make things easier for himself and his brothers."

"What kind of twisted thinking is that?" said Gideon.

Gant shrugged. "It seems twisted to us, but it sounds as if most times when Samuel didn't get his way or lost his temper about something, he took it out on one of his boys. The fact that Rachel continually refused to marry him apparently made him a little crazy. The latest confrontation with her must have really set him off. Lately he'd been going after the youngest lad with a vengeance."

"Well, I suppose it remains to be seen whether he meant any real harm to Phoebe," Gideon said, "but I for one don't believe this last stunt of his was any kind of an accident. He hasn't admitted it—Carl said he won't talk about it yet—but that iron pipe he was carrying around could have been deadly."

Gant looked at Rachel, concerned about the effect Gideon's remarks might have on her, but she seemed quietly composed. She even added a comment of her own. "He might have meant to use it only to break in, Gideon," she said softly.

"And then what?" he shot back. "Come on, Rachel, you know he had it in for you because of his *dat*. He had more in mind than breaking into your house this time."

"Even so, I can't help but feel sorry for those boys," Rachel said, her voice still low.

Gant marveled at the fact that she didn't even seem angry.

"Aaron must have had a miserable life," she continued. "Apparently, all of them have grown up troubled and mistreated."

"Don't feel too sorry for Aaron," Gideon put in. "He intended to hurt you that night, Rachel. He was after revenge. Aaron thinks you ruined Samuel's life, and therefore you wrecked *his* as well. He's as off in the head as his *dat*."

"Has anyone heard yet where Samuel went?" Gant asked.

"He's back at the farm for now," Doc said. As if to reassure Rachel, he quickly added, "But he's not staying. He came back to put it up for sale and collect the household goods and furniture. If you can believe this, he's actually calling himself a bishop again, and he's assembled a few followers to accompany him to Indiana. They'll be starting a new district there, and Samuel will be their leader. At least that's what Malachi told me. It seems that the Riverhaven Amish are far too lenient for Samuel's liking. He's going to preside over a new community that more specifically follows the tenets of the 'true' Amish faith."

"What about the boys?" Rachel said, her forehead lined with concern. "Surely they aren't going with him. They've already suffered so much."

"No," Doc said. "They're going to stay here, with their aunt. At least for now. Aaron, of course, will have to serve time once he's sentenced."

"Aaron." Rachel shook her head, her expression sad. "He's turned out to be just like Samuel, if not worse."

"Rachel, Aaron is sick," Doc pointed out. "He's sick in his mind. He needs help—badly. It could be that time away from his father will do him good, even though he'll spend it in jail."

"Don't count on that," Gant said. "All too often a fellow comes out of jail worse than he was when he went in."

At that point, Doc cleared his throat, saying, "I think we've had enough depressing talk for now. There is, however, another piece of news that you probably haven't heard yet," he said, turning to Gant and directing his words to him. "I know you like Malachi Esch and have a great deal of respect for him, as do we. I thought you'd like to know that he's to be our new bishop. The lot fell on Malachi at the service today. We need to be praying for him."

Susan smiled and said, "Malachi will be a fine bishop. He's a *gut* man. A kind man. Always has been."

Doc held Gant's gaze for a long moment but said nothing more.

Gant was surprised and pleased by the news. And although any real hope for him and Rachel would be premature at this point, he couldn't help but feel hopeful.

After Rachel helped to clear the table, she and Gant were the only ones left in the dining room. She started toward the kitchen again, but before she could get away, Gant caught her arm, saying, "Would you give me a minute, Rachel? I need to talk to you."

She looked around, as if to see if anyone was watching. "I don't know…I need to help in the kitchen—"

"Fannie's helping Susan. It won't take long. Please."

She studied him for a moment and then nodded. "Dr. David and Gideon are in the living room playing checkers. We can talk here."

"So...Malachi will be the new bishop," he began.

She nodded, not looking at him.

"Then I mean to speak with him. Soon."

She remained still as a stone.

"I mean to ask his permission to convert. Do you think I have a chance?"

Now she looked at him. "I...I don't know."

"Do you care?"

"Do I...well, if that's what you want, Jeremiah, of course I care."

"You know very well what I mean, Rachel. If Malachi grants his permission for me to become Amish...when the time comes, will you marry me?"

Her eyes widened. "You shouldn't ask me that yet."

"Why not? Surely by now you know if you want to marry me."

"It's much too soon for us to talk about marriage."

"I need your answer, Rachel."

He stopped. "A long time ago, I asked you if you'd marry me if I were Amish. At that time you told me you would. Did you mean it then?"

She brought her hand to her mouth in a self-conscious gesture, watching him. "Yes. I meant it."

"And now?" Gant pressed, finding it difficult to get his breath. "If I convert, will you marry me?"

"Jeremiah...you mustn't convert only because of me. It wouldn't be right."

"I won't lie to you, Rachel. You're the most important reason I want to convert. But you're not the only reason." He stopped and then went on when she started to protest again. "Listen to me, Rachel. I think...I *know* I want your life. The Plain life. I want what you and your family have. I want it for myself. I know I'll have to change in a lot of ways. But I also believe I can. So I'm asking you again, Rachel. Will you marry me?"

She lifted her face to look at him. He felt as if those dark, gentle eyes were searching his very soul. "Yes, Jeremiah," she said softly. "I will marry you."

Relief mingled with joy, and he moved to embrace her but then stopped.

He lifted a hand slightly and gave a small shake of his head. "I'm going to assume you want everything done properly, in keeping with your Amish ways. Right now I need to kiss you so badly I can scarcely breathe. But I also want everything to be the way you want it. So I'll wait."

Rachel smiled just a little. Then, closing the distance between them, she went into his arms.

"Just this one time, Jeremiah," she said, lifting her face for his kiss. "*Then* we'll wait."

47

No Longer a Stranger

Love transforms the heart
That once waited outside, looking in
To one that belongs and abides.

UNKNOWN

What a glorious day it was! Hints of spring were everywhere, with trees in bud and flowers poking their heads through the rich river soil. The light breeze carried a fresh, sun-warmed fragrance, so welcome after the winter months.

Rachel stood on the front porch, watching. Watching for any sign of Jeremiah.

He was speaking with Malachi today, meeting with him to request permission to convert to the Amish faith.

The weeks had dragged by ever so slowly. So often it had seemed as though this day would never come. According to Gideon, Jeremiah, too, had been as restless as a caged bobcat throughout the waiting time.

Her brother often spoke of bobcats, particularly "Captain Gant's bobcat," now that he had seen the creature for himself. Rachel hadn't forgotten Jake either. Jeremiah still puzzled over how and why the animal had turned up all the way out here that terrible night.

She had thought the creature magnificent. A lot like Jeremiah himself. Confident. No doubt headstrong. And handsome. Oh, he *was* a handsome animal! Probably unpredictable too. There again, like Jeremiah.

She was growing restless now. Anxious. Malachi was a kind man, a reasonable and fair man. But now he was also the bishop. He had to take many things into consideration, matters that dealt with spiritual guidance and tradition. Matters to be followed in accordance with the *Ordnung.* There was always a chance he would refuse Jeremiah's request, forcing him to remain an outsider.

She would go in and make some coffee. Jeremiah might be hungry when he finally arrived. Besides, she needed something to do…she needed to keep busy. She'd make coffee and cut the fresh gingerbread she'd baked only that morning.

Then she saw him. Coming up the road, seated tall on Flann, his big red horse. She stood, fixed in place, holding her breath as she watched him dismount.

He tied up the horse, reached for his cane, and came hurrying toward the house, taking the biggest, broadest steps of which she knew him capable, given his bad leg.

His expression was solemn…too solemn…until he was halfway up the yard. Then suddenly he stopped, cracked an enormous smile, and tossed his cap in the air.

"So, then, Rachel Brenneman," he called out in an exaggerated Irish accent, "do you happen to know of a good Amish language teacher in these parts? Oh and by the way, will you marry me, m'lovely?"

Rachel stared at him, too stunned for a moment to move.

When she delayed, he planted both hands on his hips, tilted his head to the side, and said, "Well…will you ever answer me, woman?"

Rachel finally found her breath and willed her legs to move, practically leaping off the porch as she ran to meet him, skirts flying, tears flowing even as she burst into laughter.

"Yes…yes…*yes!*" she cried, falling into his waiting arms.

→ Epilogue ←

River Song

Come, we that love the Lord,
And let our joys be known.

Isaac Watts

Riverhaven
Twilight in early December, two years later

Rachel Gant tiptoed through the back of the new house, intending to sneak up on her husband.

It was becoming more and more difficult to walk quietly, thanks to the ever increasing girth of her unborn baby. Mamma was convinced the *boppli* would be a boy, given Rachel's quick and substantial weight gain. Rachel didn't care whether their first child would be a girl or boy so long as their "wee wane"—Jeremiah's term—was healthy and came soon. She was eager to be a mother and just as eager to lose this excess weight.

Somehow she actually managed to surprise Jeremiah. She moved in close behind him, grasping his shoulders and planting a soft kiss on the back of his head. He was kneeling on his good leg, apparently putting the finishing touches on the newly laid wooden floor of the kitchen.

With a yelp of surprise, he pivoted on his knee and then got to his feet and pulled her to him. "And just what is it you're up to, Rachel Gant?" he said with feigned sternness. "Trying to give your husband a scare, is it?"

Rachel smiled up into his handsome, bearded face and produced the

295

cookie she'd brought him. "I thought I'd bribe you into a short walk by the river."

"Isn't it a bit cold for you to be walking about?" he said, taking the cookie and biting into it. "Mm…delicious."

"It's actually mild for December. And remember, Doc said I should walk a little every day."

"Even now? He also said the baby might come any day." He finished off the cookie, wiped a fist over his mouth, and planted a light kiss on her forehead.

"Even now. Please?"

"All right. But we'll not go far. Agreed?"

Rachel nodded. "Agreed. I wouldn't last very long on my feet anyway."

While she waited for him, she went from room to room, admiring his handiwork. She supposed some might find the new house a foolish extravagance, but she understood Jeremiah's reluctance to live in a house built by her first husband. He wanted a place of their own, a home he would raise with his own hands, his own skill. Gideon and Doc and many among the People had helped, but the plans, the design, and much hard work were all from Jeremiah. He had always wanted to build a house, he'd told her.

And now he had. He'd built it in keeping with the Plain style of living—no fanciness or frills, just a good, solid home with much planning and fine workmanship. A house with three bedrooms besides their own. "One for the boys, one for the girls, and a bigger one for Fannie," he'd said before the first wall was ever set in place. "A young girl's room for as often as she chooses to visit."

And then, of course, connected to the side of the house was his new workshop. He would be moving out of the shop in town as soon as the new work area was completed. Given the way his reputation had spread, no doubt he'd still have a good number of *Englisch* customers as well as Amish, but now he would work closer to home. The new shop was big enough for him and Gideon to be comfortable working together and was close to the road for the convenience of his customers and deliveries.

As it happened, the house Rachel and Eli had once shared would soon be occupied by Gideon and Emma, now that they were married. They had been staying with Emma's family, waiting for their own place, which they would have as soon as Rachel and Jeremiah moved into their new home.

Rachel was delighted to know her brother and his wife—and eventually their children—would be living in her former home.

She was glad, too, that soon she and Jeremiah would have a secret room nearby, on their own land, instead of in town in the carpentry shop barn. Completed only a few days ago, it was built below ground in the new barn, with a concealed door and stairway well hidden behind another small room where feed and other supplies were stored. This is where they would continue to offer protection and seclusion to any refugee slaves in need of safe harbor.

The practice of harboring runaways was never spoken of throughout the community, never acknowledged, but conductors always seemed to know how to find a station when needed. Now that a few other Amish and *Englisch* families in the area were contributing to the efforts of the Underground Railroad, the secret rooms were becoming more numerous.

Before they were married, when Jeremiah asked Rachel her feelings about providing refuge for the runaways, she had insisted he continue. She knew how strongly he felt about helping the slaves gain their freedom, and she wasn't about to interfere.

In truth, she had come to share his abhorrence of slavery. She intended to work alongside him in his work to defeat the odious practice.

Gideon, too, had expressed his desire to help in any way he might be needed. So with Asa planning to build a small cabin on the adjacent land Jeremiah had deeded to him, they would all be able to work together—at least when Gideon and Asa weren't on the road—in providing refuge for runaways. It was important work, and although it was risky work as well, Rachel felt blessed to be a part of it.

Outside, Jeremiah took her arm as they started toward the river. "Warm enough?" he said.

"I'm fine. But I imagine you're tired. You said you had a busy day in the shop, and now you've worked for hours on the house."

"We'll have some real winter soon. I want to get most of the work done and the shop moved out here before then." He squeezed her arm. "You're still feeling all right?"

Rachel nodded. "You surprise me," she said after a moment.

"That's good. I wouldn't want to bore you."

"As if you ever could."

"So how do I surprise you?"

"I never thought you'd be much for fussing. But you fuss over me all the time."

"Some things are just worth fussing over, m'lovely. You're one of them. Besides, I've never had a wife to fuss over before. I'm rather enjoying it."

As they approached the river, Rachel leaned closely into his warmth. "I rather enjoy it myself."

He stopped, leaned over, and kissed her.

"Jeremiah! Not in public."

He looked around. "Do you see someone I don't?"

She elbowed him and started walking again. "We need to keep working on your language lessons, you know."

"Malachi says I've done very well. He wouldn't have allowed me to convert otherwise."

"Oh, you have done well," she said dryly. "But you're still speaking the Amish language with an Irish accent. You can use a little more work." She paused. "And you should probably refer to Malachi as Bishop."

He waved off her suggestion with his free hand. "He doesn't mind. Doc still calls him Malachi too."

"Mmm."

They walked along in silence for a short time before he pressed her arm to stop. "That's enough walking for you. Here's our bench."

He had built a sturdy wooden bench on the riverbank nearby where they could sit during the evenings in good weather and watch the river. Rachel loved being close to the water, listening to its song, watching its flow. But she knew Jeremiah loved it even more.

"If you're cold," he said after a few minutes, "let's go back to the house."

Rachel delayed only a moment before saying, "I'm ready to go."

He looked at her. "You seem distracted tonight. Are you really all right?"

"And you seem overly anxious. I'm fine, Jeremiah. Really."

He studied her for another moment and then nodded. "Let's go then."

Halfway to the house, he said, "I almost forgot. I have news."

Rachel also had news, in truth had been bursting to tell him all evening, but at the moment she thought she might wait. She was feeling a little breathless, and her legs seemed strangely heavy.

"Tell me," she prompted.

"Well, it seems that your *Englisch* friend Ellie and the doctor are also going to have a new wee wane."

"Oh, I'm so glad, Jeremiah! That's wonderful!"

Rachel and Ellie Sawyer had become friends over the past year. When Ellie married the new doctor in town, Rachel had made one of her more colorful birdhouses and given it to them as a wedding gift. It was hard to believe and embarrassing to think that she'd once struggled with jealousy over what she'd perceived as an attraction between her friend and Jeremiah. Now she could look forward to sewing baby things for Ellie's new little one in addition to her own.

By the time they reached the house, Rachel knew she'd walked too far. Her breath was fairly labored, and her feet felt as if she were wearing bricks for shoes. She plopped down on a kitchen chair the moment she shrugged out of her coat.

"Rachel? Are you sure you're all right?"

She tried to wave off Jeremiah's concerned frown. "I'm fine. Just a little out of breath. I was starting to get cold."

"Let me fix you some hot tea."

Rachel watched her husband move with ease around the room. One nice thing about marrying a man who had been on his own a few years and hadn't always been Amish was that he knew his way around a kitchen and didn't mind doing "woman's work."

He sat down beside her and watched as she drank her tea. "Better?" he said.

She nodded, though it was a bit of a pretense. Still, there was no sense in worrying him. At least not yet.

"I have news too," she said, straightening as she tried to find a comfortable position.

"And you're just now telling me?"

"Well, it's...big news. I was waiting for the right time."

Now she had his attention. "So?"

She was enjoying this even if she was uncomfortable. "Doc thinks... he can't be sure, mind you...but when he examined me today, he thought he might have heard two heartbeats."

"Two..." He looked at her. "What does that mean?"

"Well...it could mean I'm carrying two babies instead of one."

He reared back on the chair. Stared at her. "Two?" He sounded as if he were about to strangle.

"Two," Rachel echoed, unable to stop a smile. She had never seen Jeremiah look so positively thunderstruck, except perhaps on their wedding day. "It's just possible that we're going to have twins."

As she watched, he struggled so hard to swallow that she feared he might choke.

Finally, a somewhat stunned grin broke over his face, and he made a move toward her.

In that instant, something clamped down hard in Rachel's middle, and she caught her breath.

Apparently, Jeremiah didn't notice. "Rachel...I'm at a loss. This is—"

She lifted a hand to stop him. "Jeremiah..."

He dipped his head to kiss her, but again she put out a hand of restraint. "Jeremiah, you can kiss me later. But right now there's something else you need to do."

"Aye. Anything," he said, his voice still unsteady.

"You need to go and fetch Doc and Mamma. And, Jeremiah..."

His eyes wide, he shook his head as if to clear it. "What, sweetheart?"

"You need to hurry. I do believe you're going to be a father tonight."

River of Mercy

Like a great and mighty river is God's mercy,
Flowing through God's people who believe.
His power is ours in fullness beyond measure,
Forever pouring out as we receive.

Though obstacles may rise and block its passage,
Slow it down or modify its course,
There's nothing that can halt its steady flowing,
For the Living Water is the river's source.

Life's struggles won't impede God's stream of mercy
If we trust His love to always make a way,
And the river will flow out from us to others
If we keep our eyes on Jesus day by day.

—BJ HOFF

DISCUSSION QUESTIONS

1. Gideon Kanagy has moved away from the Plain community and is living as an *Englischer* in Riverhaven while he works for Jeremiah Gant in his carpentry shop. Why, then, isn't he under the Amish *Bann* for not living according to the *Ordnung*, their unwritten rules for proper living?

2. Do you understand the reason for the *Bann*—the shunning— employed by the Amish? Can you explain its purpose and express whether you agree with it or not?

3. How do you see Samuel Beiler? What kind of a person is he? What do you believe is responsible for his tightening of the rules in the Riverhaven Amish community? What do you think accounts for his conflicted treatment of Rachel?

4. Is the embarrassment or humiliation Rachel feels after Samuel Beiler confronts her about her "wrong behavior" with Gant justified? Do you believe she actually did sin with him, or did Beiler's accusations influence her opinion of herself and her love for Gant?

5. The story told in *River of Mercy* takes place almost entirely in the winter. Did this affect your mood as you read the book? How?

6. When did you first begin to think you knew the identity of the troublemaker(s) in the story—early in the book, later, near the end, or not at all? Was your assumption right? Did anything in particular trigger your realization?

7. Dr. David Sebastian advised his stepson, Gideon Kanagy, that things have a way of working out if we follow God's leading:

"The most important thing for you, son—for any of us—is to heed God's will, though His will may not always seem like a possibility. Sometimes it won't even seem to make sense. But as I said, things have a way of working out in the long run if we let the Lord put us where He wants us. You just follow where He leads and let Him take care of any obstacles."

Do you believe that? Can you recall a time in your life when you've followed that advice? How did it work out for you?

8. Is there a particular character in *River of Mercy* to whom you especially relate? How and why?

9. Did anything in *River of Mercy* change your preconceived ideas about God's mercy or enlighten your understanding of it? Explain.

10. Did Rachel surprise you with the way she handled the approach of a likely intruder in the dead of night? How would you handle a situation like this?

11. How do you think the arrival of Silas, and Asa's eventual recognition of the boy, might ultimately change both their lives?

12. If you've read all three books in the Riverhaven Years series, who was your favorite character? Who was your favorite in *River of Mercy*? Why?

ABOUT BJ HOFF

BJ Hoff's bestselling historical novels continue to cross the boundaries of religion, language, and culture to capture a worldwide reading audience. Her books include such popular titles as *Song of Erin* and *American Anthem* and bestselling series such as The Mountain Song Legacy and The Emerald Ballad. Her stories, although set in the past, are always relevant to the present. Whether her characters move about in Ireland or America, settle in small country towns or metropolitan areas, or reside in Amish settlements or in coal company houses, she creates communities where people can form relationships, raise families, pursue their faith, and experience the mountains and valleys of life.

BJ and her husband make their home in Ohio.

Visit BJ Hoff's webpage at **www.bjhoff.com**

To learn more about books by BJ Hoff
or to read sample chapters, log on to our website:

www.HarvestHousePublishers.com

HARVEST HOUSE PUBLISHERS
EUGENE, OREGON

MORE OF BJ HOFF'S DELIGHTFUL FICTION FROM HARVEST HOUSE PUBLISHERS

SONG OF ERIN

The mysteries of the past confront the secrets of the present in bestselling author BJ Hoff's magnificent Song of Erin saga.

In her own unique style, Hoff spins a panoramic story that crosses the ocean from Ireland to America, featuring two of her most memorable characters. In this tale of struggle and love and uncompromising faith, Jack Kane, the always charming but sometimes ruthless titan of New York's most powerful publishing empire, is torn between the conflict of his own heart and the grace and light of Samantha Harte, the woman he loves, whose own troubled past continues to haunt her.

This new edition combines two of BJ's best novels into one saga-length volume.

> "*Song of Erin* contains some of my favorite characters. This story and its people hold a very special place in my heart."
> —BJ HOFF

AMERICAN ANTHEM

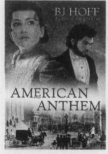

BJ Hoff offers another thrilling historical saga that will capture your heart.

At the entrance to the city, an Irish governess climbs into a carriage and sets out to confront the man who destroyed her sister's life—a blind musician who hears music no one else can hear...

On a congested city street, a lonely Scot physician with a devastating secret meets a woman doctor with the capacity to heal not only the sick but also his heart...

In a tumbledown shack among hundreds of others like it, an immigrant family struggles to survive, and a ragged street singer old beyond her years appoints herself an unlikely guardian...

So begins *American Anthem*, a story set in 1870s New York that lets you step into another time to share the hopes and dreams and triumphant faith of a people you'll grow to love and never forget.

"An eloquently told story that weaves history, music, faith and intrigue...an absolute pleasure."

—CHRISTIAN RETAILING

"The story gently unfolds with intriguing characters and the sound of music, which Hoff manages to make fly off the pages with her glorious and passionate descriptions."

—CHRISTIAN LIBRARY JOURNAL

Great reviews for BJ Hoff's
MOUNTAIN SONG LEGACY TRILOGY

A DISTANT MUSIC

"BJ Hoff always delights readers with her warm stories and characters who become part of your circle of special friends."

—JANETTE OKE,
BESTSELLING AUTHOR OF *LOVE COMES SOFTLY*

"For this Kentucky woman, reading *A Distant Music* was like driving through the eastern hills and hollers on a perfect autumn day with the scent of wood smoke in the air and the trees ablaze with color. BJ Hoff's lyrical prose brings to life this gentle, moving story of a beloved teacher and his students, who learn far more than the three Rs. I brushed away tears at several tender points in the story and held my breath when it seemed all might be lost. Yet even in the darkest moments, hope shines on every page. A lovely novel by one of historical fiction's finest wordsmiths."

—LIZ CURTIS HIGGS, BESTSELLING AUTHOR OF *THORN IN MY HEART*

"When I open BJ's books, I'm drawn into a place that is both distant and at home...as I tell my husband, I wish I could create the kinds of characters BJ does because I fall in love with them and want them always as my friends."

—JANE KIRKPATRICK, AUTHOR OF *LOOK FOR A CLEARING IN THE WILD*

"In some ways, *A Distant Music* is reminiscent of the Little House series. Each chapter recalls the details of an event or some character's dilemma. Eventually though, Hoff connects all the threads into a solid story whose ending will deeply touch readers. *A Distant Music* should find an eager audience."

—ASPIRING RETAIL magazine

THE WIND HARP

"BJ always does a great job of drawing her readers into the lives of her characters. I'm sure that there will be many who will be eagerly pleading to know what happens next. I will be among them."
—JANETTE OKE, AUTHOR OF *LOVE COMES SOFTLY*

"BJ Hoff continues the story of Maggie and Jonathan, who must endure their share of trials before reaping their reward. Though this novel is historical, BJ Hoff deals with issues that are completely contemporary...Kudos to the author for charming us again!"

—ANGELA HUNT, BESTSELLING AUTHOR OF *THE NOVELIST*

THE SONG WEAVER

"Like a warm visit with a good friend over a hot cup of tea, *The Song Weaver* offers comfort and satisfaction...and you don't want the visit to come to an end."

—CINDY SWANSON

"BJ Hoff is a master at characterization, and her stories are rich with insight. I love the historical setting and learned something new about the role of women in that society."

—JILL E. SMITH

"*The Song Weaver* is the last book in the Mountain Song Legacy series, and I hate to see it end. I'll miss Maggie and Jonathan and all the others...A very satisfying end to a special series. BJ Hoff never disappoints."

—BARBARA WARREN

And BJ Hoff's beloved
EMERALD BALLAD SERIES

BJ Hoff's Emerald Ballad series was one of the most memorable series published in the 1990s. With combined sales of 300,000 copies, these beloved books found a place in the hearts of BJ's many fans.

SONG OF THE SILENT HARP

Song of the Silent Harp, book one of BJ Hoff's acclaimed and bestselling Emerald Ballad series, begins the five-book saga of three friends raised in a tiny Irish village devastated by the Potato Famine of the mid-nineteenth century as they struggle to survive and hold on to their faith during Ireland's darkest days.

Nora Kavanagh has lost her husband and young daughter and now lives in fear of losing her home. She and her young son, Daniel, have only one hope for survival, the poet/patriot—and love of Nora's youth—Morgan Fitzgerald. But his dangerous involvement with a band of Irish rebels keeps him in constant danger and puts the possibility of a future for him and those he loves in jeopardy.

Michael Burke, a close childhood friend of both Nora and Morgan, left his homeland for America and is now a New York City policeman. A widower with a difficult, rebellious son, he still remembers Nora with love and fondness and wants nothing more than to help her escape the cataclysmic famine and build a new life...with him.

This panoramic epic of love and faith and adventure spans an ocean to follow three of BJ Hoff's most memorable characters in their quest for survival and courage and hope.

HEART OF THE LONELY EXILE

In *Heart of the Lonely Exile*, book two of BJ Hoff's acclaimed and bestselling Emerald Ballad series, Nora Kavanagh struggles to build a new life for herself and her son, Daniel, in America. She receives help from a wealthy American family and friendship and support from a British gentleman, yet Nora finds herself caught in a conflict of the heart.

Michael Burke, a strong, dedicated Irish policeman, desperately wants to keep his promise to his best friend, Morgan Fitzgerald, to marry Nora and protect her. But Nora's instincts urge her to resist Michael's proposal and follow her heart in a different direction. More troubling still, in the midst of her personal struggle, the heartaches from her homeland continue to plague her.

Heart of the Lonely Exile continues the saga of the Kavanagh pilgrimage—a journey of the soul in a strange new land, where all those who are exiles and aliens seek to finally find their true home.

LAND OF A THOUSAND DREAMS

In book three of BJ Hoff's bestselling Emerald Ballad saga set near the middle of the nineteenth century, Irish patriot Morgan Fitzgerald, felled by a gunman's bullet, strives to restore his life and reclaim his future. But even as he takes steps to provide a home for Belfast orphan Annie Delaney and nurture his love for the beautiful, mute Finola, he finds himself again locked in a fierce battle with the powers of darkness.

In America, Morgan's friends Michael Burke and Nora Whittaker discover that the land of opportunity also teems with poverty, injustice, and corruption. From the opulence of Fifth Avenue to the squalor of New York slums, he fights against not only the evil running riot through the streets but also the immoral schemes of an old enemy bent on destroying Michael, the woman he loves, and his only son.

You will be mesmerized by a drama that spans an ocean, taking you on a journey of faith and love that encompasses the dreams of an entire people seeking not only survival but also a land of hope where they can live in freedom and peace.

SONS OF AN ANCIENT GLORY

In book four of her bestselling Emerald Ballad Series, BJ Hoff continues to build the drama and excitement of her sweeping mid-nineteenth-century Irish–American saga.

In Ireland, poet, patriot, and schoolmaster Morgan Fitzgerald is locked in conflict with his closest friend's rebel son, who steals the heart of Morgan's adopted daughter. Among the streets of New York, Pastor Jess Dalton and his feisty wife, Kerry, continue to battle against poverty and persecution while taking the gospel to both the powerful and the poor of the city.

You will be swept into an epic tale of life and death, heartache and victory, all the while revealing the ancient, enduring glory of an entire people.

DAWN OF THE GOLDEN PROMISE

In the fifth and concluding volume of her bestselling Emerald Ballad series, BJ Hoff brings the exciting Irish–American historical drama to a climax with all the passion and power you have come to expect from her.

The saga finds Morgan Fitzgerald adapting to life in a wheelchair as a result of an assailant's bullet to his spine. Meanwhile, his wife, Finola, must face the dark memories and guarded secrets of her past. In New York City, policeman Michael Burke is caught in a conflict between his faith and his determination to bring a dangerous enemy to justice.

This unforgettable series began with the promise of an epic love story and an inspiring journey of faith. The finale delivers on that promise.